D0172252

echoes

LAURA DOCKRILL

HarperCollinsPublishers

HarperCollins*Publishers*
77–85 Fulham Palace Road,
Hammersmith, London W6 8JB

www.harpercollins.co.uk

Published by HarperCollins*Publishers* 2010

1

Copyright © Laura Dockrill 2010

Laura Dockrill asserts the moral right to be identified as the author of this work

A catalogue record for this book is available from the British Library

ISBN: 978 0 00 730129 4

This novel is entirely a work of fiction.
The names, characters and incidents portrayed in it are
the work of the author's imagination. Any resemblance to
actual persons, living or dead, events or localities is
entirely coincidental.

Set in Stempel Garamond

Printed and bound in Great Britain by
Clays Ltd, St Ives plc

All rights reserved. No part of this publication may be
reproduced, stored in a retrieval system, or transmitted,
in any form or by any means, electronic, mechanical,
photocopying, recording or otherwise, without the prior
permission of the publishers.

Mixed Sources
Product group from well-managed
forests and other controlled sources
www.fsc.org Cert no. SW-COC-1806
© 1996 Forest Stewardship Council
FSC

FSC is a non-profit international organisation established
to promote the responsible management of the world's forests.
Products carrying the FSC label are independently certified
to assure consumers that they come from forests that are managed
to meet the social, economic and ecological needs
of present and future generations.

Find out more about HarperCollins and the environment at
www.harpercollins.co.uk/green

For my family...
I love you.
xxx

WITHDRAWN
Albany County
Public Library
Laramie, Wyoming

Dedication

These stories are not all from my imagination; some have been retold and passed down from others and so…

With love and thanks to the following:

19:16. A special thank you to **Daniel** for this East London urban legend and for being an inspiration to me always.

Hibiki Jikiniki is for my friend and fellow poet, **Tim Clare**. Thank you for your time and exciting, revolting mind.

The Tongue Cut Sparrow A special thank you to **my mother** for the story and for your friendship … thanks for pretending not to notice when I steal your food.

That Shrewd Little Fox is for my especially talented friend and loyal editor **Clare Hey**, we've had lots of fun together creating these stories. Without you I would be in an awful pickle.

The Boy Who Cried Monster Thank you for the story, **Ryan**.

CONTENTS

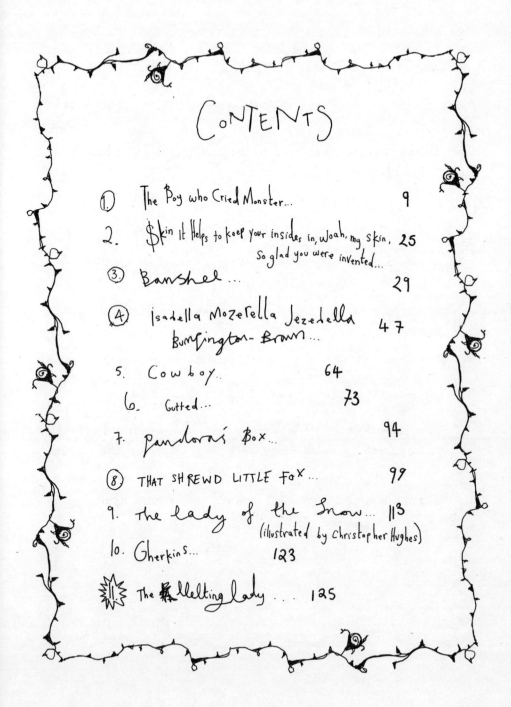

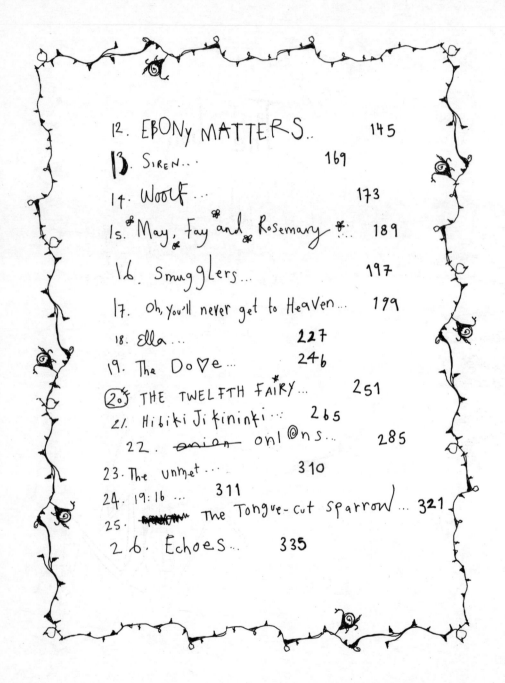

The boy who cried monster.

Off an oily main road, where not even the pigeons could be bothered to visit, was an ugly mechanical building. The building was so violently ugly that visitors were advised to bring sunglasses to shield their eyes from the hideous view. Most of the building had been deserted, odd bits of furniture lay everywhere, haunting empty office spaces, broken technical equipment, all under a blanket of dust and old skin cells as though it were the residue of a ship under the sea. Forgotten.

But at the very top of the building was an office full of professional scapegoats. Inside, the cold walls were colourless, covered with empty corkboards and organized post-it notes. Everything was stiff and dated and static, so painfully unforgiving it forced you to wander through it as though you were colour-blind. It was as though somebody had ordered everything to be painted grey.

And the eight people who worked in this office were dry and flaky – not in a tasty almond croissant way, but in a sore skin sort of way. And these people were pessimistic. They believed that the world was crumbling in; they believed everything was a conspiracy against them, gruelling, grumbling, and continuing, even though every day consisted of boredom and dullness and paranoia. And this wiry stiff party (bad choice of word) wouldn't communicate – they wouldn't know how to, they never played the radio or treated themselves, they just sat and stared and tapped away like robots. All except for one.

Albert started off at Limps as a work experience, forced by his parents to do something, *anything*, other than write his silly stories. And three years later he was still there, filing, plonking out letters, photocopying, but always, in his head, writing stories. His father said he should read more than write, he said before you even pick up a pen you have to know the history behind what you are writing about. He said, 'You can't have a tree without roots.' But Albert believed that history was created every day and roots were growing all the time, it was just a matter of where you planted the seeds.

Albert liked writing about what he already knew. He liked to write about what he saw and what he felt. He liked to write at about six o'clock when the sky was so pink and perfect he could almost see Marc Bolan rising out of it. He liked to write about the cute girl he saw on the train that day who had odd shoes on and had bent a fork around her wrist as a bracelet. He liked to write about when he was little and wanted to be a wrestler so badly he would wear a carrier bag over his body like a vest and tear it open like a raging Hulk Hogan. He liked to write about the homeless man that got on the bus and told all the passengers he had stolen ketchup, brown sauce, vinegar, salt and pepper from a café and had managed to get away with it, laughing to himself, muttering, 'Condiments, that's all you need.' He liked to write about the fat little Mexican girl with the braces on her bottom teeth who walked past him every day and the way she was always so fascinated by the little box above his house that looked like a front door where a pigeon lived. He liked to write about the weird lady with the white boots who was always trying to commit suicide and asking people if they wanted to come round and see her cooker. Or the squatters who everybody used to hate until they made a theatre in the living room of the squat and everybody loved the shows so much that whenever the council came over, the neighbours lied and said the owners to the house were just on holiday, just so the shows would continue. That's what Albert liked to write about.

Boredom. How could anybody ever be bored? But, he had to be careful because that's exactly what everybody at Limps suffered from, boredom. And it was contagious.

Once upon a shitty day, Albert had just finished a story about a wolf when he decided he was a bit peckish. Rolling back on his chair across the grey gravel carpet, he was about to stand when he saw Norman sinking his milky teeth into a cardboard sandwich, inside was all rubbery cheese and browning lettuce. He saw Sue eyeballing the computer screen so intently her eyes were beginning to bleed. He saw John just sitting, his broomstick tash twitching. Albert felt sick, watching them, he felt as though he were watching the room though a television screen.

So, out of nowhere, he began to run.

He ran through the desks, throwing the paper up in the air, over to the bookshelf, rattling the books, encouraging the files to slide out of the shelves, he picked up the plant, still in its pot, grey and droopy and he smashed it against the wall (and then he felt bad, because it was alive and had the potential to be something beautiful. He would tend to that later). Then he ran in circles, destroying anything in his path and his colleagues just watched him. Gormless.

Out came Mr Hurt. 'What on earth is going on?'

Good point. Yes, what *was* going on? He had to say something . . .

'It's a tidal wave. Outside.'

'A tidal wave?'

'A tidal wave, a flood, a . . . a . . . monsoon! Water's everywhere . . . We're going to be drowned if we don't move now, now, now. Allow yourself to be swallowed up or move, move, move!' he yelled.

'A monsoon? From where?' Mr Hurt tried to understand, but he hadn't communicated in so long it was as though he expected a feast of bats to come screeching out of his mouth.

Before he even had a chance to answer, the workers uprooted, their knees creaking out of their swivel chairs like rusty hinges, surprised almost that their bodies could do something other than sit and plonk. They ran too, they joined in with Albert, running, fast and fierce, panicking. They found their voices, realized they could scream, realized they didn't want to lose their lives, realized that they did want to have barbeques and parties, and learn how to make Death by Chocolate, they had always wanted to

go to the ballet after all and pack a suitcase and go shopping for toiletries, they did want to skive work, have a duvet day, sleep all day, and see the sea. They ran, falling, scratching their kneecaps, scraping their skin violently, the bleeding felt good, throbbing, a pulse of its own. Alive, they felt alive. They threw themselves down the concrete staircase, reckless. Some cackled, wild with hilarity, and poured out of the fire escape, grey jumpers, grey ties, grey socks in a pile only to see . . .

Nothing but an oily street.

'Where's the flood?' Norman demanded.

'The monsoon?' Sue asked, teary-eyed.

'The tidal wave?' Mr Hurt quivered. Their pupils swelling from the sunlight. Flowering as though jasmine in hot water.

'I . . .' Albert began. His heart was still drumming, adrenaline soaring through his veins.

'You mean to say you *lied*?' Mr Hurt sneered. 'You were bored and so you lied. You lied to me, you lied to your colleagues and you lied to yourself. You are a disgrace to Limps.' He shuffled his tie, pulled it close to his neck. The cluster of people looked up at him, sourly; never had they felt so let down.

'I'm sorry,' Albert said. He wasn't.

'Hollow words,' Mr Hurt muttered. 'Hollow words.'

In the evening, Albert went out and got drunk by himself. He sketched a monster on a beer mat; he was a better artist than he thought.

'Fancy a bit of colour?' the barmaid asked him, suggestively.

'I'm fine, thanks.' He spluttered his shandy over the table, wiping it with his sleeve. Albert had never been any good with girls.

'Whatever suits you.' The girl strutted off.

He saw the crayons by the till, divided into little plastic beakers, obviously meant for children. Hopelessly aching to ask for them, as a bit of colour was all he wanted.

The electronic sound of paper going in and out of a printer was driving Albert up the fucking wall. He was stuck in this office, in this block, this box, this tiny fucking stone box, with no way out. He had been looking for jobs all morning. He would be sacked sooner or later, wouldn't he? If he kept up this foul behaviour, they would just fire him. Good. He wanted to be fired. He would rather be happy and poor than get the same sarcastic pay packet, week in week out and be a prisoner to a photocopier. He saw it on television. People could have fun in offices. Ricky Gervais had fun in an office, didn't he? And everybody in *Ugly Betty*? Their office was like a circus. Why couldn't it be the same here? Why couldn't they get hot people to work here? Not to go out with, just to look at. He would fancy the funny girl who sat in the corner with the bowl haircut who threw elastic bands at his head and wore kooky dolly shoes. There could be a bitch, a geek, and a prick that everyone hated . . .

Then, suddenly, Albert found himself doing the same thing as last week, the same thing again. Leaping up, plunging to the sky, he ran, he didn't know where he was going or why he was doing it, but he did it and this time he let it rip, as though it were meant to happen, so none of the awkward talking happened again. He picked up an ancient fire extinguisher and let it blow, its hose spiralling in whipping motions on its own accord, gushing out its contents onto the drab workers. Then it seemed as though it was the right moment to let tumble out of his mouth that was open as wide as it could possibly go, 'FIRE!!!'

Now, the office had practised this. They knew the drill, they followed the clear laminated instructions as carefully as they did the 'In case of emergency . . .' sheet on an aeroplane. They knew those little pictures of tiny men hopping out of windows better than they knew themselves. And they ran. Their imaginations, having not imagined something for so long, did the dirty work, their brains gallivanted, stirring up the formidable, imagining the fire tearing at the building, screaming, already chewing up the fire exit, clawing at the window. And then they began to hear it, the crackling noise of burning, the popping of the flames as it teased the workers, drew sweat beads on their foreheads. Panic. Their heartbeats deafening, they ran fast and they ran with reason, a fear so petrifying it caused some of the workers to stumble, tripping on each others' grey limbs. They had always wanted to go horse riding, buy a scratch card, swim the Channel, they had wanted to make a jelly in the shape of a rabbit for their baby nephew, they had wanted to buy that canary in the pet shop window, they needed to call their mothers, they hadn't watched all three *Godfathers*, they hadn't found out what the most deadly spider was. They ran, pulling back each others' hair. Survival. There was so much to do, wasn't there? So much to see and hear and smell and here was Norman lying on the floor, he had slipped, clumsy, getting in the way, so they had to go over him, didn't they? Squashed or not, not their problem, they had to get out, didn't they? Crunching his body was just half of the battle, wasn't it? Part of the adventure, trampling over him as though he were a little drawbridge. And Mr Hurt bouncing up and down telling everybody to remain calm; what did he know? What did he know when there was fire to play with? Linda twisted her ankle, the weight of her meat-and-two-veg body crashed down on it, pinging it to the side and it flopped loose like a runner bean, her howl sirened through the corridor. Hurrying everybody along until they pressed the release bar and out. Fresh air, alive, alive, alive . . .

'Fire? What fire?' Sue blurted.

'I was trying to tell you . . .' Mr Hurt shushed everybody. 'The building is fireproof anyway and it has smoke signals. It was highly unlikely that there would have been a fire without us knowing about it.' He twitched, taking his coat off from the imaginary heat his mind had created.

'So where did this come from?' Linda sobbed, cowering, her tights bloody from the scrapes. She needed an answer.

Everybody needed an answer.

They all looked to Albert. Like waiting for answers at a quiz.

'Your silly fabrications have done you no favours, you have disrupted everybody's mental stability one time too many. Besides, there is photocopying to be done, that is not doing itself, now get you . . .' He was getting nervous about speaking out loud now that everybody was listening. 'Now take your . . . now take your . . . Just get inside, will you?' He slung his jacket over his shoulder, huffing, tutting, shaking his head in anger. The others slumped after him, the noise of the sirens already coming as some bonehead had taken the trouble of calling 999. Just in case. Just in case. Just in case.

Albert walked home that night. The last thing he wanted to do was cram himself on a tube with a bunch of grey nobodies, the odd whacky character trying to stand out with a crazy-coloured tie would depress him. He got himself three cans of Coke and drank them straight, one after the other. He had never done drugs; lifts like this made a world of difference.

'Albert,' his father opened a conversation. 'Son, how's work going? Sniffed out any news of a promotion yet?'

Albert put his fork down, ready to spill, he had stories to tell, to ignite, to fabricate, to embroider the truth, to spin, to say but a clear 'Yes, I think they'll promote me in the next few weeks' would be easier to digest, especially around the dinner table, especially now. His mother clamped her hands onto her chest, a deep heavy puff of relief gushed out of her, her eyes rolled to the ceiling and then to her husband, who patted her on the knee in pride.

'We always knew you had it in you, son. Now we can put those silly nonsense stories to bed.'

Yes and maybe they could. Albert was twenty-five and his room read as a child's, a loner, a weirdo. He would never get the kooky girl with the funny shoes when he lived in a land of make-believe. He would be alone forever, always, wouldn't he?

The next day at work he kept his head down. Plonked, stared, tapped, mumbled, shuffled, ate a cardboard chicken wrap. Felt sick, took a chalky dusty pill to make everything better.

The day after that, at work, he did the same. Plonked, stared, whistled, remembered whistling was barred so stopped, shuffled, awkward, went to the corner of the room to fart, ate a cardboard sandwich. Tap, tap, tap.

The day after that, he did the same, plonk, plonk, plonk, stare, stare, stare, thud, thud, thud, ate a cardboard salad, wasn't enough, licked the air, thud, thud, thud, watered the plant in the gaffa-taped pot, tap, tap, tap, tap, tap, tap, tap, tap, tap, tap, fucking tap.

I'm going to get coffee.

It was a good-looking day, why didn't they have a window? It was unbelievable, who decided that this was how the world worked? That you just *missed* the sunshine? That it was okay to ignore it? They needed fresh air, those pasty faces in that office, their skin like tracing paper could do with a splodge of daylight, could do with a . . .

A swarm of people came flooding through the streets, screaming. What was going on? Cars in upheaval, and then that noise, the road rippling, churning, cracking; cars and shops snapping like the body of a Coke can giving in to the swelling and the people turning into the air, scooping and falling like a scattering of confetti. It was unlike anything Albert had ever seen; different from his stories, his pictures, a . . . well, it was a monster. An actual monster. Oozing sticky, navy in patches, dark deep green in others, diabolical, sludgy, dripping after it was a transparent tar-like residue, like a globby snail trail. It had a tail too, this creature, sweeping the road as though the city were a calm lake and his tail the oar. It bat the buildings, knocked down street lamps, post boxes, people, animals, in long hard savage waves and it had these chunky arms covered in scales like a sea monster, that led on to mammoth hands and long spindly fingers and at the end of each spindle sat a stretched claw that was now blood-splattered and was doing the exact same job a spear would do, gutting anybody that came into its vicinity.

Albert, too afraid to even utter a word, scrambled, quick. He had noticed that although this thing was big and fucking scary, it seemed to be slightly . . . dim. Albert watched its drowsy, glittery eyes fazing over in long slow sleepy blinks and saw it seemed to be plodding, destroying with little sense of direction or care, it was though it didn't really want to be here. Swaying, fumbling, lost, sort of. Albert knew if he began to run now he would be all right, he could get home, get his family, do what he needed to do but then what about Limps? They couldn't even hear the carnival floats as they sailed by last year, they couldn't hear a storm, they couldn't hear a bird tweet, a fox cry. Why, they were trapped in their stone cube where they tapped and pushed buttons and waited for hundreds of copies of the same hundred copies to be copied. They wouldn't have time to escape, time to leave, would they? Would they?

So Albert thought quickly, he typed his key code into the security pad and launched himself up the concrete staircase, his flat shoes tapping out his urgency.

He blew open the wooden door and screamed at the top of his squeaky voice, 'THERE IS A FUCKING MONSTER OUTSIDE. HE'S GREEN AND HAS CLAWS AND A TAIL AND TEETH – *HUGE* TEETH – AND HE . . . IS . . . KILLING PEOPLE. ANYBODY, ANYTHING. YOU HAVE TO LEAVE, YOU HAVE TO ESCAPE. NOW!!'

Tap. Tap. Plonk. Print. Zuuuoooom. File. File. Shuffle. Shuffle. Bleep. Bleep.

'DID YOU HEAR ME? I KNOW IT SOUNDS STRANGE. IT'S MAD, I KNOW. I CAN HARDLY BELIEVE IT MYSELF, BUT PLEASE, IT'S BIG AND IT'S SCARY. PLEASE.'

Plonk. Plonk, blip. Blip. Flick. Flick. Tap. Tap. Tap. Stare. Stare. Stare.

Albert clawed his hand desperately through his hair, as though something were creeping up behind him. He spoke again, his eyes frolicking about, rattling in his skull, fantastically psychotic, as though he were a main part in an excellent sci-fi film, 'PLEASE!!!!'

'Go home, Albert. Just go home.' Mr Hurt gave up.

'Go home? Go home? But there's a . . .'

'It's because of ignorant people like you that things like war happen,' Mr Hurt croaked out.

Albert frowned. Confused. Bit harsh. 'Fine. Fine,' he managed and went to leave, turned around again. Tap. Tap. Tap. Mr Hurt and his stupid face turned back to the screen. And then he saw his plant on the desk, now gaffa-taped up, rescued. And he took it with him, turned to the room and its grey contents and said, 'And it's because of negative people like you that nobody believes in a story anymore, and for that, Mr Hurt, I will never forgive you.'

And he plunged down the stairs, hurtling forward, catapulted himself out of the door and then changed his flurry into a casual stroll, whistling as he popped into a paper shop, then into Costa, and got that coffee he was after. He watched the road, the mums with pushchairs, gossiping, trotting past, the man on his mobile in a rush, the schoolboys laughing with their bags of chips, the cute girl with the beret. Albert picked up his pen and began scribbling down all the ideas he possibly could, excited, he spewed out phrases so wickedly; he could barely get a grip on the pen and he scrawled . . .

And then the monster got into Limps. He ripped off Mr Hurt's head, and then squeezed his torso until his guts poured out of the open gash where the neck was meant to be, like a tube of tooth-paste and everybody was sorry then.

. . . even if it was true, if the monster was there, if it did claw its way into the office and begin slashing throats and crunch-ing bones, Albert wouldn't have minded, he wouldn't have tried to escape. It would be the most interesting thing that had hap-pened to him. Ever.

<u>Skin it helps to keep your insides in, woah, my skin,</u>

<u>so glad you were invented...</u> (that is just the title basically)
(See how its underlined? yes, that means its a title.)

The only one
to bury my bones
You bury my bones
and clean my home
When I am warm
You make me swarm
You warm my bones, you warm my bones,
  you warm my bones you do.

I'm never alone
and you are never alone.

The only one
that sees me gone
and sees me back
and makes me yawn   Oh my bones!
You warm my bones...

I'm un alone, I'm un alone
My head bowed down
and on it a crown

never a frown
when you're around
Down down down down down down - Ah.

the only one
that ties me to the ground
with all the sounds
that claw me down
and when in a crowd
it's you that stands out
and makes me tall
and makes me mad

and makes me act stupid
and makes me look sad
and when it's all over and when I've been had
I'll look back and
I'll still hear you....

Hey hey hey hey

We just couldn't get close
get close enough
you know
In bed we'd hug

but it wasn't enough
it was all elbows and kneecaps and jaws... hah!
and on the floor it was carpet
and on the sofa it was armpit
and I couldn't really take it anymore...

Snuggling in the Snuggery like they do in the films
My head on your chest
but it doesn't really work in reality, you know,
You'd get a dead arm and be annoyed and
        wouldn't speak

and I'd get a cramped neck
 and watch you fart your way to sleep - ah hah!
So I took out the mallet
and knocked you out cold in the head
You looked like a nicer person when you were dead
and I cut you open with some kitchen scissors
Mainly because, they were BIGGER
and it felt just like cutting bacon fat
and blood came out
So I put some towels down
and took extra care to keep everything intact
So that when I sewed you back

You were exact...

And now...

Climbing in like a rabbit burrowing into a hole
like a small child trying to put the quilt inside
   the duvet cover
All corners
and Once I saw your ribcage
I just knew it was the cage for me
I climbed inside like a house in a tree
it was comfy, actually.
I sewed you up from the inside and then
You just normally woke up again
                        realized what I'd done
At first you thought I was gone but when you
You were pleased and put the kettle on.

I often took late walks, especially whilst house sitting for the Barretts. They had a strange little dog called Mozart, friendly, but oddly curious, and I would walk him along the beach and on top of the cliffs. The seaside, at night, is terrifying. Thinking back, I don't know why we walked that way.

Here, in the night light, the pebbles took on the characteristics of beetle's eyes. The sea was cold and ringing, the air piercing, the wind howling, burying itself into cracks in cliffs, the loose rocks surveying the emptiness like watchmen. The subtle salt residue clung to the cliff face like left-over tears; the grass took a beating and warned the seagulls of the weather. Beacons lit the land, dusted the beach like the crumbs of a Christmas ginger biscuit. Apprehension hung in the playground like a word on a lover's lip; ghosts swung on swings, slid down steel and round on rubber, shared kisses, and passers-by breathed invisible cigarettes and bad kids smoked real ones.

Mozart ran to the heath, barking. I threw him a ball but we were both too blind in the darkness to see it. He ran into the night, I watched the end of his tail trail off until I could no longer see him.

'Come on, Mozart,' I called, searching for him. The blackness was dense and secretive. It hid the world away from me.

'Mozart, here boy . . . come now, boy.' I heard his barks but he was nowhere to be seen.

'Mozart!' I shouted, louder this time. The barks faded. I began to walk towards the heath. My mouth tasted of copper. The wind stirred and I felt pressure behind me, heavy, as though a pair of invisible hands had shoved me forwards.

The darkness had smothered me like a kitten in a trapped curtain. I scrambled but all I could see was the end or the beginning of a dense search.

Now I am as mad as the eye of a rabid crow.

As lost as a missing glove.

As discomforted as drinking tea from a neighbour's mug.

And my heart is anywhere but home.

At first I thought I was dreaming, as clichéd as it is. I saw her by the sea, a hood over her head, so small and dark that it would have been quite possible to have missed her, if I had wished to. Her elbows were working; I saw her shifting – forwards, backwards, forwards, backwards – as though she were sanding wood.

I should have let her be.

By the light of the beacon I made out the woman in some more detail. What was she doing out so late? I made my way over the stones, the air was cold, deathly cold. The sea hushed in and out, sweeping.

'Excuse me,' I began. 'Excuse me . . .'

The lady clearly couldn't hear. I went closer; the air was biting my nose, and a tear ran down my face.

'Excuse me. . .' I tried again. 'Sorry to bother you, but you haven't by any chance seen a dog around have you? My dog has gone wandering.'

Again, the lady ignored me. Strange.

I left the lady and walked away from the sea. I would go to the top of the heath and call for Mozart there; I would be at an advantage from the height. I felt oddly obscure without Mozart's company, wilting, and my panic was slowly translating to tiredness. With each hoof up the heath, I figured I could see him, his little body, wagering, but it was my mind playing tricks, until he howled a scuffed, scruffy moan from the end of the Barretts' home and he was there, chewing something in between his clawed paws.

'Good boy,' I ruffled his back. 'What you got there, boy? Let me see.' Mozart snarled as I put my hand forward. 'Come on, boy. What have you got there?'

The dog growled, angrier this time, his eyes like yellow flames put my hairs on end. I reached in again. 'Show me, boy, come on, Mo. GAH!'

The dog bit my hand, not as hard as he could have but a bite all the same. That was unlike him. I felt as though I wanted to cry from sheer shock, it was too unusual, unusual behaviour indeed.

'Okay, boy. Home.' Too tired to shout at him, and not wanting to aggravate the animal even more, I headed back to the house. We'd have tea; he always had a mug of tea poured into his bowl, sometimes he liked a slice of toast too. But tonight he didn't seem interested. He sat in the corner of the kitchen, crumpled round the cupboard chewing on whatever he had as I washed and saw to my wound. The tea I had poured for him in the bowl went from hot to warm to lukewarm to cold. I decided to leave the damned canine, and sort it out in the morning.

In bed, the wind swept the windows, rumbled the glass rooted into the ledge. I tried to sleep. My eyes wouldn't stick to their lids. I couldn't relax, my dispute with Mozart was playing on my mind, I felt the bandage around my hand, the throbbing ache beat with a pulse of its own. I had to go downstairs and see what it was he had.

I let myself out of the bedroom; the corridor was dark and cold. The floorboards felt like planks of ice under my milky trembling toes, black-wired hairs standing on end. I could hear the water boiler, filling, trickling and churning. When I got downstairs, Mozart was snoring in his corner. I squeezed in through the crack in the door, not wanting to wake the dog with the un-oiled *muuuuu* of the hinge. Light flooded in, a luminous box of shadow darted over the kitchen tiles. The dog's ribcage was going up and down, up and down, up and down. I squinted my eyes in adjustment, trying to focus, to get a better look. A slice of silver glimmered, shone at me like a chink of light. I went over. In between his paws was the object. I carefully put my hand forward, I didn't want another bite. The dog flinched. I moved back quickly, breathed, and tried again, my hand quivering in its forwards move. I grasped it – ha! – and escaped quick as can be into the hallway to look at my prize.

It was a comb. A small silver one, antique. Beautiful. Each prong as perfect as the next and the design butterflies engraved into the silver, heavy, not too heavy as to break hair, but not cheap. He was a funny old dog, sensitive old fool. Still, he could hurt himself on the comb so I decided to keep it upstairs with me. Much more relaxed now, I went to bed and lay down, within moments I was sleeping, heavily.

I awoke at around four to an alarming noise; it was Mozart, that silly dog, missing his comb. I could hear him at the bottom of the staircase, crying his needy little heart out. I thought about not getting up but he was really upset, he had a real wail going. 'Okay, boy,' I reassured. 'I'm coming.' I put on my housecoat and made my way downstairs to tend to the dog.

But the dog wasn't at the bottom of the stairs. He was asleep, sound asleep. The wails were still going, screaming now, like a crazed fox or a deranged woman. I searched the house; it sounded the same distance away everywhere I searched. Piercing, it was, screeching. The house shook, the ornaments rattled, falling off the mantel, the knifes rang in their block, the pots and pans on the ceiling harness jangled, murmurs whistled through the keyhole from the treacherous wind. My ears were bursting and I covered them with my palms as I ran round the house. Mozart was awake too now, his tail down, his heavy salty eyes the size of snooker balls. I scooped him up and took him to the bedroom where he trembled in my arms. I put him into the bed with me and pulled the blanket over the top of us. Our bodies shaking in rhythm together, squeezing him closer I felt his tiny heart flattering. I tried to calm him with my voice, soothe him with a stroke; the noise was unbearable, it made me nauseous.

Then, at last, the screaming stopped. I let out a heavy sigh. I slowly pulled back the blanket and peeped my eyes out from under the quilt. It was as though nothing had ever happened.

Until I saw her.

At the window was an old woman. Toothless, black-eyed with white wirey hair, a tatty black shawl round her haggard shoulders. She looked me dead in the eyes, her bony arm slowly lifting upwards, and that was when I realized she was hovering.

'AWAY!' I shouted.

My mouth clammed up once more. Her arms reached higher and higher until she rolled her fragile hand into the shape of a fist, about the same size as a small plum and she knocked.

And knocked.

And knocked.

Three times in total and then pointed her finger, straight at me, her nail shooting into the glass like a warning. I looked down the bandage around my hand I had used to cover my wound from Mozart – it was drenched in thick red blood. A tremendous pang weighed me down, filling my larynx with a cloggy bogginess, unsure of what this feeling was leading me to believe, it crept up on me like hands in the dark and something made me think – it was my turn.

I woke up to the sound of the bin men arguing with the neighbours. My bed was a damp nest of perspiration and muck. The white sheets had changed to a murky sour colour, the corners of the pillows like smokers' lampshades. I got up out of the dismal filthy pit and thought about making coffee. Last night's incident was nothing but a nightmare, my life was not fiction, this was not a storybook, this was nothing but a calculation of the mind.

I finished my coffee in the chair by the window. Mozart was still distressed from last night's activity and was shaking himself into a fuzzy ball underneath my footstool. This made everything only too real for me to deal with. My hand throbbing away in its bandage and I knew I needed to talk to someone about this. I decided to call the vicar. I wasn't religious but it seemed only appropriate. I found his telephone number in my address book under 'V', Vicar Doddley, written in pencil. I dialled his number and waited for the for his voice.

We met later that day at the entrance to the park. The vicar was early as was I.

'Shall we walk?' he asked. 'I know a sweet little teashop nearby.'

The vicar pushed his bicycle by the side of the river, the sunshine beaming off the spokes. The elderflowers candied the air like billowing perfume of a fat aunty. The geese gossiped over crusts.

'Something strange happened to Mozart and me last night, Vicar. I had gone to bed, and I heard this strange wailing; it was sharper than a dog cry, almost the fix between an owl's hoot and a woman's moaning more like a . . .'

'Foxes!' the vicar sussed. 'It's foxes. My wife and I had a similar anxiety until not so long ago, it is —'

'Wait,' I interrupted. 'When I looked to the window I saw —'

'Good grief, look – it's Sally-Anne Reeves, Betty and Colin Reeve's little one. Well, she's not little anymore . . . Sally-Anne, Sally-Anne, over here, my love!' The vicar jumped up and down to get the young girl's attention, 'Her parents own the little trinket shop, you know the one?' He began peering up on his stretched legs like a small yapping dog. 'You don't mind, do you, Jim? It's just I haven't seen her in such a long time! Sally-Anne, over here!'

'No, not at all.' I kicked the soil with my feet and bent down to give Mozart a stroke. Sally-Anne strode over; she was confidently flirtatious even in her walk.

'Good afternoon, Vicar, how are you? And . . .?'

'Yes, this is my very good friend, Mr Jim Beam.'

'As in *the* Jim Beam?'

I shake my head.

'I like whisky,' Sally-Anne smiled, and twisted a dark lock of hair around her finger.

'Sally-Anne Reeves, surely you don't. That's a gentleman's refreshment. Next you'll be saying you like beer!' The vicar laughed off his disapproval awkwardly, his mouth bent like a wire hanger slurping in his drool. He mopped his brow with an embroidered handkerchief and made his lips into a little funnel allowing a hoot of air to hush out of it. Sally-Anne crinkled her nose into a perky little shape that happened to be quite charming and her eyes, quite almond-shaped, looked into my soul and unpicked a few stitches. I decided I fancied her slightly.

'So where are the two of you troublemakers off to?' She winked at me, pulling me in on the joke.

'Troublemakers!' the vicar squealed. 'I don't think that we'll be seeing any trouble from me, not as long as the Lord is watching!' The vicar panicked under the beautiful scrutiny of Sally-Anne, his nimble hands locked into a prayer position before again making good use of his handkerchief.

'We're going to have tea,' I answered, not wanting to neglect Sally-Anne.

'Yes, we're having tea at the sweet little teashop in the park. Do you know it?'

'Well, I was passing through that way anyway to meet a girl-friend. Perhaps I could join your walk?' Sally-Anne smiled, her teeth as perfect as the white picket fence I could see framing the home we shall live in for the rest of our lives together.

Sally-Anne met her friend at an indoor table and the vicar and I chose to sit outside in the sun.

'She's a real beauty, Jim, honestly. From one man to another, she makes me question my faith. She brings me out in these . . . you know . . . steams.' The vicar wiped his forehead. He tried to focus on me; his blank eyes drove holes into mine. I decided it was time to draw him back to my problem.

'Right, well, in terms of foxes, I'd say sprinkle the juice of twelve ripe lemons onto your front lawn; the smell will put them off doing their dirty business outside your home, something about the citrus. By the way, when are the Barretts back?' the vicar asked, doing up the dorky little buttons on his jacket.

'The day after tomorrow,' I answered.

'Come and see me before you go, share a tumbler of Jim Beam, Jim Beam. Tell me, before you scoot, is she looking?'

'No, Vicar,' I answered. She was looking at me.

The two of us left the café and made our way towards the path home. 'Damn!' I sighed. 'I forgot to tip the waitress,' I lied, clicking my fingers for dramatic effect. 'I'd better go back.'

'No need, I go there often, I can drop in some change tomorrow,' the vicar offered.

'No, it's very rude of me. Here, take Mozart.' I quickly took Mozart's lead off my wrist and handed it to the vicar, 'I'll just run by and drop off a little bit,' I insisted, and turned my walk into a backwards jog towards the café. 'I'll catch you up.'

The door fanned open and plunged at me the smell of toasted almonds, honey and coffee. Sally-Anne's eyes hit mine like cricket balls, my eyes wanted to bleed. I acted fast, went up to the counter, tore off a piece off the corner of a receipt and hurried the waitress to find me a pen.

'Got a biro, love, but it's red.'

'That's fine, red's fine.' I snatched the pen away with such haste I forgot to say thank you as I squiggled my details down on the corner and called back the same waitress. 'That girl – that woman – over there, when you give her the bill could you also please give her this? Thank you and for the pen, thank you.' I rushed out and met the vicar.

'Was she still in there?' the vicar asked handing me back Mozart.

'Who?' I acted. I was proud of my fast response.

At home it was getting late and the darkness had already begun filtering through the sky. Mozart had decided to eat which eased my worry slightly as his instinct was usually accurate. I plucked a book from the shelf – it was a book about plants. But, much though I loved flora, I soon fell asleep.

I woke to a fast squawking ring from the telephone that startled me.

'Hello, Barretts' residence . . .'

'Barrett? I thought your name was Beam?'

'It is Beam. Who is this?'

'Well who is this? Are you having an identity crisis?' It was Sally-Anne, I could tell.

'No, no, not at all, I'm house sitting.' I didn't want her to think I was married with a family.

'I'm joking. I gathered you weren't from here, you don't exactly *fit in*. It's Sally-Anne, by the way.'

'Yes, I know. I mean, I thought so.'

'So, you're in then.'

'Yes.'

'When do you leave?'

'The day after tomorrow.'

'So I guess we're in a bit of a hurry.'

'I guess so.'

'I'll come round. Can you wait twenty-six minutes?'

'Yes. Why twenty-six?' But she had already hung up. What a bewitching woman. I pondered on the thought of such an entity being in my space, my comfy universe with Mozart and what it would feel like to have that ruptured. To tell you the truth, I couldn't wait. I jumped up to bathe, put a bottle of wine in the fridge and then lit candles. I wanted to wash the sheets from last night but I didn't want to get myself a reputation. The record began to turn and the latch released.

Sally-Anne wore a long purple silk dress, her creamy arms sat in a heart-shaped clutch in her hands. I poured her wine and she enchanted me more with her cheekiness. She wasn't like any other woman I had ever met; within moments her feet slipped naked from her heels and began squeezing my calves.

'I brought you a present,' she said. 'Well, it's more for Mozart, really. Where is that chap, anyway?' she asked innocently.

'I don't know, but I'm sure if you have a gift for him he'd like to see it.' I jumped up and called the dog's name. 'Mo! Mo!' Nothing. 'He sometimes curls up in the oddest of places; wherever there's an inch of warmth, he's usually snuggled up there.' I started to climb the house, I wasn't really in the mood for playing hide and seek with Mozart but I didn't want to disappoint Sally-Anne. I called him in the bedrooms, searched on the beds, in the laundry baskets, under the radiator and, after finding nothing, climbed up the next set of stairs. This floor was home to the master bedroom, Mrs Barrett's sewing room and the door to the attic. I peered for him in both rooms, he would normally come to a call.

But while I was searching, a vile smell started to lurk up the staircase. I peered down, it was a burning smell, bitter and it hit the back of my throat. A fire! I rushed down the stairs in a panic, 'Sally-Anne, are you okay?' The smoke flooded up the stairs in a dark groggy fog, 'Sally-Anne, have you got Mozart?' As I reached the bottom of the stairs I was hit by a wall of black swirling smoke, thick like a screen of charcoal. I began to cough in deep chesty whoops.

'Jim! Help! Help me!' came a distant voice. It was Sally-Anne calling from the front room. 'Jim! Please, come quick!'

I couldn't see what with all the smog so I got low on all fours and clambered round searching for Sally-Anne. I still couldn't hear Mozart so I had to hope his instinct led him away from the house at the first sign of danger.

'Sally-Anne, I'm coming, cry again if you can hear me so I can reach you faster. I can't see.'

'I'm in here, hurry!' she shouted.

I coughed in splutters as I concentrated the best I could. *Damn candles,* I thought as I reached the corner of the front room door-frame. I crawled as fast as possible towards the settee but was hit by the sound of licking flames from the fireplace, the crackling sound pounded my eardrums. I stayed low and found Sally's feet. I grasped them with my hands and inched my way up her ankles and calves in short sharp grasps so as to not be inappropriate. 'I'm here, I'm here, I'm here, don't panic.' I pulled myself up and reached her hands, her wrists, her arms, her shoulders. I held her close, lifted her into my arms like a child, turned with my back to the window and plummeted onto the front lawn, through the window.

I threw her off me and turned over to tend to her, picking frag-ments of glass away from us. But, to my horror, she was not the same woman! Instead of almond-shaped petals, her eyes were sunken droopy rags over glassy black marbles. Her skin, once creamy and radiant, was saggy and wrinkled and covered in age spots. Her dress, not purple silk, but a shabby dirty nightdress, her hair, tufted, mangled and snowy. I gave her to the grass in terror and ran back into the flaming house to find Sally-Anne. I used my coat as a barricade as I went in but was trapped immediately by a barricade of screaming flames. I can remember no more.

'Mr Beam, you have been very brave to have suffered this, we're terribly sorry for your loss,' the fireman said when I came to.

'It was my fault, stupid candles. Have you seen my dog any-where? I had a dog, Mozart, he was inside—'

'Yes, Mr Beam, the dog was the cause of the fire, he was

found in the fireplace with this.' The fireman handed me the silver comb. 'I'm sorry.'

'I don't believe it. Mozart is dead? Burnt? Dead? I can't believe it. He was the . . . but what about Sally-Anne?' I asked, on the brink of hysterics.

'Mr Beam, you did say a woman was trapped inside the house with you, but no woman was found, I'm afraid,' the fireman said. A line of ash under his left eye made him look like a warrior.

'I'm sure I carried a woman out, an elderly one, not Sally-Anne but an older lady, I know I had her in my grasp. I threw her onto the lawn. She was wearing a nightdress and—'

'Listen, Mr Beam, you are in a very bad state. Why don't you wait until you are at the hospital to discuss this further. You should rest now. We are going to salvage as much of this house as possible and the Barretts are on their way home.'

'No, you don't understand. Sally-Anne, she was in my house, she was there, drinking wine, she wanted to give Mozart a gift. Please, let me have a look for myself, please.'

Later, I hung myself on a willow, on the evening of the hottest day of the year, crying as the rope could not hold my weight and I fell, slippery like a cut tongue to the floor, not because I had failed but because I was and always will be in the wretched grasp of the banshee, forever in her debt.

THE END

Isabella Mozzarella Jezebella
Bumpington-Brown

Isabella Mozzarella Jezebella Bumpington-Brown was the youngest of seven sisters. Like *Little Women* they lived, except . . . err . . . they weren't *actually* poor (in fact they were pretty rich), and except they weren't *properly* artistic *really* (they weren't fussed about nice old juicy books and dressing-up trunks and baking). They liked getting pedicures and sitting in Caffè Nero and scraping their way onto the London Fashion Week guest list and were really good at wearing expensive pashminas, flipping their long blonde hair over from one side to the next and saying, 'Wix' (which I think means 'wicked').

Now, where you are about to be craned into the story something really HILARIOUS has just happened, although we aren't really supposed to laugh, because it's not funny. Well, it is, but it's bad karma to giggle at other people's misfortune. But when it's a Bumpington-Brown, it's easy to get caught up in the moment.

In two hours and three minutes' time the Bumpington-Brown girls are supposed to be flying to St Lucia to visit their parents, who now live there. Except FUCKERADA! Isabella Mozzarella Jezebella has lost her passport.

'I think you are an absolute selfish cow. You have cocked this up too many times in the past and you're doing it again,' Tillytubs grunted, her piggy nose quivering in frustration.

'Mum is going to f-reak,' Jemima snarled under her breath.

'You are un-fucking-believable, Isabella,' BeeBee shook her head in disgust, catting her eyes into dark little slits.

'I can't help but think you did this on purpose to spite me for snogging Damien. Look, he came on to *me* okay, it's not my fault I'm prettier,' Taramasalata sighed, folding her St Tropez arms into a bony square.

'Well, if you're not coming, let me get my hairdryer out of your bag.' Frillyskirtbean began digging around into Isabella's hand luggage.

'Can I please have your Ray Bans if you're not coming? Ooh and your sun oil? Ooh and your Ruby and Millie lip gloss? Ooh and your iPod?' Haggis joined in on the squabble, texting at the same time.

So off they went, all six of them, UGG boots, Paul's Boutique jackets and acrylic nails. Like a grouching, fake-tanned parade of pretty ducklings, they swanned off to check in. Isabella, stripped of her goods, went to find a quiet, un-embarrassing, un-cringifying space to call Add Lee.

'WTF?!' she texted her BFF. 'This is a long trek all day to the airport to get shunned. Random. L'

To which her BFF replied, 'WTF?! Bumped, you must be pissed. Ah well. Nero?'

And something happened to Isabella then, when she saw that dreaded word, 'Nero'. There is something drastically disappointing about packing to go and enjoy two weeks in the Caribbean sunshine, to being deserted by your siblings, and then have to spend the afternoon bitching into a supermarket box of sushi and an espresso. So, as out of character as it was (so out of character it hurt), she replied, 'Oh, random, they are letting me fly after all. Wix! See you in two weeks ;) .'

To which BFF replied, 'Lucky bitch. Have fun. xoxo'

The Add Lee driver texted to confirm his arrival. The car door shut.

'Wandsworth Common, please.'

Isabella emptied her suitcase, re-packed it for Cornwall. The Bumpington-Browns had a cottage; she would go there, in hiding, for the fortnight.

After a tormenting train ride with normal, poor people, Isabella slogged her suitcase up that torturous hill in her Primarni ballet pumps (a richy always likes to get these simple footwear on the cheap – shoes were disposable, basically like foot-shaped teabags), pashmina and all. She eventually reached the cottage.

Then, scrambling through her Burberry handbag, she fingered through old fag boxes, tampons, hairgrips and Nero loyalty cards for her set of keys. 'You *are* joking,' she grumbled, after not feeling her keys where she had thought they'd be. She bit her lip and got down to her knees. It was dark and beginning to rain, the wind blew her hair about. She turned her handbag upside down. The wind targeted its contents, attacking the loose receipts and scrappy papers. No keys. 'No fucking way.'

She looked around the doorstep for a key: under the doormat, behind the plant pot, in the letterbox. *Fuck, fuck, fuck.* She couldn't go back. How humiliating. *Fuck. Fuck. Fuck.* She kicked the wall. *FUCK. Ouch, fuck, bollocks.*

She looked through the window and could just make out the living room, the remote control, the mirror, the candlesticks, the dining room table, the alarm beeper signalling every fifteen seconds. *FUCK.* The rain began to pellet down in heavy, thick strokes; it was difficult to breathe, difficult to keep her eyes open, impossible to get out her mobile phone.

Then she remembered Barnaby at number sixty-seven. *Excellent.* At least he might be able to give her some tea, then she could order a taxi, or he might even have a spare key to the cottage. Right. On she went, her suitcase crackling behind her, sloshing in the gutter where the rain had almost begun to rise.

Doof, doof, she fisted the door of number sixty-seven, her mitten punching the door in heavy clods. Silence. *FUCK.* She tutted. 'What a shitty day.' Again: *DOOF, DOOF.* Nothing. She checked her mobile phone. *Could ring Mum, break into the cottage, ask her for the code. But she was in a bad mood, she wasn't supposed to be here in Cornwall, she'd worry, tell the police, get that smelly woman from the teashop to chaperone her home to London. No way. DOOF DOOF.* Still nothing. *Great.* She would find a hotel. It was getting late. Then, all of a sudden a light came on, it was like a flicker at the end of a dark tunnel, warm, glowing and *phew*. The door latch clicked open and released. It was a guy, a handsome one too, about the same age as her.

'Hello?' he asked.

'Hi. I was, erm, looking for Barnaby.'

'Oh yeah, right. Barns ain't 'ere.'

'Oh.' Isabella smiled politely, fake, ridged and difficult. 'I thought he . . . sorry, okay. Thanks.'

'That's a big suitcase you've got; you come far?' he asked, opening the door further. A sticky, sweet smell swam out of the door; the scruffy hallway was on display, a guitar, shoes, and a surfboard. Weed. Druggies. Just what she needed.

'Yes, London, but, it erm . . .'

'Yeah, we just rent the place off Barns, he lives a few miles away now, got into that property development and we work for 'im. S'all right. Do you want to come in for a cuppa?'

'No, I . . .' she started to protest and then a gush of relief blew out of her like a normal breath after a coughing fit. She was tired and could not refuse some warmth. Besides, her hair now sat in dreaded clumps like dripping icicles, her mascara was bleeding down her face, rainwater-sodden, her tiny shoes, water everywhere, overflowing out of the backs of her heels. It was impossible to argue.

'That would be lovely. Thank you.'

Inside the house were three other boys. Two were playing a game that Isabella just could not grasp the name of – it was pronounced in a heavy Cornish groan, 'Cul-a-Jooty.'

The boy who'd answered the door left Isabella in the living room saying, 'This is J and this is Paulie, Boys, this is . . .'

'Isabella,' she answered sheepishly.

'Isabella. That over there is Bill, his real name's Ollie but he can't olly, can't skate for shit, but he *can* bill-up . . . get it? As in, rolling up, s'ank like that.'

Bill was tugging at a bong that gargled in his hands, his head covered in a spread of gingery dreadlocks, his jeans scruffy with band names scribbled over them in heavy black marker, a hoodie with Dr Dre on it. ''S'up.' He acknowledged Isabella and sat up straighter, offering her the bong.

'No, thanks.' She waved her hand and sat down, awkward, not wanting the material on her clothing to settle on the surface. The room was not how she remembered it when it was Barnaby's living room. It was now a dark, dingy pit, the only light being the blue hypnotic flash of the Cul-a-Jooty which entailed lots of shooting. Stacks of cassettes, CDs, vinyl and video games were piled from floor to ceiling. On the walls, over the once flowered wallpaper were scraggy sun-stained posters of Carmen Elektra, Eminem, Snoop Dogg. On the shelves where Barnaby's football trophies used to sit were funny ornaments and figurines, a mini Batman and Robin and a Rubik's Cube. It was like a big kid's room. The main noise, apart from the occasional burp or grizzle was from the stereo in the corner.

'Do you like RATM?' the door opener who had now revealed himself as Stoo asked, as he passed her a cup of tea.

'Excuse me?' Isabella asked.

'Rage Against The Machine?'

'I err . . .'

'Hungry?' She was but she lied and instead suffered, watching him plough his way through eight mattresses of buttery toast, the smell mortifyingly tempting. He then sank his hot tea in one courageous gulp. 'So, like, what, like, happened?'

An hour later, the shooting noises mixed in with the whiny scruff of rappers began splitting holes in Isabella's head like a woodpecker. She was getting really tired. How the fuck did she end up here? In this dump? With these *chavs*. Ugh.

'Can I?' She held her forefingers out like a small set of scissors to encourage Paulie to pass her a joint. She smoked weed the same way you'd imagine a nun would.

'Insane,' she boasted, trying to fit in.

The floor beneath her was covered in porn magazines, dirty plates with sealed splodges of dried-up ketchup and corners of toast.

'So like, do you wanna sleep over and that?' Stoo asked.

'Sorry . . . shit,' she said. Where had the day gone? She was licked. She did not expect to be sleeping the night with tramps in Cornwall, stoned and helpless.

'I guess so. That okay?' Isabella shrugged. She knew it would be, like it made a difference, there could have been people sleeping, fucking, lawnmowering in the kitchen sink and nobody would have batted an eye.

'So, like, whass your mum and dad do?' Paulie asked. Paulie was a John Travolta lookalike. Well, John Travolta aged . . . say nineteen. He could have done that as a profession.

'My mum works for a charity and my dad is a . . . I don't actually know what he does.'

'Sceen.' He accepted that.

'What about yours?' she asked, trying to be curious, but she didn't care, she was just being polite.

'My dad's a librarian and my mum is a slag,' he said, simultaneously shooting a sea of enemies.

'Oh,' Isabella smirked.

'So, you're rich then?' J asked from across the room.

'Why do you say that?' Isabella asked.

'Well, look at you, your phone, your bag, your stuff, your way.'

'No. Most of this stuff was gifts, actually.'

'From who? Fucking P Diddy?'

'Mummy and Daddy.' And she realized, as soon as the three killer words flooded out of her spic, span little mouth, that she sounded like a complete tit. And the response was not a let-down.

Like a pack of hyenas, the boys began cracking up, frolicking. They loved it: their own personal pocket-sized posh bird as their new gadget that they could prod and push and make do funny stuff.

'Low it, boys, come on, shut up,' Stoo tamed. 'Pass over that joint, bruv.' He sucked in, his eyes drawing in, wincing. He huffed out in misty clouds. He was hot. He just was. His floppy hair, his long smooth arms and chunky wrists and those clean fingernails. He scooped his wrist round, a beaded charm bracelet shifted down his arm, and offered Isabella a toke.

'Do you have a cleaner?' J asked, unable to give up the game.

'Yes.'

'Do you have a big house?' J asked.

'It depends what you mean by big.'

'How many bedrooms you got?'

'Nine.'

'Nine?!'

The ruckus kicked off again and the questions kept coming on, strong.

'BOYS!' Stoo wafted his arm and got up, stretched and walked out the room. 'I've got the munchies.' He gargled as his voice trickled away into speckles of dust in the misty, intoxicated air. Isabella saved by Stoo yet again. *But where was he going? Why was he leaving her now?* At this desperate point of humiliation . . . this was just the rough side to getting *everything* you want, normal people – *poor people* – wanted explanations, as though telling them how and why you were wealthy would infect them with it too.

'Okay, one more . . . What's your full name? Bet it's like double-barrelled and shit.'

She should have lied, she could have said anything, she could have said half of the fucking thing and it would have lessened the load.

'Isabella . . .' she began

J paused the game.

'Mozzarella, Jezebella . . .'

Bill put down his bong in disbelief.

'Do you know what a jezebel is?' Paulie giggled.

'Bumpington-Brown,' she rushed out in one breath, embarrassed.

The laughter reached an abnormal peak, but to her surprise the boys thought she was taking the piss.

'What a joker!' Paulie smacked his leg. 'She's high!' he warbled. 'Blud, you are *fucked*!'

Isabella pouted, covered her lips in Vaseline, and then looked at her phone.

'Right,' Stoo poked his head round the doorframe. 'To the boudoir!' he instructed, looking rather proud with himself.

Thank fuck, thought Isabella. 'Can I just use the loo?'

'The *loo* is just here.' Stoo was being a real gentleman, well as gentle as a boy in khaki shorts and a Run DMC t-shirt could be.

The toilet was worse than she had expected. The pink walls were grimy with, well, grime, and had transformed into a grey peachy colour. In the cocoon of stink, she locked the door. The toilet seat had fallen off the bowl and had a new home down by the side of the bowl with 'R.I.P' written on it in marker. The bowl was covered in a waxy seal of gunk and foul design and splodges of piss and dirt. The sink was a mess of soap and pubes coiled round the taps and limescale chasing the plug and climbing all over wherever it could. The floor was carpeted in cardboard toilet roll cores, the little whispers of tissue clinging onto the rolls for dear life so as to not touch the slippery floor themselves from fear of infection. The rug was booted into a cuddle underneath the sink, like a small soaking dog it lay decorated in muddy footprints. Isabella made her exit as quickly as she could.

Stoo was waiting outside the door for her. 'Ready?' He led her up the soiled carpeted staircase and put his hand on a door handle of a door decorated in *South Park* posters.

'Now, princess, I know this is not what you are used to, but I hope it serves you well.'

He bent the handle down and pushed the door open to reveal mess, mess and more mess. There was so much stuff, so much stuff she could not even believe it. It was a like a bad nightmare or a severe example of somebody with a hoarding problem. There were stacks of boxes, of records and CDs, of videos and game consoles. It sat like Aladdin's treasure, only not for Aladdin, for a seventeen-year-old boy. Skateboards, footballs, clothes and magazines, books, textbooks, bongos, bin bags, bongs, jigsaws, sleeping bags, tents, guitars, towels, clothes hangers, television

wires, video players, deodorant cans, Homer Simpson figurines,
a bird cage, shit and shit on top of more and more and more shit,
like a dump, like a big fat dump belonging to a bag lady. And,
on top of all that, right at the very, very top, was a skinny little
mattress, a pillow and a sleeping bag. Oh, and a twisted, tangled
nest of fairy lights that were wrapped around the mess pyramid
like an attempt at a recyclable eco-friendly Christmas tree and
extension lead, plugged into extension lead, plugged into exten-
sion lead, plugged into the wall.

'Cool, ain't it?' he smirked.

'Is it always like this in here?' Isabella asked.

'Nah, you divvy, I just made it. Well, not the mess, that's
always there, but look . . .' He ran excitedly up the moun-
tain of crap and hobbled up the mattress.

'See?' he yelped. 'Come and try.
Hope you ain't afraid of
heights!'

'Erm, maybe I should just call a taxi. I think I might just stay in a hotel tonight . . .'

'Look, princess, it's half three in the morning, you've had a crazy day. Just sleep over, okay . . .?' His eyes lit up, grinning. 'Come on,' he beckoned her.

Isabella tongued the roof of her mouth. Then she kicked off her pumps, put her phone in her back pocket and attempted to climb the mess mountain. Aerials, radios, an alarm clock, roller-blades, monopoly, biscuit tins.

Stoo pulled her up by her worthy little paws and there she was. Looking down, in Cornwall, with a stranger, in a room piled sky high with mess, on a mattress, on top of it. Ridiculous. *Ridics.*

'I know it's not St Lucia but it's all right.'

Isabella laughed, and for a moment thought about maybe kissing Stoo. Just for jokes. Then she reminded herself of the fact that he was a pikey.

'Okay, so see you . . . maybe not in the morn-ing because I usually don't wake up till one, but I guess I'll see you when I see you.'

Then he hopped down, as though he did it all the time, waved and turned off the light, leaving Isabella alone under the fairy lights, prac-tically kissing the ceiling. *Oh my God!* she thought. She was like Tinkerbell, and they were her lost boys. And that actually made every-thing seem quite magical.

During the night, as she slept, Stoo let himself into Isabella's makeshift bedroom, tiptoeing, tight-lipped, and stole her coat. Aubin and Wills – *nice*. Downstairs he fumbled through the pockets, MAC receipt after Urban Outfitters receipt and then her bankcard. 'Isabella M. J. Bumpington-Brown.'

'Jesus,' he nudged Bill. 'She weren't lying, look.' He showed the card to his friends.

'I've got this feeling,' he laughed in triumph, 'it's her!'

Woken up by birdsong, Isabella stirred and stretched. What a sleep. My goodness, what a beautiful sleep. Her body felt electric, recharged, reset, alive, buzzing. She let herself slide halfway down the mountain, past a notice board, spray glue, an office chair, and to the window. She pulled back a crack of the scruffy curtain and saw the sweetest bird singing on the sill. She rubbed her eyes and climbed the rest of the way down.

'Mockingbird,' Stoo said as he opened the door, pleased to see Isabella still there.

Isabella slept at Barnaby's house for the next thirteen nights. Separate from the world in their fantasy land of rubbish she became a Snow White (except without the cooking, although she did order them plenty of takeaways). She taught the boys about coffee and they got 'buzzing' off it. She made them watch *The OC* and *Mamma Mia!*. She cut open an avocado and fed Stoo the mushy pear innards. She made them taste *real* chocolate and taught them how to count to ten in French. And they took the piss out of her iPod playlist. Stoo taught Isabella how to eat chips, beans and gravy, the significance of hip-hop and

Family Guy. On the fourteenth day she spent the entire afternoon under the Cornwall rays (well, a sun bed at the back of a local salon, to, you know, at least make it *look* as though she had been away. The deluded woman behind the counter rang the *Sun*, to inform them that Paris Hilton was in town).

Then she got her bag ready and prepared herself to say goodbye to Paulie, to J and to Bill but didn't quite know how she'd manage to leave Stoo.

'I guess I should go now,' she said at the door. Her taxi beeped from the road outside.

'Do you have to?' Stoo asked, unable to look her in the eyes. It was strange seeing her with make-up on. She had been herself when she was with him. 'Take this,' he said and slid his beaded bracelet down his forearm, wrangling it at the wrist, he let it scrape his skin and handed it to her. And she kissed him.

And then the house turned into a magical palace, Isabella transformed into an elegant princess, Paulie, Bill and J became handsome princes, the taxi became a beautiful silver chariot and Stoo . . .

No, Stoo was just Stoo. Happy, gormless and cute, that wicked, charming look in his glittery eyes. The house was obviously still just Barnaby's shitty house, the crap still lodged in the hallway. And of course Paulie, Bill and J were not princes, they were just stoned and ripping the piss out of each other. And the taxi . . . well . . . yes . . . it was still just a taxi with an angry, fat, red-faced man inside it, commenting on the youth of today. Snogging apparently costs time and a half.

You see, a kiss is just a kiss. They didn't need the earth to gobble them up and shoot them to the stars, they didn't need to pretend they were in a film; a handsome, tanned, blonde prince and an anorexic lead role with long, red, tumbling locks. They just needed a charming chav and a lonely toff.

The taxi was waved off. He beeped his horn in rage and sped away. Isabella allowed her prince to carry her suitcase back inside the house, Paulie, Bill and J staring, confused to see her back,

'I have sisters, you know . . .' Isabella giggled as she slid Stoo's bracelet onto her bony wrist, tying it in a knot at the end.

Together they began to shift the mess mountain in the room. If she was going to sleep here more often she would need a space for her wardrobe, darling.

'What's this?' Isabella said, plucking a tiny green bit of gunge off the floor.

'Ugh, it looks like . . . I dunno . . . a squashed pea,' Stoo said.

'Yuck, how long's that been there?'

'I dunno. Throw it away.'

Isabella threw the matted flat pea into the open mouth of the bin bag, the mockingbird squawking outside, the fairy lights twinkling. This was the beginning of her fairy story. That was seriously, ever so, utterly, superbly . . . *random*.

The End.

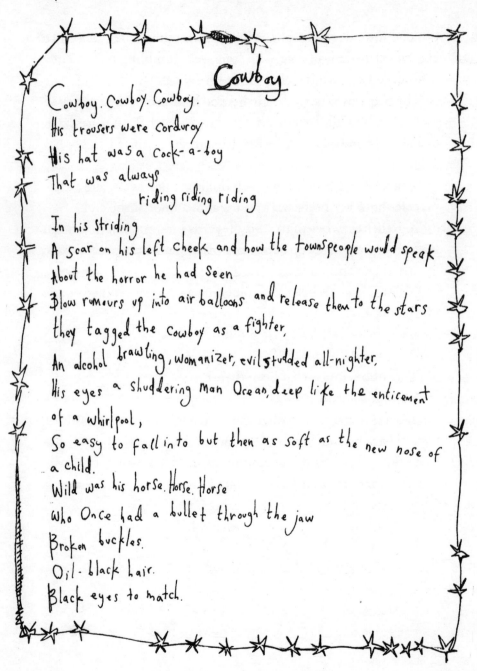

Cowboy

Cowboy. Cowboy. Cowboy.
His trousers were corduroy
His hat was a cock-a-boy
That was always
                riding riding riding

In his striding
A scar on his left cheek and how the townspeople would speak
About the horror he had seen
Blow rumours up into air balloons and release them to the stars
they tagged the cowboy as a fighter,
An alcohol brawling, womanizer, evil studded all-nighter,
His eyes a shuddering man Ocean, deep like the enticement
of a whirlpool,
So easy to fall into but then as soft as the new nose of
a child.
Wild was his horse. Horse. Horse
Who once had a bullet through the jaw
Broken buckles.
Oil-black hair.
Black eyes to match.

But to the cowboy's face the people said
nothing. Nothing. Nothing.
Only in the air was something,
Grew ~~thick~~ thick like mould on old cheese, like a disease
It was thought best by all if the Cowboy were to leave.
Like a widow he'd grieve.
Reap the streets like a follower

Trotting. Trotting. Trotting,
There was nothing he'd think of fonder
Than to just be seen.

Thursday night was crisp and dim
Bit the nails and prised apart the lines in skin.
A barn door ajar
An owner unknown
Made his cockles warm
And his bones groan
Just a little snooze, just a little snooze
The hay bales as beds were lousy

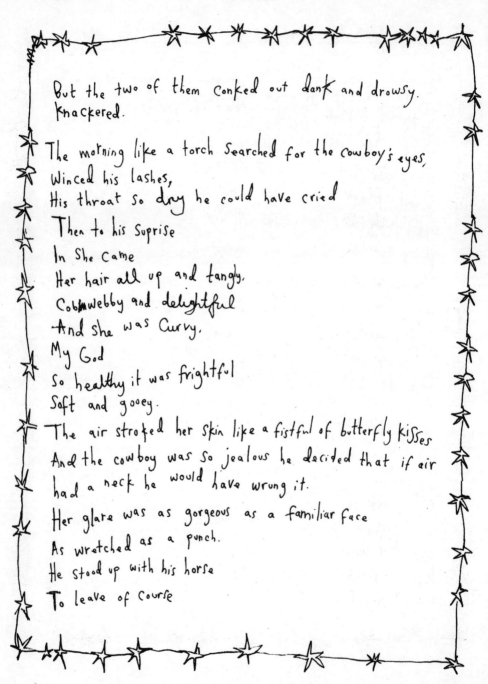

But the two of them conked out dank and drowsy.
Knackered.

The morning like a torch searched for the cowboy's eyes,
Winced his lashes,
His throat so dry he could have cried
Then to his suprise
In she came
Her hair all up and tangly,
Cobwebby and delightful
And she was curvy,
My God
So healthy it was frightful
Soft and gooey.
The air stroked her skin like a fistful of butterfly kisses
And the cowboy was so jealous he decided that if air
had a neck he would have wrung it.
Her glare was as gorgeous as a familiar face
As wretched as a punch.
He stood up with his horse
To leave of course

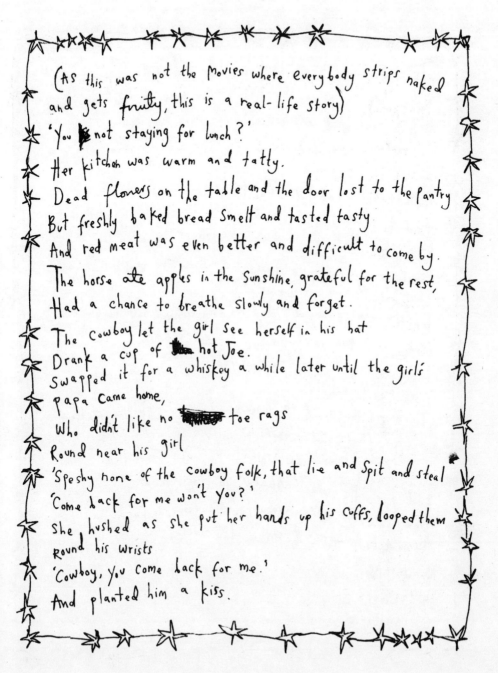

(As this was not the movies where everybody strips naked
and gets fruity, this is a real-life story)
'You ~~are~~ not staying for lunch?'
Her kitchen was warm and tatty.
Dead flowers on the table and the door lost to the pantry
But freshly baked bread smelt and tasted tasty
And red meat was even better and difficult to come by.

The horse ate apples in the sunshine, grateful for the rest,
Had a chance to breathe slowly and forget.

The cowboy let the girl see herself in his hat
Drank a cup of ~~the~~ hot Joe.
Swapped it for a whiskey a while later until the girl's
papa came home,
Who didn't like no ~~things~~ toe rags
Round near his girl
'Speshy none of the cowboy folk, that lie and spit and steal'
'Come back for me won't you?'
She hushed as she put her hands up his cuffs, looped them
round his wrists
'Cowboy, you come back for me.'
And planted him a kiss.

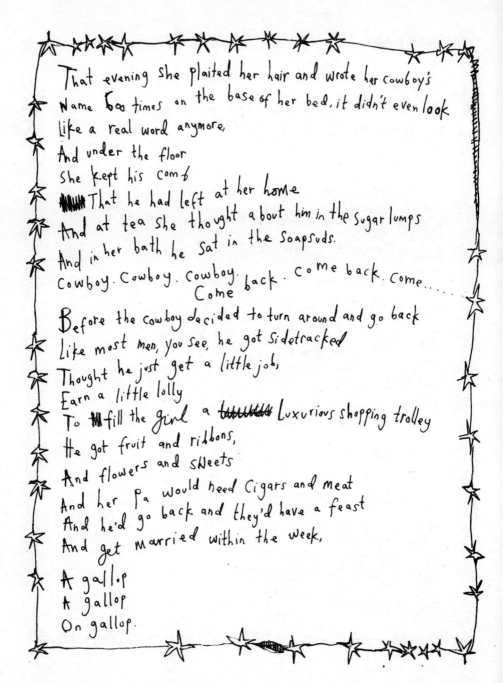

That evening she plaited her hair and wrote her cowboy's
Name ~~600~~ times on the base of her bed, it didn't even look
like a real word anymore,
And under the floor
She kept his comb
~~▪▪▪▪~~ That he had left at her home
And at tea she thought about him in the sugar lumps
And in her bath he sat in the soapsuds.
Cowboy. Cowboy. Cowboy.   Come back. Come.....
                    Come back.

Before the cowboy decided to turn around and go back
Like most men, you see, he got sidetracked
Thought he just get a little job,
Earn a little lolly
To ~~fill~~ fill the ~~girl~~ a ~~tttttttt~~ luxurious shopping trolley
He got fruit and ribbons,
And flowers and sheets
And her pa would need cigars and meat
And he'd go back and they'd have a feast
And get married within the week,

A gallop
A gallop
On gallop.

The night-time crept up its set of stairs
Creaky, uninvited
And the cowboy was losing direction,
His memory was ghastly.
His horse was thirsty
And the branches were being all flirty
Clinging to his clothes, invading his privacy.
Just as he was about to give up
He saw a lamp inside a house
It must have been love.

As the two of them hopped through the brambles,
Making a shambles of their ankles,
They made it through to the clearing
And there the lamp, with the girl he loved so
dearly.
Dressed in his most favourite colours.
Brown and red.
Had he said?

Her eyes peeled back
Lit like gorgeous fruits
She ran down the staircase
And kicked open the door with her boot

Only to see her Cowboy
Face down in the land. Still.
No sign of the horse only in the air chill,
~~and there~~ and there on the windowsill, sat her pa
~~with~~ with a shotgun
'Got that one.'

He grinned,
His sweaty head pinned to the wall,

Laces rotten,
Trodden in trousers like turnips.

A vest,
fat squeezing at the seams

He was a Cannibal's dream
And his daughter,

Only Sixteen,
Ran to her Cowboy, all bloody and horrid
And held him and cried 'I'm sorry. I'm sorry.'
Then she kissed and closed his eyes
And wiped her own in his corduroy.
His body sank
The ground employed,
Her guy.

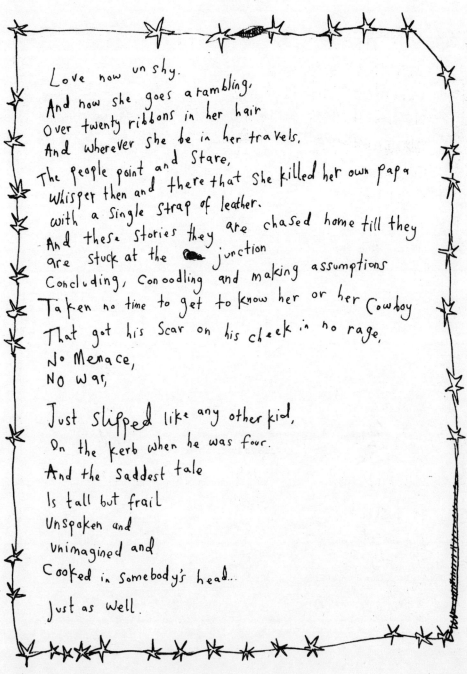

Love now un shy.
And now she goes a rambling,
Over twenty ribbons in her hair
And wherever she be in her travels,
The people point and stare,
Whisper then and there that she killed her own papa
with a single strap of leather.
And these stories they are chased home till they
are stuck at the junction
Concluding, Conoodling and making assumptions
Taken no time to get to know her or her Cowboy
That got his scar on his cheek in no rage,
No Menace,
No War,

Just slipped like any other kid,
On the kerb when he was four.
And the saddest tale
Is tall but frail
Unspoken and
Unimagined and
Cooked in somebody's head...

Just as well.

aitlyn was fat. Not plump, not chubby, or curvy, or voluptuous, or bubbly, or broad, or chunky or big boned. According to her GP, her sister and her sister-in-law, her ex-boss and herself, she was fat. She stood in the mirror and pulled at her flabby rolls, she dragged her tummy forward and inspected the pimply, neglected hunks of fat, she turned around and felt her squashy arse, the magnificent flap that swung in front of her pelvis. The skin was so taut it had gone almost transparent, blue and purple in patches, covered in silvery lines that travelled like silk worms up the shiny rivers of her stomach, her thighs and the two sandbags that hung so effortlessly in that hammock she called a bra.

She had had enough. She plugged in the tea stained, yellowed computer wire into the plug socket and waited in silence for the twelve minutes it took to come to life. The computer finally churned on and the screen lit up the dingy sitting room. After finding her bearings she managed to source the Internet button, her left hand sifting through a sharing bag of cheesy crisps, sprinkling orange fairy dust all over the mouse and keyboard. She licked her fingers wet and typed into the search bar:

too fat to think help

The list of results grew, diet options reloading one after another. Caitlyn recognized the ones she had tried, recommended, gone back to – the ones that nearly killed her, that drove her mad, the ones she hadn't even heard about. And then it appeared:

THE CREAM CAKE DIET
You *can* eat and look great at the same time!
For more information, please call specialist
Dr Ellie Sage on 07834 25590.

'Not on your nelly!' she giggled and reached for the phone. She began to dial, her chest puffing in excitement.

Two days later, she drove her chubby finger on the buzzer of a tall, Victorian building, the brickwork of a once elegant home now littered with graffiti and the papery residue of club night posters. The nearby windows boarded up or punctured with gaping holes, split rubbish bins splattered their insides over the pavement.

'Hello,' she said into the dirty intercom, 'I'm here to see Doctor Ellie Sage.'

The door released and Caitlyn, vulnerable, nervous, stepped inside. The hallway was a dismal cave of a place, taken over by mops, brooms and buckets. The carpet on the stairs was boot trodden and spoiled, blotches of blackened gum and brown coca-cola stains had seeped into the fibres. But the most overwhelmingly disturbing aspect was the smell; a brassy smell that was brutal on the nostrils and the back of the throat. As soon as Caitlyn became aware of the stench, it only got worse and she began to imagine all the vile scenarios that might have produced such an odour. Caitlyn was wary about going further; she put her hand on the banister for support and peeked her head round to get a better look upstairs.

'Hello?' she called up.

No answer.

'Hel-lo?' she tried again.

Nothing.

She walked up the staircase further, her face red and puffy, tears of perspiration dribbling from her forehead and upper lip. She thought about turning around and going home but what would she tell her sister? That she had failed again? Besides, this diet *did* let you eat cream cakes.

She went up another flight of stairs.

'Hello, I called yesterday,' she said into the darkness. 'I'm looking for Doctor Ellie Sage. My name is Caitlyn Anderson . . .?'

She had got to the top of the stairs. She huffed and looked ahead of her. She had reached the landing of what seemed to be a family home, however there was an odd sense of an unsettling sickness that resonated throughout the atmosphere, like a bad taste in the mouth. The air here was clearer but dust particles still danced like puffs of spilt talcum powder and the air was still foggy with the awkward stench of discomfort. If senses were a dial on a compass, all arrows would point to 'YOU HAVE GONE THE WRONG WAY.'

At the top of the landing there was a very small, insignificant door made of cheap wood. The door handle had broken off so a screwdriver hung out of a hole as a makeshift handle. Caitlyn read the lettering:

DR E. SAGE

Caitlyn knocked on the door with her grapefruit-sized fist and awaited a response.

'Hello,' she said. 'Is anybody there?'

The smell was quite unbearable as she stood waiting for the door to open, the cocktail of awfulness included sewage, blocked drains, burning hair, chalk and that same overriding smell of metal. Caitlyn decided to leave and started to make her way back down the staircase.

'Miss Anderson?' a northern voice called after her.

Caitlyn froze.

'Miss Anderson, are you here for your appointment?'

Caitlyn was a bit embarrassed. 'Sorry, I thought you weren't ... perhaps ... in. I knocked but ... yes ... here I am,' she warbled nervously as blood sneaked up her neck, flooding her large face.

Dr E. Sage was small and mousey; she had long, dark hair and her parting was owned by a set of orange roots. Her pale, almost vampyric skin lit up the dark corridor like a beacon.

'Would you like to come upstairs?'

The office was just as grim as the rest of the building. Caitlyn felt disturbed slightly by the yellow-tinged wallpaper, the damp circles that swamped the ceiling and the spiders' webs that joined the curtains to the beaten-up bookcase.

'Take a seat, Miss Anderson.' Doctor Sage directed Caitlyn to a battered swivel chair, the cushion was moth eaten, yellow sponge bled out of the holes. 'I believe you're here for the diet. Where did you hear about us?' the doctor asked whilst filling in a form. The biro she wrote with was so badly chewed the end had come off exposing the refill cylinder.

'Erm . . . on the Internet.'

The doctor continued to scribble.

'Now for the measuring. Please stand.'

The doctor was instructive and forward; she pushed back her chair and made her way over to Caitlyn.

'Arms up.' With a tape measure she began measuring Caitlyn's clumpy arms. 'Very good,' she muttered under her breath. 'Part your legs now please, Miss Anderson.' She got onto her knees and measured Caitlyn's ankles, calves and thighs. 'They've been under a lot of stress, Miss Anderson. Looks like you have come just in time. Your chest please.' The doctor began behind Caitlyn, vulnerable, sick with embarrassment, and moved round, her left hand still behind Caitlyn's back and then brought both hands to the front, over Caitlyn's breasts to measure.

Caitlyn knew it wasn't a good idea, but she looked down to check the measurement – she no longer knew what was big and what was gigantic. Her eyes chased the inches until she became distracted by the doctor's fingernails; rooted in each nail lay a thick heavy slug of grime and dirt, and perfectly embedded in each nail was a frame of what looked like dried blood. Caitlyn swallowed hard and, not wanting to make her discomfort obvious, looked forwards again and locked eyes, accidentally, with Doctor Sage.

'Satisfactory for you, Miss Anderson?' Doctor Sage asked.

'I think so . . . yes, quite, thank you.' Caitlyn forced a smile that made her want to scream. The doctor must have eaten something messy, chocolate cake perhaps? It happened.

'Step onto the scales please, Miss Anderson,' the doctor demanded.

'I'd rather wait till next time if that's okay, it's just that I . . .'

'Do you take weight loss seriously, Miss Anderson?' Doctor Sage tensed her square jaw and shook the head of the scales. 'We must weigh you otherwise we cannot test our progress, and that's what we want isn't it? Progress?' The doctor's lips pulled in like the opening of a drawstring purse.

Caitlyn nodded and slid off her flip-flops before stepping onto the scales. She had not been on a set of scales in over a year and knew by the feel of the clothes she could still just about squash in to that she was at her biggest ever. Doctor Sage wrote down some numbers and nodded. Caitlyn watched a moth obsess over a light bulb.

'You must also take these every day, twice a day.' The doctor handed Caitlyn a box of beautifully made cupcakes, they were like something out of a magazine. They sat proud, oversized, with cake sponge pouring over the paper casing. Each had a shiny, ruby red cherry sitting perfectly on the top of the finely iced topping. They were the most wonderful, delightful cup-cakes Caitlyn had ever come across.

'You having a laugh?' Caitlyn giggled.

'Twice a day, every day,' Doctor Sage confirmed.

'They are so beautiful, I don't want to ruin them by eating them,' Caitlyn laughed.

'Do you take weight loss seriously, Miss Anderson?' Doctor Sage growled.

'Yes Doctor,' Caitlyn nodded.

'Then please sign this contract, here and then here.' Doctor Sage handed Caitlyn the contract and a second mauled biro. 'Do you have the cash?'

'Yes.' Caitlyn anxiously handed over the purple wad and signed the contract; it was only a signature, wasn't it?

'See you next week then Caitlyn.' The doctor snatched back the contract, opened up the door by the sharp end of the screwdriver and let Caitlyn, who could not quite digest what she had just experienced, go.

When Caitlyn arrived home that day, she opened up the box of cakes and marvelled at their beauty. They looked even better in her own home than the stomach turning office of Doctor Ellie Sage. She took a picture of them on her camera phone and sent it to her niece and nephew. She picked up the first cake; the weight of it was perfect, and she could feel just by holding it that it was baked to perfection. With her sausage-shaped finger she scooped a load of the sugary icing onto the tip and carried it to her mouth like a truck offloading at a barge. It tasted like angel dust as it dissolved onto her slippery tongue leaving just granules of delightful sugar. She peeled back the edge of the paper and sunk her wardrobe-sized mouth into the fluffy cake. It tasted like a Sunday afternoon, like vanilla bean taken straight from the pod, like sleeping in new pyjamas and ironed bed sheets. It tasted like falling in love, like jumping on a trampoline, like laughing so hard your belly aches, like almond and sugar and sweetness beyond anything you have ever known. It was divine. Each bite was swallowed gorgeously, the mixture sat in her belly, pregnating her beaming body with a placebo of energy and happiness; this was the best day ever.

Caitlyn ate normally throughout the rest of the day. She watched television, put the washing out and brought it back in a few hours later before deciding to have her second cake. This time she sat down to eat it – she knew how to enjoy this one properly. She had read an article once, where this hot guy only liked sleeping with big women, they don't get it often enough so when they do, they really go for it, was his reasoning. *Git*, she thought. She slowly unwrapped the casing, as if undressing the man from the article, she imagined unbuttoning his smarmy shirt, pulling it off his chunky self-righteous shoulders as she plunged, for a second time, into the cupcake. Her nose tingled with the sugar rush. Fabulous. That taste rippling on her tongue made her see herself jumping into the sea in a bikini she looked great in, she could taste the cinnamon on the roof of her mouth swallowing her, tippling her upside down, she saw herself sipping a cocktail on a balcony of an expensive hotel, the sun on her hair, laughing hysterically as the exotic flavours exploded in her mouth; mango fruit, pineapple, coconut, saffron and love and love and love. She flipped her head back onto the sofa and indulged. The phone rang, but Caitlyn let it ring out.

That night, whilst in bed, Caitlyn dreamt of the woods, she pictured herself being chased by rabid wolves. The wolves were angry and frantic, they snarled and they spat. Their ears darted back in fury as they nipped at the back of Caitlyn's heels, snapping at the back of her dress; she ran to the trees and tried to climb but she was too unfit, too big, too bulky, too heavy to pull herself up. She tried with more effort but it was no good, she kept falling further and further, as each finger came away from the branch she had gripped onto, she started to fall into the open dribbling mouths of the wolves and then . . . she woke sweating, breathing heavily, panicking. And then the most awful pain struck in her stomach, it was a sharp stabbing pain that made her sit up in surprise. In agony, doubled over, she made her way to the bathroom and sat down on the toilet. She hadn't even sat for more than a moment when she realized she was going to vomit. Still sitting on the toilet she leant over the sink and allowed herself to throw up. Within moments she began to be violently sick, her food came up but then so did a vast amount of blood. All she could do was vomit. As it continued to come up, the blood became almost blue, it spiralled down the plughole and splattered onto the taps and the tiles like the evidence of toothpaste a parent looks for to check that their messy child has brushed their teeth. The spots like freckles, no like chocolate chips, disgusting, food was disgusting wasn't it? The thought of the food made her throw up even harder, furiously, she didn't want to be fat, she didn't want to be like this. She was sick of herself and that made her more sick, she was sick of the sly comments of passers-by and that made her even more sick, she was sick of the way people pulled their chairs in at restaurants when she walked past them, when people always felt the urge to tell her she had lost weight when she hadn't, she was sick, sick, sick. Caitlyn's eyes filled with water, she spat out the last metallic taste from her mouth and was glad it was over. With bleach, she scrubbed the sink white again, brushed her teeth and went back to bed, exhausted. The pain had gone.

When she woke up, Caitlyn put the previous night's occurrence down to stress. She made herself a cup of tea and ate her first daily cupcake; the first bite was even better than she had remembered. Like a drug this time she bit, hard, aching for it, and how did it feel and taste so good? She saw herself at the bottom of a candyfloss machine spinning, pink and frothy like the head on a cappuccino and lovely and light, she was so lovely and light, like the shoe of a slight ballerina. She saw herself smart and smug like the red heart on a jam tart on a picnic blanket. And then as though she were a cage of doves, the door was unlocked and how she flew freely, innocent and gone, away, and out and into ecstasy.

However, that night again the same thing happened. Caitlyn woke to a sharp stabbing pain. Already familiar with the symptoms, she ran to the bathroom and allowed herself to throw up. Blood came out again, but this time followed by what appeared to be chunks of meat. When Caitlyn had finished throwing up she looked closer at the meat. She hadn't eaten anything meaty in the last couple of days; she picked a piece up and held it in her hand, wiping the stringy snot off, inspecting it closer. Must be from a while ago, she decided. Meat can carry in a human's body for up to seven years, and this was a big old body. She picked up the cleaning cloth and, as before, scrubbed the sink, the taps, and the bathroom mirror. The sockets of her eyes were leathery with smoky brown patches underneath and her mouth was encrusted in a reddish residue, she looked like a monster, she splashed her face with water.

The next morning Caitlyn invited herself to visit Doctor Ellie Sage. She pressed on the buzzer and asked, as before, to see the doctor. The door released and Caitlyn let herself into the dingy hallway. As well as the junk that was there before, some other odd bits of crap had moved into the rotten hall: a bicycle and a number of different sized suitcases, spilling over with clothes that looked dirty and stained. The same disturbing smell haunted the shabby corridor. Caitlyn bumbled up the staircase as fast as she could and then she knocked on the door with the screwdriver.

'Hello, Doctor Sage, it's me, Caitlyn . . .'

Caitlyn waited outside the door. She could still taste the blood in her gums. Her stomach still panged with a chalky acidic ache. Eventually the door opened.

'Good morning Miss Anderson. Please, come in.'

Doctor Ellie Sage's professionalism seemed strange in comparison to the squat that the office was laid in. Caitlyn followed the doctor in.

'How is the medication working for you, Miss Anderson?' the doctor asked, sizing Caitlyn up.

'Well, that's just it, the cakes are lovely, really they are, but I keep getting these pains, I'm not sure if I'm allergic to something in the ingre—'

'Yes, that's normal. Anything else?' the doctor asked.

'Well, yes, actually. I've been vomiting,' Caitlyn said shyly.

'Yes, and anything else?' Dr Sage looked vacant.

'Vomiting blood.' Caitlyn shuddered at the memory of the chunks of meat that had come up. Flashbacks of meat, separating slow and gloopy in long sticky hunks, she pictured the body of the dead rat that kid in her primary school had dissected and stapled to the notice board. The insides were so grey, why were they so grey?

'Good.' The doctor began fishing through a filing cabinet.

'Good?' Caitlyn asked. 'How is that good? That's not normal.'

'It means the medication is working. Are you eating normally?' the doctor asked and made some notes.

'Yes, it's just the vomit, it's terrible and then yesterday . . . last night, some meat . . . it looked like meat anyway, came up and . . .'

'That would have been your kidney, Miss Anderson.'

'Pardon me?' Caitlyn's face bleached, her knees jellied.

'Onto the scales please, Miss Anderson.'

'No, excuse me, kidney? I'm sorry?'

'It's all part of the medication.'

'But that's my kidney. I'm sorry, I'm not quite sure I know what's going on, excuse me, I need to get out of here.' Caitlyn pushed past the doctor who gripped her chubby arm.

'Do you take weight loss seriously, Miss Anderson?' she said staring her cold eyes into Caitlyn's, the whites of the doctor's fingers began to show.

Caitlyn searched for an answer and nodded, stepping calmly onto the scales as if somewhere in those rounded folds of flab, a bone had been struck and it hurt.

'Very good. You have lost six pounds since the first time you met me. Do you understand that that is nearly half a stone?'

'Of course I understand. That's incredible, a miracle, but I've eaten the same . . . how can that be?' Caitlyn's colour came back to her cheeks.

'You see, keep this up and you could be losing up to two stone per week. That's eight stone in a month!'

'Oh my goodness, I could be my ideal weight in a month and a bit!' Caitlyn cheered, clapping her globe-sized hands together.

'You see, this is why this diet is the best diet; it's the only diet worth doing. We also promise that the weight will not be regained.'

'But that's all I lose isn't it? Just a kidney?'

'What do you mean?' the doctor frowned.

'That's the only organ, that you know . . . will . . . you know?'

'Be deposited? No, everything will go.' The doctor ended the conversation, jotted a few lines down on her clipboard and smiled shortly, as though this were a normal doctor's check-up.

'Sorry?' Caitlyn stopped.

'Yes, it's the medication, that's all you need now.'

'Is this safe?' Caitlyn asked the doctor.

'Do you take weight loss seriously, Miss Anderson? I mean, by all means, go to your GP, get her to put you on a calorie-controlled diet and see how far that gets you. Or stick with the Cream Cake Diet and watch the weight slip off.' The doctor made more notes, her eyes refusing to meet Caitlyn's.

'Okay, well, I guess I'll be back next week.' Caitlyn acted on the impulse to leave and removed herself from the strange office.

'Yes. See you then.'

Caitlyn stopped by the shopping centre on her way home. She wandered through the clothes shops, gazing at the clothes that she had never managed to fit into. Halterneck tops, mini skirts, boob tubes, tight dresses, knee-high boots, a bikini. She stopped off at Gregg's and got her usual – two cheese and onion pasties, a sausage roll and a yum yum – and told her usual lie at the counter to make herself feel better about eating too much. 'Kids, eh?' she tutted. 'Mouths to feed.' The lady behind the counter smiled politely.

At home, Caitlyn went to the cupboard and got out her cream cakes, they looked as wonderful as the day she had received them. It was a bit worrying, she thought, the way they didn't decay, they were always perfect each and every time she looked at them. They were like props, stage cakes or something. Caitlyn thought back to an old friend that used to help her with will power, who told her that the worst foods were those that didn't rot. Fresh was the best way to eat; food with a long shelf life was stacked full with preservatives and e-numbers. Caitlyn knew this, but only a few weeks left, she thought, what harm could it really do? She ate her two daily cakes one after the other, popping them in like small truffles. Wow, she really was like a lady of leisure, she was like the women in the Galaxy adverts, lying back, breaking off chocolate as though it were cubes of air and the way they did it with such bitchiness, really rubbing it in, it was like punching a thousand women in the face. And glory, glory, glory, sweetness, she folded, melted, rippled, swam into a sea of sweet syrup, went underneath and never wanted to come out again.

Caitlyn began to anticipate bedtime as she started to feel sleepy on the sofa. She made her way up to bed and felt the same agonizing pain, earlier than usual, her insides were churning. She ran to the toilet and vomited. Blood gushed out of her mouth as though she were a fire breather; the mineral iron flavour burnt her throat, tore shreds of the inner fleshy bit in her neck as though she were swallowing squares of Velcro. Tears ran down her face. Caitlyn cursed herself. How had she let her body get so big? Where was her discipline? She threw up more and more. In moments, adrenaline had full control of her body and she was rushing off of the experience, enjoying the feeling of punishing herself, like picking a big scab, feeling morbidly pleased when her intestine began tunnelling its way out of her mouth, snaking its way into the toilet like an overgrown Cumberland sausage. Caitlyn's eyes widened, she thought she was dreaming. When her body stopped convulsing, she lay on the bathroom floor, dark spots of blood on the rug, an orangey stained bib of blood on her nightdress and all round her nose and mouth. She felt satisfied.

The week went by fast and each night the same thing happened. Caitlyn was feeling worse and worse inside. Everything ached; she could no longer go out as everything hurt too much, nothing was comfortable. Still, she ate the cakes religiously as she

rapidly began to resemble a set of bagpipes. Her empty skeleton
rattled like a broken birdcage. But still her fat wrinkled around
the frame like half-cooked bread, heavy and sloppy. She moved
like a slug, slow. She got a taxi to see Doctor Sage who helped
her up the smelly rotten staircase with a set of sticks.

'You look great!' Doctor Sage hissed.

Caitlyn did not.

She had lost: two kidneys, one intestine, an appendix, one
womb, one bowel and a bladder. Her face was the colour of off
milk; charcoal rings circled her sunken dreary eyes that looked
tired and haunted. Her hair was coarse and frazzled; her teeth
were blood stained and grey.

'How much weight have I lost?' Caitlyn got straight to the
point, barging her way through the flimsy door.

'Now, let's hold on. How do you feel?' Doctor Sage asked.

'How. Much. Weight. Have. I. Lost?' Caitlyn gripped the
doctor's desk aggressively.

'Make your way to the scales if you are able, Miss Anderson.'

Caitlyn used her arms to slowly launch herself up and sloped
towards the scales. She took two steps and then fell face for-
wards into a soggy heap on the office floor.

Doctor Sage took her mobile out of her pocket and dialled a
number. 'Hello, Gregory? She's ready.'

Caitlyn's body was moved by a makeshift crane made of canvas,
springs and odd bicycle pieces. It hauled up the entirety of
Caitlyn's now modest structure and held her in mid air. Next
the crane was pushed on wheels that squeaked un-oiled yelps by

Doctor Ellie Sage, Doctor Gregory Wimpole and his assistant, his younger sister, Rosie, to the next room along.

This room had been made to seem clinical. However, the white-washed walls, no matter how whitewashed they were, would never manage to conceal that this was once a child's bedroom. Seventies choo-choo trains and helicopters could be made out underneath the watery white blanket over them. The furniture in this smaller room was minimal, a simple operating table with an improvised lighting system overhead made up of torches, odd bulbs and L.E.D lamps.

The crane clumsily angled Caitlyn's droopy body onto the table, where it was met by Doctor Gregory Wimpole and released from the harness. Rosie immediately removed Caitlyn's flip-flops, her necklace and the tiny gold sleepers from her earlobes, these all went into an old Woolworth's bag and Caitlyn's initials were scribbled onto a slice of already torn-off masking tape and then dumped to one side. Rosie then unbuttoned Caitlyn's curtain of a dress until she lay sprawled with the dress around her, simply as a swaddled frame, that miserable heap of a body.

The once white bra and knickers were browning, dirty and unwashed. The sustainability of basic things such as cleanliness and personal hygiene had gone out of the window when this diet had come into play. Nothing mattered more than those cream cakes and this diet. Rosie was instructed to cut off Caitlyn's underwear with a pair of scissors; she did so with sloppiness and disgust. The garments were put into the carrier bag.

Doctor Ellie Sage sanitized Caitlyn's body with alcohol from a canister full of cloudy fluid; it flooded over the dead woman's body like a rumbling tsunami washing out a landscape. Doctor Wimpole plunged a scalpel into Caitlyn's chest and tore downwards cutting through the skin like those cheese wires that the deli man has at the back of Sainsbury's. The carcass gaped open like a giant gash revealing only the colour red, split like a tear in a beanbag. As many of the organs were now missing, removing the rest was simple; each organ was taken out messily with little strategy and was then discarded onto the dated brown carpet. Within moments blood circled the unwanted tool. Welcoming it to the grossness of the house that had guilt in every drop of cement, every inch of wallpaper and on every fibre.

When Caitlyn was finally completely gutted she was nothing more than a dishevelled balloon, her nimble bones seemed so frail, how did they carry that humungous weight?

The crane was then fastened around her body and she was picked up a further time and moved into the third and final room. The evening was peeping through the window. She was covered in salt, put into a waxy body bag and zipped up. The door was shut on her; Rosie put the bag of her belongings, including her coat and dress into a suitcase.

The doctors and their assistant went down the distasteful staircase to their higgledy piggledy kitchen where they boiled a kettle and prepared for dinner. They ate microwave meals and drank sweet, milky tea, none of them even thought to wash their hands. They slept in what used to be a sitting room in uncomfortable single orphanage iron beds that made tinging noises throughout the night. They slept well, as always.

At around 4 a.m. a transit van arrived at the back door of the horror house, a tall masculine woman with a pretty face rat-a-tat-

tatted on the back door and, with the help of Doctor Wimpole, carried Caitlyn's body to the van where she was thrown in and driven away for good. The suitcase with her belongings inside was transferred to the hallway with the other cases, the bicycle, and the mops that were never used. Caitlyn was driven to Oxford. She was stuffed with apple and rosemary, with mint, onion and sausage meat. She was basted in extra-extra-virgin oil and pricked with tiny crosses on her pre-salted skin then charged with garlic cloves, capers and sliced black olive rings. Her nails were removed with a tiny scalpel and were thrown in the fire – as simple as throwing seashells back into the sea. Her teeth were kept as they were valuable and could be sold on; there was money to be made in the lucrative teeth business. Caitlyn's eyeballs were de-socketed and a blind maid then curled her hair with hot tongs. She did an excellent job and placed a crown of dried roses upon Caitlyn's fickle head. An orange sat inside her mouth for decoration and to keep her meat moist. She was cooked for twenty-six hours in an outdoor stone oven. The neighbours admired the smell and fantasized about having cooked something as wonderful themselves.

Roast Caitlyn was served to a table of eighteen with goose fat potatoes, honeyed carrots and shallots, pancetta and chilli cabbage and a red wine sauce. They carved her from the bottom up, tore crusty bread over her ankles and ridiculed her podgy face, mimicking the orange that sat inside her mouth.

Whilst her heart beat in a suitcase somewhere far away, pleading hopelessly.

The End

Pandora's Box

The box sits on the mantle,
I move it to the stairs.
I sit with it till the sun goes down
and when it comes up again.
I bite my nails off,
roll them into circular shells.
I drink three coffees
and finish off last night's dinner as well.
I'm wasting time.
I cannot sleep.
I cannot sleep.
Only sit by it and wait
the key burning ~~into~~ into my palm
and chase my fate away.
The kitten cries for milk...
I deny it—
I cannot remember the last time I fed her.
She leaves, walks out on me in a huff.
She's had enough.
She thinks I'm sick.
She's a bitch.

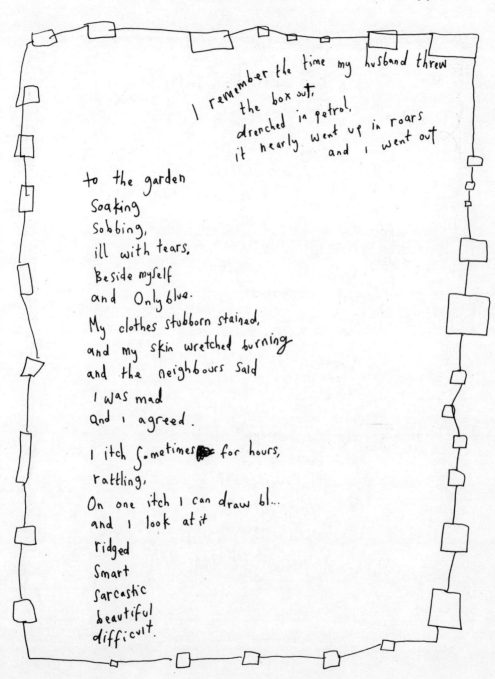

I remember the time my husband threw
the box out,
drenched in petrol,
it nearly went up in roars
and I went out

to the garden
Soaking
Sobbing,
ill with tears,
Beside myself
and Only blue.
My clothes stubborn stained,
and my skin wretched burning
and the neighbours said
I was mad
And I agreed.

I itch sometimes for hours,
rattling,
On one itch I can draw bl...
and I look at it
ridged
Smart
sarcastic
beautiful
difficult.

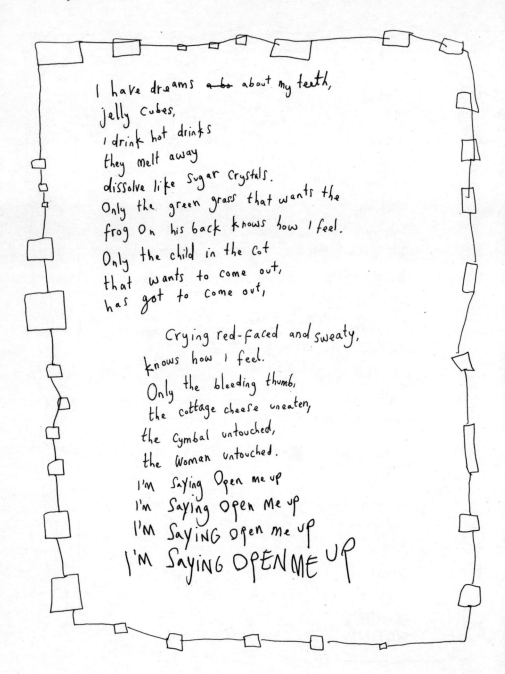

I have dreams ~~a bo~~ about my teeth,
jelly cubes,
I drink hot drinks
they melt away
dissolve like sugar crystals.
Only the green grass that wants the
frog on his back knows how I feel.
Only the child in the cot
that wants to come out,
has got to come out,

      Crying red-faced and sweaty,
knows how I feel.
Only the bleeding thumb,
the cottage cheese uneaten,
the cymbal untouched,
the woman untouched.
I'm saying open me up
I'm saying open me up
I'M SAYING open me up
I'M SAYING OPEN ME UP

The reservoir,
tangling on its own
and the birds on the electricity cables.
Hoping for a flash.

> The house
> I wander in a maze,
> urgent,
> gaze at the garden,
> an elepha....
> You're hiding
> I love finding you
> I <u>always</u> find you don't
> I?
> Tell them how I always find you.

I cannot keep a secret,
I'm gasping,
Shutter mouthed
and look at the size of my eyes.
Whatever you do
whatever you do
whatever you do
whatever you do - This is all you can do...
but a little bit inside
of us...

and the dirt
and grit and
it hurts me,
Split like ✳
    the smile on a peapod,
and i rot
as shiny as a silver apple
and those maggots
and those worms,
laughing
vgly.
The lid flaps Open,
the crow wing,
    bloody terror.
Now i see you
Malice
despair
disease
cruelty
Cruel
and all over like ▬▬ Eve,
my fingernails ✳
in bits
and the evidence
on my sleeve.

THAT SHREWD LITTLE FOX

A tale of betrayal, deceit and wretchedness

In a kingdom so great and enchanting lived the rich. Here they wined and dined and gossiped and worked and never wondered about the poor people of the villages surrounding their kingdom. These people they never thought about were so poor that they had to live in the forest in shacks made with their bare hands. It had been a tough year for the peasants, the rich people had not needed the minimal work that they usually required each month, for a snoot could never get his or her hands dirty, it was much easier to pay the poor to do a spot of painting, bake fresh loaves every morning, repair a set of shoe soles – and so times were very difficult. Plus, a drought that year had meant many of the relied-on crops had not sprung, and without crops food was scarce, there were no rabbits nibbling on the corn and no rabbits meant no meat. The rich people suffered only mildly from the drought, once in a while a small query would be thrown into conversation around an awkward, oversized dinner table to break the silence,

'How are your crops doing, Sir Everett?'

The poor people had to make do with anything they could find: bruised apples, bitter blackberries, stale oats. It was a very miserable time.

One day, the trumpet was heard – it was the foxhunters on their monthly gallivant. The clunking heavy gallops of the horses could be heard from the peasants' village, followed by the snivelling snarls of the bloodthirsty scent hounds. The peasants each went into their homes and brought out nets and rope – all hoped on catching a fox for themselves; fox was still meat, and they were hungry peasants after all. The pounding hoofs became louder and louder, a grumble in the earth vibrated like the beginning of an earthquake. The peasants fought with their families over who was the most agile, who was fastest on their feet, who was bravest. They waited.

And so the foxes came.

Mostly red foxes, not many, sixteen perhaps, threw themselves into the peasants' village. They ran fast with no direction or knowledge of what they were doing, their yellow eyes bloodshot and rattling around like the eyes of madmen. Bumbling peasants put out their nets; one was caught, then escaped, the energy was too much to be trapped in a single net, shame.

The next family caught it, the same fox.

Unbelievable.

The fox bit the mother's arm.

OUTRAGEOUS!

What a liberty!

She let out a squawking cry, but still dinner would be served.

Another shack caught a larger fox, two big hands of a big brother fell onto the fox's back and squashed him into the ground. Result.

The family cheered, some clapped hands, and the fox was brought into the shack howling for his freedom.

Four out of the sixteen were caught.

Eugene and Mary, a young couple who lived in the forest, had caught a smaller male fox.

Gosh were they happy – catching a fox earns you a little respect from neighbouring shacks. Mary was so proud of Eugene; he caught that damn fox in a second, now they wouldn't go hungry. She prepared a fire the moment the fox was brought inside and was already deciding what herbs to stuff him with.

'He is a small brute,' Eugene sighed.

'Yes, but there are only the two of us,' Mary said. 'What shall we do him as? Hot pot? Stew? Pie?' Mary's pretty mouth began dreaming of devouring the fox already.

'No, no, let's have him as he is,' Eugene grinned.

'Let's see him then.' Mary asked.

Eugene had the fox in an upturned wicker basket.

'Close the door then, Mary,' Eugene instructed and slowly lifted the basket and there, cowering in the corner, was the sweetest, bug-eyed, little, fluffy fox you ever did see. The red of his fur was glossy and healthy, his pricked perfect ears, instead of darting forward, were floppy. His soft paws cuddled his tiny body that trembled with fear.

'Oh, Eugene!' Mary put her hand to her mouth.

'Mary, come on now . . .' Eugene stopped as he could see Mary was softening like butter on hot potato.

'But look at the poor thing, he's frozen, he's so afraid. We can't eat him. Please?' Mary begged her husband.

'Mary! This is the way the world works, rabbits are cute and fluffy and you eat them, don't you?' Eugene was getting frustrated. But, in a weird way, Mary did have a point: the fox was sweet. However, he was hungry, it would just be stupid to not eat him.

'I want to look after him!' Mary said. 'I want to raise him as though he were mine, and if you kill him, you will just have to kill me too!'

Eugene wanted to argue, but was just too hungry, and so it was: the fox lived. Eugene would just have to go hunting for rabbits and badgers during the night to feed them now. The fox was lifted from underneath the basket. He was ever so timid; his little body shook in fright as Mary lifted him up to her chest and stroked him, he soon began to purr, like a cat.

'See, you love me, don't you?' Mary presumed in a baby voice. 'And I love you. We love each other, don't we, Kissykins?' Mary stroked his back, and patted his bushy tail, 'Oh, he has the softest tail!'

Then she decided to bathe him in warm, soapy water. He looked even sweeter wet, his soppy ears went flat and soggy and his eyelashes pronged into spiky forks. Eugene wasn't happy; this fox could have lice or diseases. It was quite disgusting actually, the way she was acting, it was as though she had been drugged. Eugene began to strop around the shack, slamming pots and pans, smacking his feet onto the stone floor with his boots, making it clear he was annoyed. But Mary wasn't the least bit interested.

'You are just adorable,' Mary cooed, pulling the fox out of the basin and laying him onto a towel. The wet fox shivered and then shook his body, splashing flecks of sogginess everywhere. Eugene winced.

'Mary, that's my towel!' Eugene cried.

'It's not going anywhere,' Mary hissed. 'I thought you were going hunting anyway – we're hungry.'

'Who's hungry?' Eugene asked, relentlessly furious.

'Kissykins and me.'

'Kissykins?' Eugene asked.

'Are you deaf?' Mary fired back.

'For God's sake,' Eugene took his knife and left, slamming the door behind him.

'He's mean, isn't he?' Mary said to Kissykins in a baby voice. 'We don't like him, do we?'

And to that Kissykins shook his head in response.

The sun was beginning to come up when Eugene returned from hunting with a badger, a rooster and two rabbits. He had done a wonderful job but when he opened the door to his shack he was horrified to see Mary snuggling up to the fox in their marital bed.

'Mary!' he shouted. 'How dare you put the fox in our bed? I allowed you to keep him, but this is too far. What is wrong with you?'

'No, Eugene, it is you that has something wrong, you insensitive pig. Now, seeing as though you have woken up Kissykins and me you can jolly well put the hot water on.'

Eugene ignored his dozy wife and began undressing, his blood-spattered hands needed cleaning, but oh, how he wanted to ring that little fox's neck; he would do a good job of it too.

The next couple of days were unbearable for Eugene. Kissykins now wore a bonnet and often held a rattle that Mary had made him from dried sickle seed. Eugene did worry. Occasionally, Mary would have a scrape on her face, a set of scratches on her arms and legs and teeth marks on her neck – it was apparent that Mary's friend wasn't quite as gentle as she had thought. And Mary was beginning to look different, uglier somehow. Her hair was knotty and wiry and she smelt unclean; she had not changed her clothes since Kissykins had arrived. Eugene loved his wife very much, and did not want their married life to turn into a disaster. Each and every night, Eugene would be forced to sleep in the rocking chair as Mary and that damned fox would boot him out, claiming that there wasn't enough space for three. Eugene had had several outbursts, but Mary would not budge. Kissykins was here to stay.

So Eugene tried a new tactic. As though they were a mother and father he got a babysitter for Kissykins – a local spinster named Edna who lived across the forest. She would look after Kissykins for nothing, she needed the company and was flattered to be asked. Eugene would prepare a meal of roast rabbits, he would marinate them in rosemary and thyme, and he would cover them in flat leaves and fungi and serve them up with turnips and beetroot in a chive and parsley sauce. They would drink elderflower wine and make love and forget about that shrewd little fox for good.

Mary was delighted when she walked into the shack to see it spic and span, the candles lit, and a makeshift table with their places set out. The wild thistle in the centre made the shack appear almost elegant.

'This is extraordinary,' Mary beamed in delight as the food was brought to her place. She cut the perfectly cooked rabbit, and chewed and swallowed and drank and chewed and swallowed and drank and chewed and swallowed and drank and chewed and swallowed and drank and chewed and swallowed and drank and chewed and swallowed and drank and chewed and swallowed and drank until she couldn't hold it in any longer.

'Where is Kissykins?'

This was the straw that broke the camel's back; up went the table, the rabbit thrown in the bin, the thistle went up into the air, the vase smashed into a thousand tiny pieces. Eugene punched his head with his fists in fury.

'That bloody fox! Can't we just have an evening alone?'

'I was just wondering where he was, that was all.'

'Yes, but it's constant. Besides, look at you – you're covered in scratches and teeth marks.'

'He does less damage to me than what you're doing to my home!' Mary screeched.

'It's OUR home!' Eugene shouted as he kicked the watering can.

Mary hid behind the rocking chair. She knew Eugene would never hurt her, and she would just wait until his silly sulk had calmed down.

'Fine, do you know what? I'll go and get him, if you want him so bad. I shall go and get him for you. Will that make you happy? Will it? Will that just make you the happiest princess in the world?'

Then he opened the door and charged out into the open, dark forest, all that could be heard was his angry grizzles and shouts. He was not a happy man.

Eugene knocked onto the spinster's door. No answer. He knocked again, harder this time.

'Edna? Edna?' he began. 'Edna? Are you inside?'

The shack was silent, ivy swamped the front, and holly bushes giggled secretively either side of the door.

'Edna, it's Eugene. I'm here to collect Kis—' He stopped. It made him feel physically sick to say that stupid fox's name. 'Edna, are you in?' he called and knocked again.

Edna had one window at the back of her shack, a little box-sized window that was usually covered with a tea towel. Eugene scrambled over the plants and shrubbery and got to the window;

the tea towel was not there. Eugene put his head straight into the shack.

'Edna? Edna?' he called. And then he saw what looked like a foot. Eugene focussed his eyes and re-focussed again, yes it was a foot, had Edna collapsed? He ran round to the front of the shack and held both hands onto the doorknob and pushed, with all his weight, the door open. After forcing himself inside he was terrified. Edna lay in pieces on the floor of her tiny home. Her head was covered in blood and scratches, teeth marks and bruises on her calves and ankles, some of her body was missing, some had already been devoured as in places, bare bone shone like glow sticks. Her clothes were a puddle of blood and something that smelt like fox piss.

'Oh God, Mary!' Eugene scrambled out of the spinster's house, did a Hail Mary, ran towards his own shack, right across the forest, in his mind visualizing all the wretched things that vile beast could be doing to his wife. What if he was too late? What if he had already ripped her apart? *Ignorant, foolish idiot,* he thought. How stupid he had been! That fox is a wild creature, he is not a human, he does not know how to love.

When he reached his shack he barged inside and saw Mary sprawled naked on the floor on her back, eyes rolling into the top of her head in what appeared to be agony. The fox was in between her legs, eating her insides.

'You beast! Scram!' Eugene cried. 'Get out!' Kissykins jumped up, startled, and so did Mary, annoyed.

'What are you doing, Eugene?' Mary screamed, manically searching for something to cover herself up with. She looked tiny, vulnerable, so thin. She shot Eugene with her empty grey eyes as though he were a father that had just interrupted a juvenile fumble in the dark with a first boyfriend.

'The fox, that horrible beast, he was trying to eat you! I saw him, there in between your legs attacking y—' And then he realized. 'What on earth? You mean to say? You were? The fox was? You were?' Eugene took several steps backwards, unsure of the obscenity and horror of what lay before him. He put a hand to his mouth and began to gag. Tears in his eyes, he shook out of anger and frustration at himself. He couldn't understand this; he would never be able to understand this. Only a few days ago this was his wife and now she was a ratty-haired, scratched-up mother of nature, he did not recognize her. With his hands he covered his eyes.

'Eugene, I do love that fox so. Besides, look at all the meat he has brought back for us, he must have attacked a wild bear or something – we won't have to hunt for weeks,' Mary grinned, coyly. The meat lay in slabs on Edna's blood-stained bed sheet, the fox must have dragged the treasure back himself, that shrewd little fox.

Eugene should have just left right there and then, left his zoosexual wife to fuck her brains out and wash it all down with a nice juicy hunk of human flesh. But he could not – for there was something he just couldn't leave behind: that shrewd little fox, with his smart little mouth, his hollow eyes and that strong sense he was giving off that indicated that he knew exactly what he was doing. No conscience knocked about in that empty funnel-shaped skull, only the calculating, manipulating monstrosity of his vile behaviour and it had to stop.

Eugene grabbed Kissykins by the scruff of his fluffy neck and slit that fox's throat with his rusty penknife right there in front of the eyes of his lover, the blood lashed a line over Mary's face and nipples. She screamed.

'You have to kill me now you evil, evil man,' Mary instructed her husband. And he wanted to, by Jove did he want to, but instead he managed to conjure up one of those impressive lines like they say in the movies:

'I would, but you're already dead.'

Kapow! Then he shut the door – that man shut that door – and walked into the depths of the forest. He didn't really know what to do, but at least he had escaped that crazy wife of his and more importantly, that shrewd little fox.

Mary was devastated, inconsolable. She buried Kissykins in the forest and visited his grave every hour. She searched for Eugene often, calling his name into the empty abyss of the woods, sometimes in anger, sometimes in agony, sometimes in desperation, but he never came back. She cooked herself up a meal the next day with some of the meat Kissykins had brought home. She made a pie, a splendid one with thick shortcrust pastry and a sticky glaze on top. Whilst eating the pie, Mary began to choke. She punched her own chest, coughing and panicking. She breathed in and out, harder and harder; her face went from white to red, from red to violet, she fumbled about with tumblers on the shelves that smashed around her as she tried to manage to grasp a glass of water. Her face went from red to violet, from violet to blue from blue to white again. Edna's toenail had lodged her way into that woman's throat and was the death of her. Edna had always thought cutting toenails was an unnecessary activity.

THE END

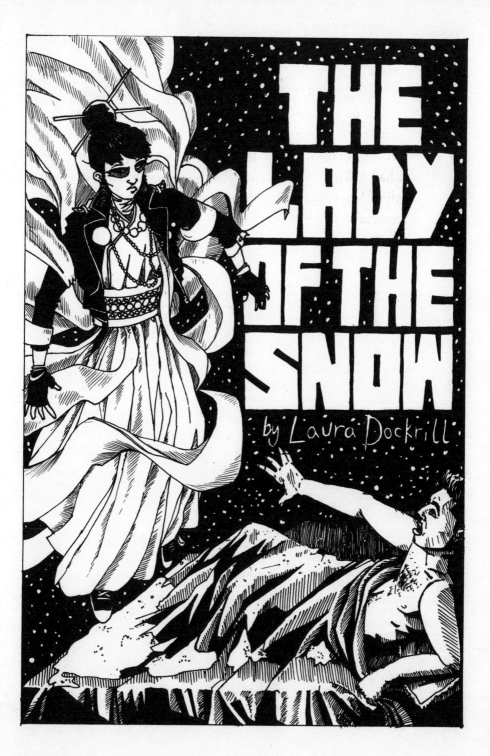

THE LADY OF THE SNOW

by Laura Dockrill

On this night the weather was dreadful. Rain fell from the skies like small rats. Denton and Marcellus were leaving the Crooked Hen. Old friends, they had a lot of catching up to do, but the publican has called time.

'Hey ma'am, do you know anywhere where two old buddies could catch a nightcap?' Denton asked.

'You could try the Elvis up the street, it's a cheap hotel, but they serve liquor until late.'

THE E VIS, the L was unlit.

The gentleman drank, talked of where they had left off. Denton told Marcellus he was about to ask his girlfriend to marry him. Marcellus told Denton that that was a good idea.

In the Elvis a glass was never empty. The music haunted shifty lonely hearts, songs from their juvenilia, where did it all go so wrong?

1.45 am: both guys are too drunk to drive home and decide they are going to sleep the night in the Elvis. Marcellus talks to the lobby maid who points him in his drunken waddle to the receptionist, who is used to the drunk and the desperate.

'I only got one room left and it's a double.'

'You have nothing with twin beds?'

'There are cushions up there, lay them in the middle. Besides, the heater's broke in that room anyway, so you might wanna cuddle up after all.' The receptionist snorted in a 'Hey, I'm a pig' kind of way. Her mascara clumped up like spider legs, her drippy red painted mouth twitched.

Marcellus handed over his card and completed all the forms, signed his signature, sucked a complimentary mint (it was stale).

When he got back to the table, Denton was missing, Marcellus scanned the bar, the lobby, and the tables and saw him leeching onto a babe. Japanese, petite, giggly, girlish. Denton leaned in, nibbled at her neck, took her hand, put it on his face, began climbing his huge presumptuous hand up her dress. *Swine*, Marcellus thought.

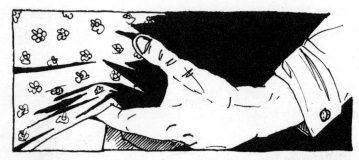

Marcellus gave the room number to Denton on a slip of paper and made his way up to the room. The tiny door screeched open, the cigarette-stained carpet pressed under his boots. Marcellus took a shower; a bar of soap, obviously designed for a toddler, snapped in half immediately – the towel just about covered his dignity.

It was awfully cold. Marcellus put his boxer shorts back on and got under the bed sheets. The mattress springs coiled, re-coiled, squeaked. The bed smelt of dirt. Marcellus put on the TV, flicked off the lamp.

3 a.m.: an intoxicated Denton folds into the room, knocks over a lamp and clambers into the bathroom. Throws up. Spits for an eternity. The tap goes on. Takes a piss. Grumbles something about the double bed and about being a homosexual and gets in. Snoring within moments.

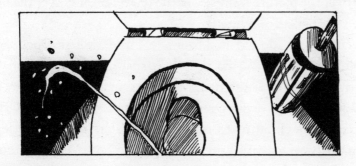

A drip is heard from the tap, wasn't quite tight enough. Marcellus sits up, shivering, steals back some quilt. Denton is naked and reeks. Marcellus checks the time. 3.57 a.m.

The doorknob turns.

A shadow sits under the door.

Japanese bitch, Marcellus, thinks. Denton gave her the room number, didn't he? Cheese dick.

The doorknob moves round further.

'Denton, Denton, wake up, your whore's at the door.'

Denton is out. K.O. Marcellus goes to switch the lamp on but is struck by the sudden icy air. It freezes his hand almost instantly. And snow begins to fall in the room. Snow falls from the ceiling, through the light socket and into the light bulb, snow falls over the picture frame, over the television and over the bed. Fine soft, pellets of white.

Marcellus is too terrified to move. His dark hair is peppered in blobs of white and he is still. A shadow arches round the doorframe and over the bed. Marcellus' eyes are locked to the shadow that now hangs over Denton like a grey cloud. Within moments the cloud turns into a woman: the Japanese woman from the bar.

In one movement, she pins down Denton's arms with her kneecaps and puts her hands over his. Then she takes a breath and locks mouths with Denton.

Marcellus is stunned. Dreaming. Fantasizing. It had been a while since he had been with a woman and he had consumed a lot of alcohol that night – it was possible that his imagination was on a chase. But within moments the kiss became violent, the lady began sucking and sucking and pulling and dragging the life and soul out of Denton. The lady pulled and sucked until it was physically visible that Denton was becoming tinier and tinier. His once merry red face was whiter and whiter, his body and hands became transparent, took on the skin of a new-born animal, or a pickled jellyfish. When the lady had finished sucking, she swallowed her breath and then turned to face Marcellus.

The lady frowned.

'I assume you do not wish to die like the man in the bed next to you, so I will leave you as you are if you go now and you never repeat what just happened to anybody, ever. You swear now.'

Her eyes fixed onto Marcellus' white face.

'SWEAR!' she stormed.

Marcellus swore and the lady faded into cloud, into darkness, into nothingness and the snow stopped.

Denton's skin lay on the bed and began to erode in smoke, as though it had been covered in acid.

Marcellus trembled and ran out of the room and out of the hotel and into his car where he drove away as fast and as far as he possibly could.

Several years later . . .

Marcellus is walking his dog. He stops in a paper shop and buys a newspaper and then sits outside a small café where he orders a coffee and a pastry. A lady walks by, Marcellus's dog barks, the lady stops and strokes the dog.

'You have a lovely dog,' she says.

Within a year the two are married. They paint their house toothpaste green and iron their bedclothes. In the evenings they massage each other's feet and impress each other with their views and ideas.

Ten years later they have two children, a new dog and a goldfish called Electric.

Now it is a Tuesday, a jasmine tea evening. The kids have gone to bed, the dog is by the fire and the fish is resting.

'We should go away.' Marcellus snaps the silence.

'Uh-huh,' his wife nods into her sewing set, looks up for a short smile.

'You know, that face you just made, that grin, you've done that before, it reminds me of somebody, I can't think . . . it's the way you sit there with the light of the fire by your face,' Marcellus says.

'Do I? Jennifer Lopez? Angelina Jolie?' His wife smirks cheekily, as she loops the thread around her pinky.

'No, neither of them. It's . . .' And then it unravels, folds in his mind, slate by slate, his memory clunking into place like the locking of an automatic car. 'I can't believe I never told you this, it's quite a strange story actually. It was a long time ago, I was with an old college friend I hadn't seen for years, we went out drinking and then ended up in a hotel . . .'

Marcellus went on with the story. His wife was displeased from the off, what with mention of old friends, booze and hotels (which only meant one thing: women and that always set her ears burning). And the story got thicker and he told his wife everything from the cheap soap right to the double bed and then to what happened that fatal night. But with everything he mentioned and talked of, from the falling snow to the lady that sucked Denton's life away, his wife only seemed to get crosser and crosser, her frown twitching into a mangled grimace.

'Marcellus, you traitor, it was me. It was me. I vowed you to never speak of what happened that night to anybody and you have just told me! For this sin and what you have done you will lose everything.'

And in an instant Marcellus's children and furniture evaporated into smoke and vanished up the chimney, followed by his wife. Grey smoke pummeled out of the fireplace and filled the room and choked Marcellus to death.

The house empty, only the shadows of secrets lingered and an engraving on the wall of the fireplace:

'A secret we earn

Is a secret in turn,

If it then taught and learnt . . .

The teacher will burn.'

the end

Gherkins

Gherkins.
He loved them.
If anybody ever said "would you like my gherkin?" he'd kiss them.
He went to prison
for robbing a chippie
he didn't do it very quickly
because he was nervous
and his face went all prickly...
and in prison
he couldn't eat them
but when he got outside
his mates made him a gherkin cake as a suprise
how he's missed them,
    but then in Brixton,
he saw a girl in a green trackie,
he put his hands around her mouth and took her back to his flat where he...
            put her in the shower for an hour
            and scrubbed her with a scourer
            he beat her head against the tiles
            which knocked her out for a while
            and she woke up to the lid screwing on the jar.
Dead now and pickled,
everyday more shrivelled
and the peppercorns on her skin like moles
and the people said,
'Suicide, what a suprise! It is the saddest of sins!'
If only they knew what that strange man was upto-
pickling young ladies like gherkins,
        So next time when you're dressed in green, blue or black
        Don't think of yourself as a style icon-
        think of yourself as a snack.

cluster of reporters clung to the Webbs' house. The neighbours stood outside in their dressing gowns smoking, gossiping, blaming, assuming. A little piglet of a lady trotted round with a tray of banana bread; she'd cut the slices into cubes to make the bread go further. The policeman flirted with her and she pouted back at him in her tuna-coloured lip gloss. She was tacky as an eye shadow palette that comes free with a teenage magazine.

'We always knew she was a weird one,' she tutted to an officer.

'Most of the time, one does,' he snuffled, suffocating in a wave of her toilet cleaner aroma. 'We just have to hope it's seen the same way in court. But, I guess, with such supportive neighbours as yourself, it should go down the right way . . .' He grinned, winked and popped a block of banana bread into his mouth.

The siren of a police car polluted the chattering streets like somebody lighting a fag in a lift. People moved to allow it to reach the gates of the house, which had been locked.

A policewoman came to the door, went back inside and returned with two blanketed children. Dressed like ghosts ready

for a Halloween party, they walked with blind trepidation fol-
lowing the woman's lead. The audience assembled outside gasped
in horror at the sight, audible shivers shooting down their spines
like the sharpening of a knife.

　　'What went on in that house?'

❧〜❧〜❧

'We always knew she was a weirdo . . .'

Helga Webb or, as she was commonly known, 'droopy face',
'candle head', 'the melting lady' was watched, all the time. The
right half of her face was all right, skinny and dirty but there
was some resemblance of a face at least. It was the other side that
horrified the neighbourhood. It sloped downwards as though it
had been melted or was constantly being blown down by a hair-
dryer. This meant that her left eye was always bang shut tight and
her mouth hung down like a heavy bin bag, leaking saliva and
dribble. Her nose was so collapsed – the muscles as worn out as
the soles of ballet pumps – it caused her to breathe
in heavy, husky vacuum sucks. Everybody always
knew when the melting lady was approaching.

　　'She don't help herself,' a local lady snapped
from the Launderette as she rolled two socks into
a tight ball. 'The way she carries herself. So shady
looking.'

　　The lady was right, she *was* so shady looking
what with her bent back, she was in a constant 'F'
shape, a higgledy-piggledy jigsaw of odd bits and

bones and put together all wrong, as though she was the prod-
uct of three different dolls that had been taken apart and put
together again by an inventive child. She shook when she trod.
When she spoke or when she moved, her walking stick rattled
on the floor, her swampy carrier bags worked like an instrument
for the wind to harp into.

You would have thought that when she took on her brother's
children that somebody would have gone over to check if every-
thing was okay. Maybe to check if she was sure she could manage?
But she was too weird wasn't she? Too dangerous. She just wasn't
right in the head. That was it, she just wasn't right in the head.

The neighbourhood got used to her behaviour. But what a
weird sight it was, seeing this odd triangle of a woman shuf-
fling about the aisles of a supermarket with two angelic children
clutching onto either side of the trolley. The children would
excitedly choose the sweetest of treats –
gingerbread hearts, sacks of pink marsh-
mallows, metre stick blocks of creamy
chocolate and tub after tub of ice cream.
And then as they'd near the checkout,
whispers would flow from the cashiers,
and the shuffling sound of the swapping of seats would ensue,
'But I had to serve her last time!'

At night, she'd go around alone, leaving trails of breadcrumbs
on the pavement, from the woods to her home as though she
were trying to lead the children away into the wilderness; she
clearly was in no fit state to care for those beautiful children. We
always knew she was a weirdo.

'She's not fit to be a carer.'

Hansel, aged twelve, had grown into a courteous, kind and healthy (well, slightly chubby, maybe) young man. The social services paid him many a visit, and every time he greeted the suspicious rep with a slice of delicious cherry pie or a frozen yoghurt stick, always making the effort to shake their hands, presenting his clean cut fingernails. He'd always invite them in and show them his electronic train set or demonstrate how excellent he had become at making popcorn.

'Listen for the pop!' he'd say, charmingly.

Gretel too gave them no reason to worry, although slightly small in stature, with a shy and elfish nature, she was amazingly creative. She was always making people cards and pop-up books, her art

work could always be found on a paving slab in chalk – often flowers, trees, or mermaids. One time she drew a picture of herself and Hansel, running far and fast – their faces a grimace of panic and terror – and behind them a lady, bent over with a coat hanger for a back, half of her face, appeared as though it were melting.

'There was something going on...'

Hansel and Gretel were rushed to the police station. When Hansel was questioned, he answered in long, eloquent phrases, dropping in words that were beyond his age. His impressive manner just added fuel to the fire, as tears swam to the eyes of the witnesses. The fact that these two children had home-schooled themselves just made matters worse. Hansel, what a little hero.

Gretel was also brought in to give a statement about what had happened that very night in that house. However, she rolled her huge eyes up to the corner of the room, humming the melody to a song that nobody recognized and only answered with a tiny, 'Yes' when the police officer asked her if she would like a biscuit.

'Along came a butcher ...'

Hansel, Gretel and the melting lady left for the shops on a Monday afternoon. Gretel skipped ahead, scraping a stick along the fence, Hansel helped his aunt with her bags.

'It's not right,' the butcher from across the road mumbled to his wife. 'That traitor of a man, dying on his family like that. Look at those poor children, they don't even go to school.' He huffed, lighting his pipe.

'Geoffrey, I don't think he would have *wanted* to have di—' his wife, Sue, began.

'Makes not a pinch of difference. Could you imagine me expiring if we had kids, leaving them with a nut bag like that? I bloody doubt it, makes me sick.'

'Dear, I don't think that they had a choi—'

'Makes me want to go in there and see what it is exactly that's going on. It's far too quiet for me.'

'Forget about it, Geoffrey, it's not our business.'

A moment of stifling emptiness suffocated the room; the only noise was the gentle hum of the oven.

'That Hansel, he's a good kid,' the butcher started. 'I could use him, what with the shop. He's strong too, he could make a good butcher.'

'Geoffrey, what are you saying?' Sue asked, her ski slope nose hoofing into the air.

'I'm saying, all my life I've searched for a reason to make a difference, and I feel as though that reason has just popped into my life. I've watched those children grow up from afar – goodness knows how they did it with that maniac. Now it's time a father stepped in.'

'Oh Geoffrey,' Sue flung her arms around his tree trunk of a neck. She held her empty stomach and sobbed helplessly. Her mind raced, already picturing making cookies with Gretel, flying kites, having bears around a small table for a tea party.

Geoffrey threw her arms off him and manoeuvred his tank of a body to the telephone.

'Now listen for the buzz word Gretel.'

'*What's a buzz word Hansel?*'

'*The word you are listening out for.*'

'*Is it "buzz"?*'

'*No you silly child, the word is not "buzz" but if you want, if it makes it easier, it can be, for this time, "buzz".*'

'*Can it be "butterfly"?*'

'*Will you remember "butterfly"?*'

'*I always think of butterflies.*'

'*Fine . . . "Butterfly" . . . so when I say . . . let's think . . . "Gretel, look at that BUTTERFLY on the window ledge," you open the oven door.*'

'*How do you know that there will be a butterfly on the window ledge?*'

'*I won't know and there probably won't be one.*'

'So why are you saying that there is one?'

'Because "butterfly" is the buzz word, remember.'

'Yes I know. So I pretend?'

'Yes. You pretend.'

'Like when snails hide in their shells and pretend they are stones?'

'Yes, like when snails hide in their shells and pretend they are stones.'

'All right. What if the door doesn't open when I pull it?'

'Why wouldn't the door open?'

'It's heavy.'

'It will open, all right? It will. So when I say "Gretel, look at that BUTTERFLY on the window ledge," what do you do?'

'Open the oven door.'

'Exactly.'

'And what do you do Hansel?'

'I push her in, don't I? In the oven of course.'

'Watching and watching and a bit more watching . . .'

The next day, Sue peered from her window as Gretel scribbled hearts onto the pavement in soft, pink chalk. Sue watched until her longing eyes screwed out of her head like telescopes, they could have broken through the glass. Gretel stood up to attention on the other side of the road, feeling eyes on her like ants crawling up her body. Sue pushed the curtain over her eyes, but not wanting to terrify the child, came outside, offering her reassurance.

Her arms folded tightly over her chest, she began, 'Good morning.'

Gretel did not answer. Her glassy eyes watching Sue.

'What are you drawing?' Sue asked. Moving forwards, she crossed the road and stood a few feet from Gretel. How pretty she was, like a small puppet and smelling of vanilla and sickly innocence. In her world of make-believe she was dressed as a princess, a pink dress, a crown, a wand, a scattering of beads and pearls around her neck.

'Oh, hearts? How very pretty.'

'It's for Valentine's day,' Gretel said assertively. She knelt; her white woollen tights gained two pink blushes on the knees.

'Woopsi . . .' Sue giggled, brushing the girl down.

'I suppose your aunty will wash these for you?' Sue probed, not ready for the answer as the words deceitfully gushed out of her.

'No, I will. I wash all my clothes.'

Sue flushed. Evidence, that irresponsible aunt, what a creature! Gretel started on a new heart.

'But how old are you, darling?'

'Eight.'

'Don't you think that's a little young to be washing clothes all by yourself?' Sue's eyes washed over in a greedy colour.

'No, I do all things by myself.'

'So what does your aunt do?'

'She locks us in a cupboard.'

'... And waiting and waiting and waiting ...'

Geoffrey sat in a stiff armchair, pulling a thread of bacon fat out of his teeth, a shrivelled Sue sat on the corner of the dated sofa, crumbling.

'So you're certain Sue, that's what she said?'

'To the word.'

'Well, I'll be damned. I knew there was something fishy going on in that house. Good work, Sue.'

'What now?'

'We've just got to get the ol' welfare over there and start talking to them properly. If the little'un says anything even close to what she said to you, they'll be out of that house like a shot and then we'll apply for custody.'

'But what if they deny us?'

'Why would they? I have my own business, you've got a few O levels, you're at home so the children won't be neglected. Damn, we recycle and everything for Christ's sake!'

'It was just her little face when she said it, I wanted to take her right then.'

'I know, I know, but we've got to do this the right way.'

For the next few days, nobody left or entered the Webb house. The door remained firmly shut, the last warning had been dealt and the toy box, for that day, was officially closed. Sue couldn't take it and soon became sick with worry and desperation; she couldn't eat or sleep. She just sat, plugged into her seat by the window like an air freshener, occasionally sighing out huffs of anxiety and watching, always, watching.

Sue pulled her hair out. With no proof or evidence and with a nagging voice at the other end of a telephone repeating, 'Well every time I've been over there the children have been in exceptional health,' it was difficult to have a point to argue. Until ...

Sue was just about to flick the last lamp off in the living room when she saw the melting lady bolting out of the house, gripping Gretel firmly by the arm, her bony fingers trapped over Gretel's mouth to stop her from crying. She walked fast with the girl, who reluctantly traipsed after her, her small milky hands trying to release her aunt's prickly grasp.

'Geoffrey!' Sue whispered, snatching her husband's meaty arm. 'Look!'

'That devil woman has gone one step too far!' He picked up the first tool he could find, a fire poker, and mechanically stood and went to the front door,

'Geoffrey!' his wife called after him. 'Think!' she pleaded.

The butcher pulled to a halt, how he wanted those children. Restraining himself, he put the poker down and held his wife close and then carried her upstairs.

'Nicely does it ...'

Gretel was drawing on the paving slabs the next morning. Oh, how it gladdened Sue's heart with an enormous relief to see her there, scribbling away. Sue wrapped a shawl around her shoulders and went out to her.

'Morning,' she said through a gaping dummy smile.

As usual Gretel ignored her. Sue tried not to be discouraged by this and reminded herself that the girl, like a piece of clay, needed warming before she spoke.

'What are you drawing today?' Sue asked.

Nothing.

Air.

'I've just seen a fox in my garden, a big one with a big bushy tail, would you like to come and see?'

Gretel looked up, her white blonde hair framing her slight face, her rosy cheeks sweet as plums. On her left eye sat a big purple bruise, as though she had pushed a handful of blackcurrants onto it.

'My goodness! Erm . . . maybe another time?' Sue squirmed as she ran backwards into the house – a stampede of racing heartbeats jolting through her body – and telephoned her husband immediately. Proof, how's that for proof?

Secretly pleased about the black eye, the butcher proudly sat, cocky in his stiff chair. 'Can't believe it, got my proof! Ha! You can hide words but you can't hide actions, not like that!' He shook his head aggressively, punching his mammoth, spotted fist into the arm of the chair; a worn patch lay underneath it. 'Just a matter of time now.' He took a long slurp from his pint of milk and smacked his lips together. 'Just a matter of time before that coward is captured.'

The truth of the matter was, nobody in the neighbourhood could visualize that tiny melting lady punching the child in the face. For she seemed oddly tinier than the children put together, bony and crinkled like a small clothes peg. What damage could she do? Still, when fury enters the brain of a maniac, the body is capable of the unthinkable.

Released from questioning, Hansel and Gretel were waved to go through health checks and general procedure before being, without a single living next-of-kin, moved to a new home. What with all the moving around and the harrowing experience of losing both mother, father and now aunty, the prospect of a foster home seemed out of the question. The butcher and his wife waited, every day seemed a lifetime. However, their case was strong.

'A cause for celebration . . .'

Within two brief weeks of filing and mumbling conversations, of pointing fingers and strange contradicting arguments and statements, Hansel and Gretel were moved into the butcher's home. Sue met them with a banner, giggling, hastily tearing their jackets off like a hungry monkey unpeeling a banana. She moved them through to the dining room, putting on her poshest voice, she invited them to sit and face a spread of roast chicken, sausage rolls and prawn cocktail (old-fashioned, I know, poor thing). The linen napkins folded into swans, a bowl of rancid potpourri created the centrepiece. The children considered the food in disgust.

'We don't eat this,' Hansel grunted.

'Excuse me?' Sue squeaked, giggling in nervous chugs.

'We like cakes and pastries and sweets and chocolate.'

'No, no, no, dear, later, plenty of time for cake later.'

'No, no, no, dear, to you, Sue,' Hansel fastened Gretel's mouth shut with his abrupt firmness. 'We do not eat this,' he added, his mouth opening wide and long; as a smooth smile lit over his rounded face. Gretel shrunk into her chair, she searched the floor for a trapdoor, anything.

'You'll never grow up to be a strong butcher unless you eat well, Hansel. Don't you want to be a strong butcher like your father?'

'He is not my father.' Hansel bolted.

Sue began to weep, her eyes filling rapidly. She folded her hard, starchy, styled hair behind her ear in an attempt to rationalize the situation. 'Well, why don't you have a bite? Just cut a slice of the chicken and taste it. Here look, I'll feed Gretel, you'll see . . . come here pretty lamb.'

Sue waltzed round the table, trying to remain calm. The butcher, in his best suit, perspiring, was already angry that the boy had dismissed him so readily.

'Here we go,' Sue patronized in a baby voice and forked a piece of the chicken meat into Gretel's mouth. 'See, moody boy, she's eating it, just like a good girl—'

And with that, Gretel slowly let the chicken eject itself from her little mouth onto the table. It came out all gloopy and grey. Gretel still silent and numb, the green residue under her eye from where the punch had been exaggerated, her look that was cocky, unimpressed, and evil.

'Right, so that will be no dinner for anybody then I'm afraid,' Sue huffed and began bustling about. 'The two of you can both go to your rooms if you're going to be difficult,' she said assertively, referring to all the rules she had read and remembered in her parenting guidebook.

Then Hansel let out an odorous groan and snarled, 'Feed us Sue.' Hansel fiercely raised his voice with a fearlessness that shook the picture frames of long dead family pets.

'Listen to me, boy. Just because your silly deranged aunty gave you those sugary snacks doesn't mean I'm going to do the same,' Sue persisted.

The butcher clammed up, unable to speak, is this really what parenting was like? His clothes had never felt so tight. And he couldn't move, why couldn't he move?

'HA! That old hag couldn't tell *us* what to do! We ate what we wanted when we wanted and when she tried to make us do differently, she paid, and you Sue, will pay in exactly the same way.'

Sue clenched her teeth and started again, nervously, 'Oh for heaven's sake, Hansel, what films have you been watching, you funny little man? You'll scare your sister if you're not careful.' Sue glanced at Gretel, she sat as still as a pebble, those unforgettable eyes, relentless.

'Okay, we'll have it your way, just for today, we'll clear up here and then we can go and get some food somewhere else, an Italian restaurant or something? Eh, Geoffrey, why don't you book us a table at the nice little Italian?'

Sue had broken the first rule from the parenting guidebook – stick to your guns, and never go back on a rule; still, it was only the first day, wasn't it? The butcher panicked, Italian, good idea, change of scenery.

Sue leant over Hansel's place to begin to clear away. She reached for the chicken and Hansel gripped her forearm heavy and hard, his fingers white on the tips with pressure, locking, he said, 'No, Sue.'

'Geoffrey . . .' Sue shrieked in terror, as Hansel picked up a small carving knife and slit a deep violent gash into Sue's arm, the skin bursting like a line down a broad bean pod, the blood fruitful, black almost, ran free. Sue cradled her aching arm, a stinging fiery sensation screaming through her body, rinsing through her like a bottle of tequila. She cowered, sticky blood began trickling like molasses onto her peach jumper, then onto her tartan skirt, her white tights, all blobby and gluey. What a mess.

The butcher wanted to do something but was para- lysed in shock, like trying to scream in a bad dream. He was dumb, clumsy, drunk and frozen, puppet-like as the children pulled his arms, linking them round his colos- sal body. 'Come on butcher,' they sang, 'let's get some real food.' And, like a zombie, they led him out of the dining room, through the hallway and out of the front door, Hansel fishing for his wallet on the way out. Sue on the sofa, quivering.

❧~❧~❧

After we saw the plume of grey smoke pouring out the chim- ney that day we knew something had gone terribly wrong, the

burning smell was unmistakeable. It was as though that mad old
hag had tried to roast a whole hog, fur and all. Nothing smells
the same as burning hair – the way it snatches away, shrivelling
into a coil.

'Once we found out that it was the melting lady that had per-
ished in the oven we thought the children must have done it out
of desperation. They had to, after she had been locking them in
cupboards and beating them they way she did. She never sent
them to school you know, can you believe that? That's neglect
if you ask me.'

After a dinner of jam doughnuts and candyfloss, toffee apples
and chocolate chip muffins, the children watched cartoons on
repeat until the early hours of the morning, refusing to be told
when to go to bed. Gretel watched from a shadow Sue clean
and tend to her arm. She sat propped up on the bed, wrapping
a bandage round the sore, her tears splattering onto the dress-
ing, her throat clogged up as though full of curdling clotted
cream.

'That poor melting lady,' Sue sniffled to her husband. 'All
those years of abuse and isolation from everybody. She didn't
lock those children in a cupboard to punish them; she locked
them in a cupboard to protect herself! Because those children
are not children, they are demons! What are we going to do?'

She fell onto the bed in a scatter of tears, her body wildly
convulsing. The butcher lay motionless, unable to move; mute,
he stared at the wallpaper, running his eyes around the flowers.

Hansel snuck up behind Gretel and put his chubby paws onto her shoulders. 'Do not feel sympathy for her, Gretel,' he whispered into her tiny ear. 'If you dare trip up again like last time with that big mouth of yours, making friends with the neighbours the way you do, I will give you a second and nastier black eye.'

Then in a deranged, unsettling frenzy, he clawed her hand into his, squeezing it in reassurance, as though they were the only people in the world that counted.

THE END

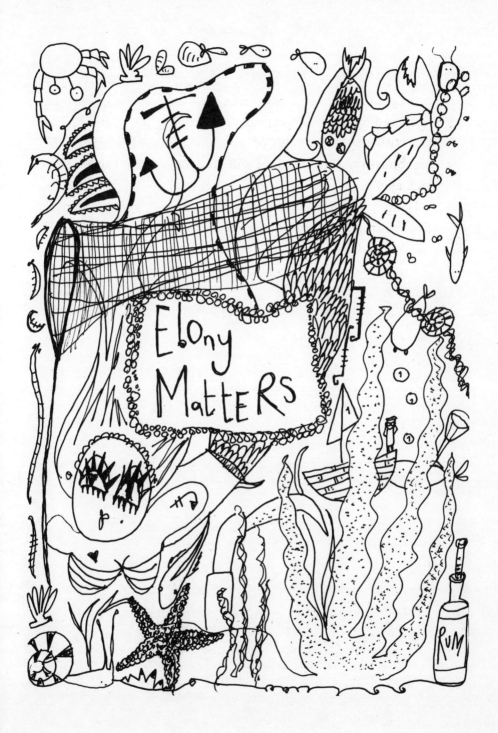

E bony faced the window, her toothbrush hanging out of the corner of her mouth like a cowboy's cigarette, utterly obnoxious. She let the toothpaste foam and allowed it to dribble from her lips and slide down onto her collarbone. Paralysed in cocky, gorgeous loveliness, she must have known how good that looked, and how it shot Ava through the heart. Ava's eyes drilled into the glass; if looks could kill, there would be carnage.

Ebony. Ebony.
Do you even know me?

In the washed-up land of Scatterbrook-on-Sea lived a fish-monger and his daughter, although to use the word 'daughter' seemed ridiculous for Ava was the most boyish non-boy that had so far ever lived.

Every morning Ava would wake up at 4.30, go for a run, come home, sleep for a further twenty minutes, shower and be at her father's fish shop for 5.30, usually dressed in the same clothes as the day before underneath a pair of bloody gut-stained overalls and a woolly bobble hat. She smoked, she spat, she rapped and she bit her nails and blew the cuttings about the fish shop. When it came to lunch she needed at least three bacon rolls just to keep her standing. But, like a boy, she wasn't growing lumpy bits or muffin tops, she was strong and anchor-like.

Her father was the opposite; he was weedy and wheat-like, his waist was an extra seven self-made, hole-punched, belt-pinch of nothing, his clothes hung off him the same way they do off scruffy schoolboys about to start secondary school, swamped in their uniforms bought too big in the hope of making them last the full five years. His bottle-end glasses and sandy soft hair made him look vulnerable and pathetic but nobody ever dared threaten the shop purely through fear of confrontation from the infamous Ava. Ava had already put three of the local boys into comas, only two are awake today and they are less than half the people they used to be.

The Codfather was everything a fish shop should be: cold, watery and smelly. Sometimes Ava believed she would still be there in hundreds of years; embedded in the walls like a caught crab she would freeze, barnacles on her hands and feet, her skin drenched in sea salt, her eyes hacked out by the seagulls. Her hands, they could be open scallop shells and seaweed as her hair and . . .

The small bell above the fish shop door tinkled, interrupting her thoughts, and in came her father.

'Any customers whilst I was away?' Pugley asked.

'No,' Ava grumbled.

'Staring into space isn't going to pay the rent, Ava-bean. Did you get started on the cleaning?'

'Erm, no.'

'So what have you been doing?'

Pugley came around behind the fish bar and stood next to Ava. He looked down to where, on the stack of white paper and with the blue fountain pen, Ava had drawn a congress of what appeared to be naked women, of all shapes and sizes, in such definite detail it was embarrassing for the both of them. Ava slammed her hand over the drawing to hide it from her father's eyes. He was humble and a bit of a prude and just said, quietly, 'Get the mop when you're ready.'

Ava and her father got on famously, sharing jokes and enjoying each other's company. They listened to the radio, rolled fags and once the shop was closed they often drank beer together. It was on one of these evenings that Pugley struck up conversation.

'Ava, I've been thinking.'

'At last!' Ava teased.

'Ha, no, but really . . . I just wanted to speak to you, just briefly, just a thought, really, an idea I've been having . . . about you.'

'No, I'm not smoking pot if that's what you're going to say. I gave that up.'

'No, no, not that, it's about you. When I was your age I was quite a lonely person, I didn't have many friends, I was always thought of as —'

'You still have no friends, Dad!'

'Well that's my point. I didn't have many friends and I still have no friends now. You see, loneliness is infectious; it is a poison that eats you up from the inside out. I'm awfully fearful that I may have – not on purpose – filled a tall glass of that poison for you and now I am watching you slowly drink it.'

'What are you on about, you old dog?' Ava bunched a fingertip's worth of tobacco and began grooving it into her Rizla paper. Pugley circled the top to his beer and felt his whiskers.

'Ava . . . you need some friends.'

Ava ignored her father and continued rolling the cigarette. She could have rolled forever, her fingers became clumsy, the tobacco began to escape.

The sea, the sea,
how boring is the sea
when there is nobody to see the sea with?

'Ava?'

'What?'

'Did you hear me?'

'It was hard not to.' Ava continued to roll.

'I just don't want you to be . . . I just want you to be happy.'

'I am.'

'I know, but a solid friendship is vital. I don't know, it's just I'm getting on and once I'm gone I'm worried you'll just let that stubbornness of yours get the better of you and I want you to meet people, that's all.'

'Yes, well, I don't want to meet people, people suck.'

And after a subtle pause Pugley spoke, 'Yes, you are probably right, people do suck.'

The evening inked through like a developing photograph, clearer and clearer and calm. Ava sat on her bed and threw her heavy boots off onto the floor. She undressed and took off her bobble hat; a long sheet of beautiful, black hair folded down her back, sweaty and knotted from where it had been stuffed under that tiny hat. In her underwear she sat on the bed and lit her lamp and a cigarette and leaned to the window; her peepshow was about to begin. As always: Ebony Matters.

Across the garden, second house to the left, top window, the pink stars sellotaped to the glass, the purple curtains; she had never changed that window.

Ebony, I can't stop thinking about you.

Ebony had the most wonderful arms, she was like the girls in the adverts that wore dresses with no straps, her collarbones were perfect, aligned, even and sharp. Her shoulders were the same as pine doorknobs, smooth and rounded off. The best bit about watching Ebony Matters undress was the way Ebony knew, knew, knew, a thousand times over, that somebody, somewhere was watching her, and the same way the eighteen years of her life had injected her with a striking prettiness, they had also tutored her to be a natural performer; elegant, sneaky and coy she gave all to her audience of one – whoever they were.

Ava was as still and as numb as a tooth. But her eyes could not keep still; they were wild, flickering, jolting and obsessed until the light went out and the only noise to be heard was from an owl.

Up early the next morning, Ava ran around the same route she ran the morning before and the morning before that, hooting out hot puffs of air as she panted around the streets. She squatted outside the front of Ebony's house and thought about Ebony. Ebony, Ebony – what Ebony's bedroom floor was like, what colour was her bed quilt? What shape was her mirror? Did she fold her clothes? Did she iron? Did she wake up in the night or think of Ava? Did she ever think of Ava?

'Fucking brat,' Ava muttered and tears began to squeeze out of her eyes. 'Fucking ungrateful, spoilt brat.' She wanted to knock on that door one hundred and seventy-nine times until somebody with a comprehensive, articulate, concise answer said, 'Ava, the reason why Ebony has not replied to your letters is because of blah, blah, blah, and so and so and so . . .'

Then she could move on, but for now, there was a constant urge to get through to her, it was like writing to the Queen only without the polite formal secretary response – it was agony.

Pugley was already at the shop taking the beards off the mussels.

'I already said, stop doing that, it's a waste of time, people

can do it at home themselves,' Ava sneered as she stormed in
through the back door and flicked the kettle switch on.

'With a bloody great supermarket selling swanky prepared
mussels in garlic and white wine sauce why would people
bother walking that extra seven minutes out of town to us to
get their mussels covered in crap? Think about it, Ava. Why are
you late?'

'I'm not late.'

'Yes, you are.'

Ava, never late Ava, went to the clock, 'What? It's nearly
eight o'clock. How did that happen?'

Confused, she put on her bloody overalls and went to cut the
lemons, completely baffled.

'Okay, how long till those lemons are ready?'

The sea, the sea, how boring is the sea?
How boring is the sea
when there is nobody to see the sea with?

That night Pugley and Ava walked home together. Within a
moment of being indoors, the harsh cloudy fog of cooked
salmon was already wafting up the staircase. It made Ava
want to chuck her guts up. She was sick of fish. Pugley
was sick of fish too. They usually ate it disguised
into something else, hidden under mashed potato
like vegetables for a fussy kid, or stirred into a rich
pasta sauce. Ava met her seat at the table with a displeased huff.

'Right, it's exactly the same idea as a shepherd's pie but it's
made with fish instead of mince.'

'Is that not just fish pie?'

'Err. Well, if you want to look at it like that, then yes, I suppose it is . . . just with peas.'

Ava pushed the TV on and the pair of them sat, gormless, zombified into the screen, their eyes flashing with the white fuzz. A grind of pepper, a sprinkle of salt, a splodge of tomato sauce.

'I'll wash up,' Ava said, 'before I die from a mercury overdose.'

Later that night, Ava lay flat out on her bed with the curtains peeled back. She could hear her father downstairs snoring, the snooker on in the background, the gentle tap of the balls kissing one another. Ebony came to her window, she gave it away in a chink of her eye that she was making sure Ava was watching. And when she was satisfied she had an audience, she began to undress. Ava blew a swirl of smoke out of her mouth and rested her rollie up on the window ledge. Ebony was so magnificent, so magnificent it was wickedly wonderful. So cruel it made her cry.

The following morning, with a small fountain pen and on a heavy stack of white wrapping paper, Ava spiralled into a daydream. Her boots had begun to stick to the fishy, gummy floor; there were no customers. She wanted to write to Ebony, she wanted to say something. Explain? Maybe she could explain herself, for once.

The sea, the sea, how boring is the sea?
How boring is the sea
when there is nobody to see the sea with?

The fish shop door swung open and a charging, angry man with a red face, fuming, barged up to the counter.

'You! YOU! You dyke, you freak!'

A violet-faced Mr Matters came round the counter and plucked terrified Ava up by the neck of her hoodie. Pugley ran around and pulled him back by the shoulders but Mr Matters was far stronger than him.

'What the fuck even are you? I know what you've been up to, you little pervert and I'm fucking serious: if you don't leave my Ebony alone, things are going to get fucking scary for you, right? If I see another one of those mental letters to my girl I'll chainsaw your face off. Right?'

'Oi, oi, oi, Mr Matters, you're hurting her, let go of her now!' Pugley pulled Mr Matters' arms off of his daughter, grasped his head and spoke, nose-to-nose, so close they shared the same spit. 'Let go,' Pugley mouthed. 'Now.'

Ava was released and quickly scurried to the corner of the shop, trembling, compiling together whatever she could of her tattered self.

'I'm warning you, sort it out. I mean it, Pugley. You're a good man, you don't want trouble.'

And with that he left, the door swaying in grief, the shop looming with a dark dreary sense of accomplishment.

'What's that old fool on about? Letters? Ebony? Well what does he think you'd want with her? The way he was going on as though you are harassing the girl. You wouldn't do anything like that.'

Ava gazed at her crumpled father, as soggy as a cloddy digestive, as defeated as a lost paper bag tangled in a tree. She wanted to speak to him properly, the way people speak to each other in films, in long indulgent sentences. But he knew already, no words were needed or wanted for that matter.

'Yes, maybe you would,' Pugley sighed. He straightened his overalls and went to the back room, within moments the radio was on and Ava drowned slowly in the sound.

That evening the pair of them ate halibut in silence. Pugley didn't bother to disguise the fish, he didn't have the energy.

They didn't talk.

Upstairs she undressed and got into her pyjamas; she wanted to feel small again, like a child, innocent and ignorant. She wanted to remember Ebony as the pretty girl that lived behind her who played shadow puppets with her, and put up a little sign in her window at Christmas that said, 'Stop here, Santa', who shared a tin can on a string as a walkie-talkie, who passed an S.O.S in the middle of the night that read 'HELP ME'. When school was shut for summer, the padlock on the gates, Ebony would creep outside, playing in her Wendy house, sunbathing, decorating star-shaped cookies. Once she found out that Ava knew how to make mud-pies and blow up frogs by sticking straws up their bums and blowing as hard as you possibly could, she knew Ava was magical and she wanted to be with her every day.

That was before the hairs began to grow. Then, as the pair of them got older and they were with other people at school, she acted as though she didn't even know who Ava was, as though Ava had been deluding everyone, making up shit, fantasizing about any communication with Ebony. And Ebony would laugh too about Ava, join in on the spitty, nasty conversation about her, and sometimes add fuel to the terrific fire by saying she once saw 'it' through her window when Ava had come out of the bath. Never a fluent lie, never a consistent story, but who cares for consistency when you are ten years old? Once it was confirmed that Ava was never going to have a period, when her hands had become hard and big, when the pores opened up like spouting cress ready for the thin spirals of hairs to pop through on her chin, that was when the rumour went round that she was turning into a man. Because, she was, wasn't she? She was turning into a man, a man that liked women.

Ava got into bed and tried to close her eyes tight shut. She didn't want to watch Ebony. The idea of it was wrong; the whole thing was wrong. She rolled over, and then turned onto her back, and then round again, and then over, and then sighing she threw a pillow off the bed, and then she kicked her duvet off and then on right up to her neck and then off and then on, and then she brought the pillow back up and flipped it over and over, and wiggled and wiggled and itched and itched and scratched and itched. She closed her eyes and saw Ebony brushing her hair and opened her eyes again, then she closed them, tight this time and there was Ebony walking her dog. She opened her eyes up, tortured, closed them: Ebony washing the vicar's car for a fiver, Ebony rollerblading, Ebony going out on a Saturday night, to meet people, to dance, to talk, to have *fun*, to be a slut. Bitch. Bitch. Bitch. And then she sat up and let out a ravenous yell and swiped the curtains apart. Ebony's light was on, and there was Ebony by the window undressed and Ebony was not alone. In Ebony's room was a man. And they were kissing, right at the window, engulfed in a moment of pure intensity. Right there, right there for Ava to see. Right in front of her. *Right in front of her.* Shameless. How dare she? *How dare she?* Ava punched the wall violently she broke two fingers and cursed.

Pugley decided to have a 'taste and sell' day. He had learnt this sales technique from the Cheese Emporium across the road and found it, overall, a successful day. Pugley thought the occasion would also give Ava a chance to meet some new people and bring the two of them back together again. He had given out flyers and, he believed, had drawn an excellent picture of a posh person tucking into a prawn cocktail. The banner read 'Make all your *fishes* come true . . .' which he found to be very funny indeed.

Ava stood behind the counter at The Codfather in a *Godfather* t-shirt, only with the 'G' crossed out and a 'C' replacing the 'G'. She was *mad*. She was in a riot. She aggressively gutted a fish for the mayor. Snarling, she ripped the silvery skin, as if slicing open a letter. She let the purple blood spill onto her wrist and she wiped the splatter onto her overall. She clenched her teeth and tore the spine out of the fish.

'Are you going to take out the fine bones too?' the mayor asked, intrigued, attempting to get the locals fired up about the art of seafood.

Ava gritted through her teeth. She ignored the mayor but clenched her knuckles tight around the knife. *Ebony you slut. Ebony you fucking cheating bitch.* A few customers peered over to the counter, nosily staring as they shoved king prawns and winkles into their jammy mouths. Pugley tried to remain calm as he began on a history of Scatterbrook-on-Sea.

'It may interest you all to know that Scatterbrook-on-Sea used to be compared to some of the most popular beaches, such as Brighton and Hastings . . . but without the money!'

A clutter of false awkward laughs fluttered into the air.

The head of the fish lay on Ava's board, his eye glassy, glancing at Ava, watching her, judging her. The mayor intensely popping his chubby face through the glass as though she were a fish in a tank, trapped, watched. *Ebony you are ruining my day, stop destroying everything. Go away.* The mayor, grinning, his gold filling glinting, his don't-mind-me hands shoved in his pockets. The head of the fish, assuming, he wouldn't stop assuming, that pearl of an eye, watching and watching and watching and then the fish head, it took a breath as though it had something to say and then his lips they began to open up and in one move she stabbed the knife into the fish's head.

'FUCK EBONY MATTERS!' she screamed.

'Excuse me?' the mayor asked, shocked. Pugley rushed over, excusing himself from his storytelling.

'Ava? What's the matter?'

'The fish, he looked at me, he was watching me with his eyes,

he was about to speak . . . I could see his lips quivering as though
they were going to . . . I'm sorry . . . I don't know what I . . .'

Ava ran out of the shop, easing through the crowd of frozen
customers. She threw her apron off, tumbled it into a ball and
ran. She had to speak to Ebony; she had to see her, to ask her
who that stranger was in her room. She had to know everything,
why she stopped being her friend, why she didn't want to make
booby traps in the garden anymore, and sit in dens and make
poisonous concoctions and feed them to the sheep. Why had she
started ignoring her, gossiping about her and then letting men
kiss her on the lips – how had it come to this? Whilst running
she let her tears run with her, spraying out and into the air like
silk scarves on a lady in a fast car. Driven, she controlled herself
and thought positively. That was right, she didn't want a period,
she didn't want breasts or hips or full lips or long fluttery eye-
lashes. She wanted to be square and flat and strong and sharp.

She wanted to be that man in Ebony's room, stroking Ebony's arms and standing in the window with the stars sellotaped to the glass. She ran to Ebony's house and when she reached it she knocked stiffly on the door.

No answer.

That fucking bitch. She should have left it, but she was too angry, too possessed to let go. She knocked again. *Pow. Pow. Pow.* That fucking bitch was blatantly in there, wasn't she? She ran round the back of the house, urgent, desperate and she pulled her hoodie down over her elbow and smashed through the living room window. She undid the lock with her hand and pulled up the frame. Now she was in the house. Like a thief she felt unwelcome and outrageously wrong.

Minding the glass, she tiptoed towards the hallway. She heard the scratches of a dog's nails clipping on the kitchen surface, slow clapping taps. She hated that dog, he was so old and slow, and how Ebony loved him. He showed himself. Arthur. Who calls a dog Arthur, anyway? It's weird. Arthur leapt forward the best he could, his soft joints rickety and unsteady as he leapt onto Ava and then began to bark dusty chugs. 'Shush up,' Ava instructed and pointed a finger at the dog, who came back more fierce and excited. 'Get off me!' she demanded and tried to push the Labrador to the floor, but again he came back, his grey gums and his tongue all cracked and hot and gummy like a sheet of greasy gammon. His slobber began building a heavy web over and around Ava and she lashed out and punched the dog in the face. His thick, heavy body plodded to the ground like the torso of a horse. Her hand aching, her knuckles bruised. Arthur was dead. She nodded to take it all in, to soak the sadness up. Ebony would be ruined.

She made her way upstairs. She reminded herself that what she was doing was all right, correct, that she had a definite legiti-mate reason to be at the Matters' house, snooping, alone. She opened the first bedroom. It was the parents' room, she could tell because it had all that fitted wardrobe rubbish in it, all plastic-covered hardboard and shiny handles covered in ugly roses. Mrs Matters' hairbrush lay on the side, the hair still locked inside the prongs.

The next door was the bathroom. Toothbrushes, cracked soap, the toilet handle, the toilet paper, soft. The rug, the bath, the Aussie shampoo, the Dove, the sweetness, the cleanliness, the hairs in the bath, long strands and this excited her. And then the door. An 'E' on the panel, and then a cluster of sticky silver stars, must have been there since she was small and a poster of that actor from *Twilight*, suspended by Blu-tack. Ava grouped her palm round the doorknob, let her hand gobble it up, pushed down and twisted.

The heat of the room was stifling, what with the sunshine pouring in. Ava saw her own bedroom across the garden, shabby, scruffy, a swelling of damp on the surrounding brick, pigeon shit on the windowsill and a scattering of cigarette ends. Ava looked at Ebony's bed; neat, tidy, her clean clothes washed and in piles on top, pink socks, a grey blouse, underwear. But Ava did not want to touch anything; she just wanted to look, as though she were at an exhibition. The best exhibition in the world. She went over to the dressing table; the mirror with all the necklaces and beads hanging from it, the make-up, the blusher brush, the hairspray, the deodorant, the hairgrips and colour palettes and hand mirrors and a mix tape. And then the drawers, the books, the shelves, the stuff that made up who Ebony was. The floor, the purple carpet, the stripy rug, the bin, the snotty tissues, the magazine, the Twix wrapper, the wallpaper, the wall mirror, the Polaroid. Ava and that man. Who *was* that fucking man? Then she heard the alarming cue of a key twisting in a lock and the door opening. 'Hi!' a voice calls up. Ebony.

'Looks like no one's here . . .' she hears Ebony say. 'Do you want a drink?'

Who is she talking to, that sneaky cow?

'Yeah, okay, what you got?'

'Erm, let's see . . . orange juice?'

Ava began to panic, she rushed around the bedroom, the wardrobe was full of clothes and shoes, everything was so neat, there was nowhere to hide, to go, and Arthur, what happened when they saw Arthur and the smashed window and . . .?

She heard them coming up the stairs, plodding in racy steps. Ava scooped her body under the bed and blew out in relief, the door flew open and then Ava sucked in again as she felt Ebony's body bounce onto the bed followed by a hefty masculine flop. Ava's pupils widened as she felt the pressure over her, like an umbrella of concrete, she wanted to die. Feeling the writhing satisfaction above her was smothering. Ava's heart was racing, sweat beads squeezing out of her forehead and turning her from hot to cold and back and forth and hot to cold and back and forth until she was so close to exploding. And then – another key in the door.

'Ebony!' Dad was home.

The two on the bed collected their clothes and in a flurry of swearwords and bumping bodies, Ebony opened the door to her heated bedroom and called to her father, 'Just coming . . .' she called. She hissed, 'Paul, get your shit together, will you, for Christ's sake?' Ava, under the mattress, her spine, scoring a squeeze into the carpet. And then the scream.

'Oh my God! I don't believe it . . . I don't believe it . . . I don't . . . Arthur!' Ebony's tears shook the house like a train gushing by; they came out in tortured beats. Ava smiled.

She hadn't seen herself as a killer; she didn't fancy herself as a dog murderer. However when they saw the gash in the window, they would know that this was deliberate.

'Paul, I think it's time you left, if you don't mind,' Mr Matters instructed Paul. The boy was speechlessly excited anyway, his cheeks still flushed, his pupils dilated. 'I'm gonna take Arthur outside,' Mr Matters reassured Ebony and threw the tablecloth over the dog and his bloody gold fur.

Fuss, gabble, choice, blame, fast and the heavy urge of urgent steps and leaving and left and the door shut and the click of the door accepting the latch and shut and over and in the house Ebony and in the house Ava. Alone.

Ebony, such a spoilt brute. The right thing to do would be to dry the bloody carpet, to dab it with a dry cloth and then rinse it and then get those blood stains out. But no. She didn't see it as her job, instead she felt awfully sorry for herself and began to cry. She sent a few text messages to some friends and then she collapsed onto the couch and she cried. Then she picked up the remote and managed, just about, to wrap herself up in a blanket and to put on *Supernanny*.

Ava watched her from the staircase, her nostrils flaring, her heart jumping out of her skin furiously, pounding. What to do?

What to do? What to do? What to do? She stood to attention, she would just grasp her, she could just slowly, quietly, put her hands round Ebony's mouth . . . and then what? Murder her? She didn't want to kill her, did she? Scare her? Kiss her? Love her? What did she actually want? But before she knew it her legs, had, without her confirmation, begun walking towards the couch. Ebony's back was so small, darting up and down in grief, snuffling, controlling her tears. Ava's eyes crooked as she got closer and closer and closer and closer and her heart thumping, stormy intense drumming bangs, palpitations, furious, venomous palpitations and her hands so ready, so ready to damage and destroy and smother and Ebony's hairs raise on her neck, her sensor is up and she, in one swift glance, looks round and Ava's heart stops . . .

The doctor said it was permanent. No running, no working and certainly no smoking. Ava was far too young for a heart attack. She should live on a healthy diet of white meat and vegetables, nuts, fruit and plenty of water. For now, it is advised she should not leave the house. She should not leave the house. She should not leave the house. She should not leave the house. She never left the house.

Sat before Pugley was a fully grown man. Heavily built, bearded, thick hairy eyebrows that splayed out like the hands of grasping claws, big nostrils, big hands, big feet, flat chest covered in tiny black twists of hair, and no hips, no waist, only a stiff jaw. Pugley cut Ava's hair every so often – if he didn't cut it, she would leave it, let it tangle. Pugley would also run a big bath for her twice a week – if he didn't, she wouldn't wash, the same went for food and drink and reading and watching the television and listening to the radio. Without Pugley the only thing Ava felt compelled to do was to work out as much as she could before she was told not to. She had a strict routine that she followed religiously when Pugley left for work. And then she would lie on her bed and think. There was always so much to think about. In her dark room, the door shut, the strong rotten smell of body and bed and sleep festered over her like left-out cheese.

In the evenings she ate with her father, whom she now loomed over like a crane over a tiny bungalow. She took up so much space; her energy was like a vacuum. She sucked the atmosphere up and gave nothing back, and Pugley got on with it as though a wolf had eaten up his little girl and just carried on with her inside of him. Washing dishes, wiping surfaces, changing the arm on the clocks.

Her last check-up, the doctor said, was a success; he had noticed and recorded definite improvement and Ava was encouraged to leave the house again.

'I don't know how,' she said, barely even moving her lips, her voice was dark and deep.

'Yes you do, Ava-bean,' her father reassured her.

'No. Look at me.'

'You're lovely,' he charmed, his eyes watering at the block of scruff before him. It was in Ava's eyes that he saw his child, his little girl, his friend. 'But maybe you ought to, I don't know, have a think about . . . erm . . . who you want to be . . . if you get my . . . err . . . drift.'

'Yes, Dad, I've got it,' she smiled. Pugley always was so prudish, and was getting on a bit now too, his hair garlic white, his old eyes, he had turned into a curled prawn and was relieved when Ava said, 'Can you show me how to use a razor?'

The song of a seagull was heart-warming for Ava as she finally left her front door. Her father proudly held her arm as she stepped out, her pupils stretching, opening like the fusion of jasmine watched and remembered. Her beard had been trimmed, her hair had been cut, her nails filed and cleaned. A strong smell of aftershave trailed after her. Her walk was strong and steady, her passive energy proved to be quite contagious and passers-by seemed confused and oddly appreciative of the handsome, well-groomed man that nodded to them as they went about their business. The rumour was that the heart attack had killed Ava.

And at work, the girls would come, just for a peek, non-fish eaters would queue up outside, just to watch this handsome beast of a man using a cleaver and gutting the belly of a sea bass, taking the head off a trout, the legs off a prawn. Ava would receive telephone numbers, sweet comments of 'My friend thinks you are proper fit,' a married older woman, holding an everlasting grasp over a carrier bag, her eyes locking into Ava's. Ava would bite her lip and look away.

Ebony never did come back to The Codfather. Nor did Mr Matters. Their house was sold to a small family. Rumours were that Ebony had had a baby.

One day a girl came in, her hair a long tail of whipping blonde, curled around her face and swung down her shoulders; she was looking for the library. Pugley said there was no library.

'What a waste of a journey,' the girl said.

'Not entirely,' Pugley blinked a shiny wink as Ava came out of the back carrying a barrel of ice chips. He sat the barrel down and wiped his forearm across his hot head.

The girl ran her tongue over her teeth and Ava nodded, 'All right?'

The fish was glossy and wet, glistening and glassy eyed, the lemons fresh, mini open wounds of citrus, the radio hummed gently, the beards on the mussels remained. The future was open and waiting.

THE END

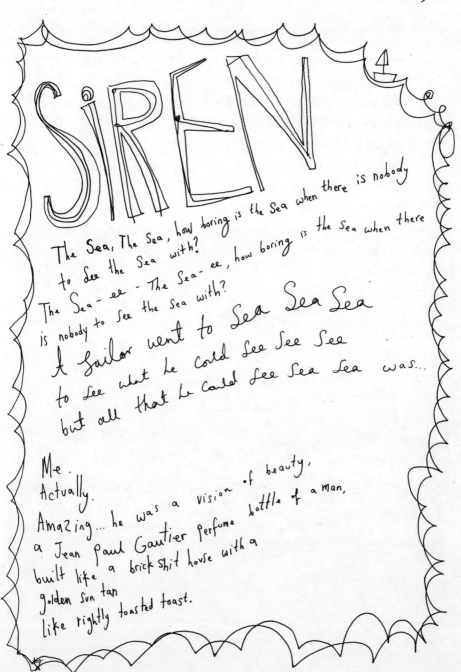

SiReN

The Sea, The Sea, how boring is the Sea when there is nobody
to see the Sea with?
The Sea-ee - The Sea-ee, how boring is the Sea when there
is nobody to see the Sea with?
A Sailor went to Sea Sea Sea
to see what he could See See See
but all that he could See Sea Sea was...

Me.
Actually.
Amazing... he was a vision of beauty,
a Jean Paul Gautier perfume bottle of a man,
built like a brick shit house with a
golden sun tan
like rightly toasted toast.

The bit I loved about him the most was his garnish of gingery ruffle that had been

grumbled

by the ocean, sweating and rippling like from the splashes he had just appeared. His

moist arms bulging up and down and up and down and up, as though he had

taken the trouble of previously stuffing them with mango fruit or hamsters.

I took the little sailor boy down to a seafood restaurant and let him smother me in

langoustine and watched as he unravelled the prawn so delicately and he headed

prickly face down into a basin of fish platter and sucked the legs apart, I

watched his ravishing jaw tear flesh and the excitement exploded my

HEART. The creature, the innocent beast, sank the wine, and I

his feast. So raw and reckless, I fondled my necklace, only to choke

myself a little to prove that this was not a trick. I was lovesick.

We ran to the pier, peered down a little bit, didn't really see anything we

really liked, So we headed for the hills, as the wind beat our legs we kissed and

rolled and tears slid down our bruised cheeks and we danced home, up the path, to

the front door, we couldn't wait anymore, as the gust blew into the house, we

had the place all to ourselves and decided to have...................

A staring competition.

We stared until our pupils went red until they widened up and dried up quick, huge like eyes of sobbing pigs like empty pig-dily, the milk froth turned to dust, the rose water went dank, but I could only yearn, I'm not sure me didn't stop. We didn't blink either as the coffee ran over a tarred black swimming river, the bulm, the burn. To think to think was an afterthought one that of I could have held my eyeballs up to get a better look. If I wasn't there, I wasn't there when the paper was pressed. Dead! If I wasn't so awfully dead! On the table, the salt. The jam. The bread. And four totally absorbed details rolling from two stubborn heads. I often hit brick walls, I didn't blink. The ache sucked at my retina and drank my soul, but I didn't stop. The pain was unbearable, at times. How many hours or afternoons we even sat there, I...

'DA-D, WE-'RE HO-ME!'

A chaos of fumbling hats and scarves, an emporium of colour, fluoro, the worst kind, yellows, pinks, sparkly wellingtons, bobble hats, flower bags. Tripping up, the dog splashes heart-shaped mud marks on the floor, like a tap dancer his footsteps echo.

'Hi girls,' Felix pulled his shirt on, slides the worn photograph of Beano under the dinner mats. The kitchen, so exposing, no place for games. 'Hi Jenny.' He kissed his wife; she aimed for the lips and got half of them and half a prickly chin.

'Dad, today I made a you out of a toilet roll and this green string, see?' Maya, so small her hands can't even scoop round the loo roll properly. Her cheeks hard with cold, her nose squashed and icy.

'Dad, today we had to bring in a piece of music, and I didn't bring any.'

'Okay, that's okay, Garnet.'

'No, that's not okay. I'm in trouble.' Garnet was excellent at making everything seem as though it was his fault, she had learnt that from her mother.

'She is in trouble, just a little punishment, nothing serious.'
Jennifer stroked Garnet's hair. 'Go and take your coats off, girls.'
Jennifer poured herself a glass of water, grey with tiredness.

'What a day.' She released. Rubbing her eyes, her stripy jumper
worn, her hair in a loose plait. Felix scanned her clothes, the
mismatch, the Gap injection that seemed to have infected her,
shot her like a cupid's arrow, for a relentless affair with stripes
and block pastel. Felix supposed it was better than the baby
sick, the porridge, oaty, milky smell that used to trail after her
like a bad memory. She had really started to remind him of a
rice cake and how had she, without him even knowing, man-
aged to become a hippy? Right under his nose. She made him
feel sick.

'I got some cous cous from the health shop. I thought I could
do a bit of salad, some veggie ke-bobs, maybe?'

It always annoyed him when she snapped words in half like they were celery sticks, especially when she thought she could mould the English language like it was a piece of play dough, like she was some sort of down with the kids youth worker. Ke-bob. *Please.*

'Yeah, sounds good.' Felix gulped, already tasting the rotten lukewarm chickpea. 'I might, actually, if you don't mind, erm, maybe have some meat kebabs with mine.'

'*Meat?*' she shrilled.

'Erm, yes, lamb.' Bad idea. Bad idea. Bad idea. Is she going to cry?

'No, okay, go to the butcher, I guess. Get yourself some MEAT.'

'Well, not if it's a problem, I won't but I sort of fanc—'

'No, no, your show, your decision, do what the fuck you like.'

She kicked the dishwasher shut with her Converse. Ironic.

Glad to be out of the house, Felix walked to the butcher, his iPod stuffed in his ears, his new piece. It needed more depth. He needed a new piano. He needed a new life. Beano. What about Beano? Everything was such a mess. Felix, what with all the music in his ears, the situation, got out his phone and texted him.

'BEER LATER? WANT TO SEE YOU.'

The smell of blood hit him before he reached the shop, iron and cold. The scattering of sawdust powdered the pavement like fake snow. All those carcasses, empty, like oversized deflated balloons. And inside those fat, ugly men and women, podgy, cranking as though they were decaying meat and their saggy south London drones, the fake cress. Pathetic. Was he doing this to remind himself he was a man?

'WHAT TIME? WHERE?'

Swinging the bag with the meat he read the text, quarter relieved Beano had texted him back, quarter pleased, half feeling guilty and shit. The piece still needed more . . . *oomph*. Beano, he played the violin beautifully, perhaps he could really bring the piece to life. No, not fair, stupid, don't mix work and pleasure. Fuck, that was how he ended up married to Jennifer for Christ's sake, and look at him now.

When he got back home, Maya opened the door, already in her pyjamas, must have got yoghurt down her front as usual.

'Mum's got a Mooncup.'

'A what?'

'A cup that you get in and it takes you to the moon.'

'No, it's not, Maya. You don't know anything. It's a special cup from the moon, invented on the moon that gives you moon juice,' Garnet corrected, folding her arms in spite.

Felix peered into the eyes of his little girls. Both tangly hair and tiny hands, dinky upturned noses and freckles like the speckles on a new egg.

'I think I erm, forgot to get some erm . . .'

Another walk, he needed more time. Jennifer, a Mooncup, what next? Was she going to leave him for a bongo? The house was stifling, the kids, the kids, the kids, the stepping on chalk, watching it crush into the carpet, pink mush under his foot, the dried crayons on the radiators, the mushy apples, the constant sticky film that resided on the kitchen table and that never-ending, ever-remaining, sarcastic stench of piss, wet wipes and cottage cheese that seemed to be everywhere all the time. He wanted just one evening, one evening that wasn't immersed in storytelling and tickling and crying and make-believe.

'I'M ABOUT NOW. YOU?'

Being with Beano was about as make-believe as Felix could get, the guy was nineteen and was as loose as a wizard's sleeve. But oh, how Felix adored him. He made him feel alive, as though everything had, finally, at last, clicked into place. Beano was broke, careless and had no responsibility, all of which Felix was attracted to.

'FORTY-FIVE MINS. COME OVER THEN?'

Forty-five minutes, forty-five minutes? How would he get away with that? Text Jennifer, explain he needed a walk? She already suspected he was having an affair, although she didn't know he was in love. She didn't know it was with a bloke. Perhaps she thought he was too dull for all that. He probably was.

'FINE. SEE YOU THEN.'

Felix hated the Frog and Pumpkin, his local pub. He hated it because they thought they were doing the right thing by trying to be like an old man's pub but it was run by twenty-two-year-old toffs who had just been ejected from their eternal gap years and were used as the fresh wheat-grass faces to stand behind the bar and put on mockney accents. This place *belonged* in Bethnal Green, it deserved to, what with all the effort: the sticky tables, the open fire, the acceptance of dogs.

'All right, mate?' the toddler asked from behind the bar; half his head was shaved, tattoos crept up his arms, ships, mermaids, hearts. *You are not an old man, get over yourself.* 'Oi, you're

that composer aren't you? Felix Woolf? I came to watch you
with my girlfriend a while back.'

'Er . . . yes.' Felix smiled, rolling his worn wallet open.

'We came to see you. I play the bass, see, my girlfriend plays
the flute, she . . . Sorry, what can I get you?'

'A glass of red, merlot, thanks.' He smiled shortly, his eyes
on the bar.

'This okay?' the boy with the tattoos asked, holding the
bottle up close for Felix to see.

'I'm sure that's fine, thank you.' He waved the bottle away as
though it were a snotty tissue.

'Nice choice.' *As though he knew*, thought Felix. *However, he
had come to see him play, he had taste. How pretentious.* 'See,
my girlfriend she plays the flute, and . . .' He scales the wall for
a good clean glass, the *best* glass. '. . . her music teacher, I think,
correct me if I'm wrong, is your missus, Jenny?'

'Yes, she does teach. Your girlfriend could well be one of her students, she teaches at our home just round the corner.'

'It was funny, we used to come and see you play when I was at college and everybody thought you were, you know, *bent*.'

'Really? Did they?'

'Funny, 'cos you're not.'

'Yes, it is funny.' The rash began creeping, the anger boiling, and the worry flurrying. *Bent? Bent?* He wanted to cry and, without meaning to, he sort of did. Collecting himself, he zipped up, drained his glass, pushed forward a £10 note and left. He would just have to go and wait outside Beano's. If he wasn't in, he wasn't in, and he could buy himself a bottle of wine and sit on the doorstep. Already indulging the image he had conjured up: the damaged composer, gay, drunk, in denial. Perfect.

He unscrewed his wine on the walk; the plumy, aging earthiness flooded his mouth like blood. His phone buzzed in his pocket. Jennifer. *Fuck off, will you?*

He reached Beano's flat. What a shitty wreck – he loved it. The blue door, the paint cracking on the ridges, the letterbox rusty, the door numbers odd and one hung upside down. There was no excuse for a front garden, instead just a block of unforgiving concrete. Brutal and grey, the odd weed had squeezed its way through for air. Felix checked his phone, only fifteen minutes to go, that shouldn't pass too slowly.

But he didn't have to wait. Beano came to the door. 'All right, Wolfie?'

'How do I look?'

'Pissed and old.'

'That bad?'

'Listen, I can't hang with you long – I got a customer coming at seven.'

'A customer?'

'Weed, baby, weed. Come and get your sorry bitch ass inside.'

The key in the lock. The door shut.

Felix fumbled for his glasses, rubbing them clean with the duvet cover.

'Let me try on your glasses.' Beano snatched them away and slot them on his nose. 'Do I look as boring as you?'

'No, you couldn't possibly.' Felix kissed Beano on the lips.

'Right, Wolfie, you got to get home to your Mooncupping hummus-making dyke of a wife and I got to get shotting. Anything else?'

'Please cancel.'

'I can't. I have to eat tonight.'

'I can give you money. Please, let me stay the night.'

'And what's your wife going to think?'

'I'll think of something.'

'No, I have to work, this guy is a big customer, he's a madman, he's fucking dangerous. Get your clothes on.'

Felix took a long gulp from a cheaper darker bottle of wine that Beano had given him. The bitterness was sickly.

'What your girls gonna think?'

'They'll be in bed soon.'

Beano pulled up his jeans, sprayed some deodorant under his armpits. He was so thin his ribs popped out like the edges of an old radiator.

'You might want to splash this on you too, papa.' Beano threw the can over to Felix, who let it fall at his feet and clumsily picked it up; the spray missed both pits, hissing into the air.

'Please let me stay with you.'

'No, come on, leave now, get your stuff, look it's five to already.' Beano leant down and began helping Felix to get his shoes on, Felix swayed and drifted sideways. 'Come on, old man.'

'Don't call me that, respect your elders.'

'All right, calm down, I'm only playing.'

'Well don't. Why don't you play me the violin?'

'Not now, I'm working, come on.'

'Do you love me?'

'Yes, I love you old man, just like a grandpappy.'

'Stop it. I'm serious.'

'Yeah, you're all right.'

'Let's run away together, come on, me and you, *come on*.'

'Can we just do this tomorrow?'

'You and me, all by ourselves, just us. Imagine that – not a care in the world.'

Beano led Felix to the front door where he unclicked the door; he had several locks that all needed undoing.

'Why are you treating me so badly?' Felix began to fall apart, sinking to the floor, becoming heavy, clutching onto Beano's trousers.

'Eh, dude, get the fuck up off the floor. You're acting like a dick.'

'Why are you doing this to me?'

The Jeep pulled up outside the front of the house, the lights poured into the windows. Felix reacted like a vampire in sunlight.

'You're acting pathetic, Kip's here, now so you'll have to—' Felix fastened his elephantine musician palms over Beano's mouth and held stiff.

The music was still pumping from the Jeep; deep muffled bass lines, a squeaky rapper jibbering over it. Then nothing. Footsteps hoofing the pavement, the car door snapped shut. Keys jangling, the noise of the alarm whopping on and then off.

The gate clacked open, the feet up the concreted front, dush, dush, dush, and on the door, nack, nack, nack.

And again, nack, nack, nack.

'Oi, Beans, open up the door, boy. Yo, Beans, open up the door, brother.'

Felix had his hands still tight around Beano's face. Beano was struggling to answer the door. Felix held tighter before throwing him to the floor.

The door fell open, stiff, from Felix's foot stopping the back of it. An arm appeared out of it, Felix's, covered over in a sheet. He produced a cellophane bag of weed.

'What's going on, Beans? I didn't come here for your drugs. Why ain't you opening the motherfucking door up?'

Felix snatched back the weed. *What DID he come for?*

'I'm sick,' Felix managed to screech.

'You're sick?' The massive man spoke strong, violently spitting the 'ick' back at the door.

'Yes.'

'Well, why didn't you say earlier?'

'It's just come on.'

'Okay. Man, if that's how you feel, that's how you feel. Get better soon then, all right?'

'Yes, thank you. I will.'

His feet were heard plonking out of the front in huge dusty steps, the gate released and shut again. The alarm whooping, the music started again, that silly music, the engine bubbling, the car tyres sped away.

Felix shrunk in relief. His entire body rinsing out through fear. What was he after? The enormity of the man still in his eyeshot, impossible to erase, the bulk and girth of his size, he could have swallowed him up whole just by a look. Still, he was gone now. Sobering up, he went over to Beano who was in the hallway, keeping low. Felix, as sneaky as a child, went over to him, crawling.

'Beano. I got rid of him, that beast of a man, he's gone. Beano . . . Beano.' He rustled his body, no movement. He shook him, hard, with vigour this time, his arms floppy and bendy like rotting carrots. 'Beano . . .' He came up to his face, patting it, tapping it, flicking his cheeks, his eyes, blowing on his face, pinching his eyelids, lifting up his eyelids and then blood, blood on his hands and oozing out of Beano's head and ear, hot and fast. His jaw creeping open, as soundless as a goldfish. Felix waited for a word to spring out of it. He knew he had pushed him, but that hard? Had he pushed him so terribly hard? He must feel for a pulse, he must call for an ambulance, must think, for once, must think, who to call?

Jiggling, nervous, he panicked. After all, effectively, he had killed Beano, hadn't he? But energy rushing through him in short, sharp bursts, blowing his veins, jittery, he tried to think of something. And then Beano's phone began to ring, hard, shrilling rings that cut. Relentless, it rang:

KIP MOB

Flashing. Again and again and then Felix's phone began to ring, and then, out of nowhere, a brick came crashing through the window. It soared through, glass splattering into the house, the shuddering violent gash made Felix jump to his feet in an attempt to escape. He ran to the kitchen, the one window was as small as a cereal box with a vent chugging through it. The bathroom window was even smaller, the same scenario. Shit. Just enough time to put the TV on, drown out some of the awkwardness.

The door seized open. Footsteps, spongy on the foul rug, the static sound of a coat, scratching, buzzing, and *Deal or No Deal* the constant melody, an audience clapping. Rapture. The footsteps went to the brick, picked it up, the smell of suspense, enough to make you gag.

And into the bedroom he went, the massive man, he knew his way round. He saw the bed, the shaped sheets, fresh with pungent dirtiness and the sweetness from Lynx. And in the bed a bump, a bump of a body of a man, scooped up in the blanket.

'Eh, Beans . . . if you didn't feel well, why ain't you saying earlier?' The man sniffed out evidence and said his name again. 'Beans . . .'

'What?' Felix mumbled from under the blankets, he lowered his tone, droning it into a South London gripe.

'What the fuck's up? My boys – they just thrown a brick through your window, they know how pissed I am with you . . .'

I don't trust what's going on, Beano, something dodgy's going on here. I got a right mind to shoot the whole place to shit.'

'No, come and sit down on the bed,' Felix managed.

'Well, you sure sound sick. I don't want no lurgies off you.'

'Shit bruv, look at your feet – they all wrinkly and big and old-looking, you really sick? What you got?'

Felix slowly drew them in, he never liked his feet, all veiny and extra large, not like Beano who was slight and cute and dinky. . .

'Yes, but you see bigger feet means a bigger package and all the better to pleasure you with Kip,' he gulped, hoping he got the nail on the head, half hoping that wasn't why he had come, he didn't like the idea of sharing Beano with anybody.

'Yes, I guess. I wanted to feel that package today, before you got all sick. I could get used to you having big old cheesy feet.'

Felix wanted to die. His heart fell through him, dropping like a stone in the sea.

'And your hair . . .' Felix had forgotten to stuff it into his duvet shield, it sat, propped out of the top like the stalk of a pineapple. Felix tried to snuggle down to cover it over. 'It's all grey and greasy and long and old-looking. You even got flecks of dandruff there, what's going on with that?'

'It's stress, money problems, but look, this way I look wise and knowledgeable, like George Clooney. He's handsome, everybody likes him, you might like that? All the better I'll look sitting next to you at the theatre.'

Kip liked that, the theatre.

'You'd go to the theatre with me? Like a date? Thought you weren't interested in going out with me? When you're better we'll . . .' He stopped for a moment. 'Listen, you better not be fucking with me, okay? I asked you out before and you said no. I don't want no bullshit. And look at your hands . . . they're so big and pale, is that from the illness too? Why are your hands so big?'

'All the better to strangle you with!'

Felix launched out of the blanket, his hands driving forward, clutching until they clamped around Kip's neck. He grabbed tight and with a power he did not have in him until he saw Beano's blood – it gave him utter absolute control over the trunk-like neck he was narrowing.

Still, Kip was bigger than he had expected, Trojan-like. His hulking hands slapped round Felix's and pulled the opposite way, dragging furiously, grinding his teeth into his big purple gums, his eyes watering, his heavy dreadlocks slapping against Felix's arms in a frenzy of madness and then he stayed still, placid and even nodded once, allowing the deafness to fasten his ears shut and let him go, peering at the heavens the entire time before booming heavily onto the bed. Felix came with him in a gust of disbelief and relief. Over.

He let himself into his house. Dummied. He felt as though he didn't live there anymore. He felt like a trespasser, invading during the night. The girls' jackets hung up on the coat stand, their scooters were lined up neatly. The dog was snoring, a tap dripping. *Must get that fixed*, he thought, and went upstairs to bed.

The End.

May, Fay and Rosemary
or
Three sisters and a sledgehammer

O nce upon a time there lived Nana Swan and her three granddaughters. The eldest and fattest was May who was kind and loyal. The second eldest and second fattest was Fay who was sheepish and shy. And the third and final daughter was the youngest and thinnest and most special – she was thoughtful and imaginative, her mind like a flickering storybook; her name was Rosemary.

One day Nana said, 'Girls, I would like to make a big pie. Could you please fetch me some blackberries from down by the railway. But remember, whatever you do, don't step on the tracks – those trains come fast and are gone.'

What with Rosemary being so slow, the idea seemed a chore. Still, buckets and gloves in hand, the three of them rattled down the cobbled road. May led the way followed by Fay and last of all came a distracted Rosemary.

The railway sides were a tangled, overgrown, thorn-ridden cage and the only opening was the tracks themselves, rusty and hard and hot from where the sun penetrated them throughout the day. The floor was a sweeping sandy blanket, ashy and dry, Rosemary thought the ground would make a perfect base to a cheesecake if it wasn't actually sand and dirt and was instead a scrummy crumble of ginger and cinnamon and biscuit. The sun was setting low and that made it hard to keep eyes open. Only the foreseeable future of a tasty pie made the chore sweeter.

When the three of them reached the railway tracks, May put down her bucket and gloves and began to dictate, just like she always did, brushing her pistachio dress down, freeing it of scummy yellow dust.

'I'm going to pick the blackberries to the left of the track. Fay, you are going to pick the blackberries to the right of the track. And Rosemary, as you are thinnest and appreciative of the most precious things in life, you can pick the finest, plumpest, untainted blackberries from in between the tracks.'

'Well that is rather nice of you to say so but Nana Swan told us not to go on to the tracks, May,' Rosemary said, eyeballing a grass snake sashaying through a bunched bush, winding in and out and folding.

'She meant the other tracks, these tracks are perfectly safe,' May insisted, fabricating, winking at her cowardly sister Fay, who begrudgingly did as she was ordered, though she knew only too well her sister's goblin designs.

Rosemary doubted her sister, as she wasn't quite sure what other tracks she meant. However, if anybody knew how tasty the blackberries underneath the train tracks were, it was she. And she couldn't resist.

Her ignorance was terrifyingly endearing and her loyalty towards her menacing big sister was pitiful. May knew a fast train was set to pass the tracks in exactly six minutes. That cruel sister, so sick and tired of dreamy Rosemary, was planning to squish her to a pulp.

Then suddenly a TRIP, TRAP, TRAP, TRIP, TRAP, TRAP came from underneath the tracks and out popped the most ugliest, nastiest, beastliest troll Rosemary had ever seen.

'YOU,' he roared, 'are picking my blackberries. These berries belong to me!'

'I didn't know,' cried Rosemary. 'Please forgive me, troll.'

The troll was fat and oily. His hair was spidery and stringy. His eyes were red and glassy. His teeth were black and dead. And in his hands he held a sledgehammer, heavy, old and beaten.

'As a punishment for eating my treasured blackberries I am going to gobble you up!'

His red eyes flickered as he prepared to launch his clawed

hands over Rosemary, his sledgehammer hovered over her pretty head.

'No, wait!' cried Rosemary. 'Don't eat me. I'm bony and sharp and small and difficult. It would be like eating a snail. I have a sister, Fay, who is much older and fatter and in comparison would be like eating a quail.'

'Hmmm . . .' The troll rubbed his chin and raised his eyebrows. He inspected Rosemary closer; she *was* rather skinny and he didn't want to fill up on cartilage.

'Send her over and then you can go,' the troll agreed.

And with that Rosemary let out a big scream and allowed her small nimble frame to slip though a gap in the tracks. Guilt-ridden Fay rushed over to the tracks, knowing full well there were now only four minutes until the fast train would gush by.

'Rosemary . . . are you stuck?' Panicking, she peeped down the gap in the tracks.

TRIP, TRAP, TRAP, TRIP, TRAP, TRAP and the troll appeared in front of Fay.

''Tis right,' he nodded grittily, 'you are far fatter than your younger sister.' He sneered and then released Rosemary, booting her so hard she launched into the air and flew over a neighbouring fence.

'I'm going to gobble you all up!' He threw his sledgehammer into the air, his red eyes glowing, beads of greasy sweat trickling down his forehead.

'No, wait!' cried Fay. 'Don't eat me, I'm not fully grown, I look chubbier than my sister but I'm mainly blubber and bone. It would be like eating a quail. I have a second sister, who is much older and fatter and in comparison would be like eating a whale.'

'Hmmm . . . a whale?' The troll's mouth watered and he brought down his hammer. 'Send her over then you can go.'

And with that Fay screamed a piercing howl that startled May and made her jump out of her skin.

May ran over to the track, and peeped down the gap in the tracks only to hear: *TRIP, TRAP, TRAP, TRIP, TRAP, TRAP.*

The greasy groggy troll stood beneath the tracks, dribbling and bobbing up and down in excitement. As soon as he saw May, the troll released Fay, booting her so hard she launched into the air and flew over a neighbouring fence.

'Your sisters were right, you are much fatter than them. I'm going to gobble you up!'

He threw his hammer into the air, angry and hungry, and as he did, Rosemary appeared out of nowhere and grabbed the other side of the hammer holding it down with a strength she did not know existed. Then Fay pushed the troll to the ground and held his fat slimy wrists in place.

The sound of the train coming closer mixed with the sound of the troll's fury.

May watched in horror and amazement as tiny Rosemary propelled the hammer into the air and brought it down onto the troll's stomach where it squelched like a fist punching a heap of dough. The troll let rip a terrible roar of pain as blood and guts splattered over Rosemary's face.

The whistle of the train screamed.

Although already tired, Rosemary took the sledgehammer into the air for a second time and sunk it into the troll's chest. His ribcage snapped like a matchstick house, bone diced into the air like woodchips.

The sound of the train wheels, metal on metal, screeched down the track.

Rosemary took the rest of her strength and hit the troll a third and final time, right in his grimy face – it split into two as simple and as neat as a dropped watermelon. Maggots wriggled free from his vile groggy head.

The train was now in sight, rushing towards them.

Rosemary slung the hammer to the left of the track and she persuaded her sisters to slip through the gap in the tracks.

The train was now up close, drawing down on them.

Rosemary slipped down into the nest of blackberries.

Fay followed, easing herself in and collapsing onto her little sister.

But May, the eldest and fattest, could not slip through. She squeezed, she sucked, she panicked, she cried, she itched all over as sweat and worry scratched her like a feather onto a nostril. How she flapped as her sisters pulled her feet and hips and called her name but the

train
ran
over
her
fast
and
was
gone.

Her blackberries crushed onto the tracks like kisses.

No songs, no dance, no time to play,

Only Rosemary and Fay and no more May.

The End

Smugglers

Cruel he creeps the forest, weak,
And shatters 'neath
The mountain peak.
~~the~~ Young and unclean where lovers go
to take a ~~girl~~ girl from the town.
And here were caves
where smugglers sport
a fondle, a snort, a rape, a ~~snort~~ snort,
Wet fingers spool
into the ~~rotten~~ gin-spoilt pool.

Monks walk the candle out blue,
Chased down the green stained afternoon,
their pupils so wide,
the saucers of spies
bloodshot mornings—evening cries.
And the ships come home and ~~offload~~ offload in the night.
Such luxuries of such delight,
tea, tobacco, whisky, ale
'tis funny how a Smugglers' pocket never fails
and that red socket.
The man is always pale.

Put out the last puff of ~~good~~ Man's Currency,
Caught in the web of the poor man's hostility,
and beaten from blue to black and black to red
and a dreary rainbow bends over each ones head.

These pirates!
These pirates!
Have no God
Only the Spirit of their grandfathers gone.
Wives, daughters and sisters
wait with the thimble, the kettle,
a stitch, a whisper, a scatter of petals.
And the richer — get better
the lonely — get sick
The lost — get engraved onto stone on the slip
of the hill,
Where ~~the lost~~ the dog barks now
is only the hollow chant of empty souls and
that is all.

'Come on, have a slice of coffee and walnut cake.'
'I don't want any,' the local murderer sighed, kicking off his shoes and resting them on the poof. The cat, Garlic, jumped up onto his lap, her paws padding his jogging bottoms, reminding him of the fact he was a slob.

'Why don't you go out and murder some of those Girl Guides? That will cheer you up,' his mother suggested.

'I'm not in the mood,' he huffed, picking up the atlas from the side and flicking through the pages.

'You dig yourself into these pits,' his mother muttered and nudged his feet with her shin so he would move his legs and, with a dramatic sigh, collapsed down beside him. 'Here you are, petal,' she said, handing him a cup of hot liquid.

'What's this?' He smelt the liquid.

'Miso soup,' she smiled.

'What soup? It smells like fish.'

'It's Japanese. The doctor told me it's good for digestion. I don't know, thought I'd try it.'

The local murderer had a sniff and put the mug on the side,

disgusted. He dropped his murdering head onto his mother's shoulder. She opened the paper up.

'What page is your column again?'

'Page nineteen.'

'Hot water bottle and lavender, that's my trick. Shall I draw you a bath?'

'No. I'm depressed, I don't want to wash.'

'Here we are. Look at your photograph, that's not a nice one, why don't you make them take it from your best side? You're far more handsome on the left. Listen: "Our best-loved culinary hero cooks up comfort food" and then look at the picture – you looking like some depressed poet.'

'Mother, leave it.'

'Let's see . . . beef wellington . . . Why don't you make exotic recipes?'

'What, like miso soup?' the local murderer snubbed.

'Well, I don't know, beef wellington is a bit boring. Why don't you try a green curry? Something *exotic*?'

'Oh, turn over, can't you read this when I'm not here? What else is in there?'

'Missing people . . . Oh, isn't it awful. Do you recognize her?' the murderer's mother asked, muttering empty chalices of nothings that she believed were the right sort of noises to make when indulging in a page of missing persons.

'No.' The local murderer sipped the soup out of boredom.

'Him?' his mother pointed.

'No,' the murderer huffed.

'Well, what about these two?'

'No. No. No. I don't recognize any of them.' Agitated, he threw a pillow to the floor. Garlic hopped off after it.

'What have you been doing then? Clipping your bloody toenails? There are four missing people on this page and none of them is thanks to you. Ridiculous.'

'Leave me alone, I'm depressed.'

'So you say. Did you book Garlic's vet appointment?'

'Yes. Did you pick up my suit from the dry cleaners?'

'Yes. I did, like a good mother.'

Across the way the Girl Guides were setting up camp for the night, a muddle of missing toothbrushes and a squealing siren after the sight of a black widow spinning in the opening of a plump girl's tent.

'Those bloody torches, the flashes keep bouncing off the television,' the local murderer grunted.

'Leave them alone, they're having fun. You shouldn't have that silly telly on, anyway. It'll send you barmy.'

'Well, they shouldn't be allowed torches. Stupid Brownies. I hate them.'

'Let off. Just because you're in a bad way doesn't mean nobody else can have any fun. Stop spying on them anyway, you're behaving like a psycho.'

Annoyed, he picked up a box of matches, lit one, let it burn to the quick, until the end was frazzled and curling. The pathetic smoke plumed up in curdling claws. The smell disbursed.

'Stupid boy, act your age.' His mother snatched the matches away, and slapped the murderer's wrists.

'Oh, you'll never get to heaven,'
'Oh, you'll never get to heaven,'
'In a baked bean tin,'
'In a baked bean tin,'
''Cos a baked bean tin,'
''Cos a baked bean tin,'
'S'got baked beans in!'
'S'got baked beans in!'
'No, you'll never get to heaven
In a baked bean tin
'Cos a baked bean tin
S'got baked beans in.
I ain't gonna
Grieve, my Lord, no more!'

'Let's tell a ghost story now,' Alex suggested, throwing the torch under her chin like an oversized buttercup. She took her lip balm out of her pocket, soft from the heat of sitting so close to her body, and ran her finger loosely over her lips.

That was when she saw her. Away from the group, by a few feet, near the tree, in the dark, illuminating the night like a milk bottle, her red hair flapping about and her hands over her mouth, tight, and those stiff eyes, beckoning, calling to her. It did not scare Alex, only caught her, froze her; she paralysed her mind and switched everything else off and tuned in. The girl – she wanted to play, she wanted to feel.

'Alex? Alex? Are you even listening?'

'Sorry, I was . . . it was . . . I'm miles away.'

'Well, can you not be miles away when I'm talking to you?' Badger, the chunky, naggy group leader muttered, folding her stuffy arms over her chest.

'I thought you were going to tell a ghost story,' Harriett nudged, grinding her teeth together. All eyes always looked to Alex for entertainment.

'Well . . . okay . . . I . . .' Alex began. Alex was, in her own words, 'Not here for the religious crap, it's to keep me on the straight and narrow.' She was like a spider, in the sense that she was more scared of everybody else than they were of her. The most baffling member of the group, she was opinionated, fiery and always had to have the last word. She combed her hair into a plaited spiral on top of her gel-slammed head, her nose piercing twinkling messages across the navy air.

'Make it quick, Alex,' Badger kicked her jaw out and began peeling a beaten satsuma, the skin coming off in rounded curls.

'She comes in many forms . . .' Alex was a good storyteller and rolled her eyes to the back of her head as she began her ghost impression, 'She is known 'cos whatever form she comes in she will always have a lock of red hair.' Alex's voice began to tremble as she glanced over to where she saw the figure who had now vanished. Alex rubbed her left eye sleepily.

'Go on . . .' one of the other girls mooched.

'Okay, okay, I just want to get this right. This girl, she was young, like us, her father was a hunter, her mother . . . a prostitute!'

'Oh shit, she was a jezzy!' Harriett squawked.

'That's quite enough of that!' Badger tapped Alex on the wrist and attempted to bring the story to a premature end, but the girls whining and pleading made her give in.

'The girl's mother worked as a prostitute in secret, to save money for her daughter to go to school, her husband thought she was doing charity work at the church. That chick was about as religious as a dyke on Halloween. She also had many men chirpsin' her, crazy for her, who after one night in bed with her had fallen head over heels in love. And, although her job was a secret, she started to get a bit baited up when these men started to follow her and their fascination turned into an obsession . . .'

'Freaky.'

'Shut up, Sam. Anyway, after a while, the mother had begun to think one of these men was kind of tick . . . Like, she began fancying him,' she translated for Badger, who was pretending not to listen or care, 'and then they started to have a bit of a 'fing going, and the mother no longer took money from him for her services . . .'

'As a hoe?'

'Yes, as a hoe. And they began to fall in love, he would bring her presents and promise to take her away to Malibu, New York, the Canaries. Anyway, this guy – let's call him Leon – had shot some deer or summit and wanted to bring it round as an offering of love to his prossie.'

'That's a whack present.'

'He knew she was poor and that.'

'How's a dead deer gonna help a poor person?'

'Food, you nut,' Alex pushed her tongue to her chin and crossed her eyes over dramatically.

'Nah, mate. I ain't eating no deer.'

'ANY-WAY, his prossie weren't in, woz she? She was out doing the old how's yer father, shubzing up with someone else, and the daughter answered the door. The daughter had well good manners and was like . . .' – Alex swiftly went into character – '"Oh hiya, how's you? Come in for a brew and a coconut ring." She invited him in and gave him a cup of tea and a coconut ring. Leon did not know his jezebel chick even had a daughter let alone a baby father and so he began to bawl into his teacup and then couldn't help but explain who he was and how he knew the girl's mother. The girl began to bawl her eyes out too and held Leon close, explaining everything would be all right. Greazy. Gravy. During this, the father – remember, he is a hunter – came home and saw the two of them. Out of rage, he picked his axe up and shanked the man, assuming he was trying to get jiggy with his daughter.' Alex used the torch as a prop for the axe, holding it high over her shoulder and bringing it down in forceful hacks. 'The daughter screamed the truth at her father, told him about the prostitution, the affair, hoping to explain that she was innocent, but he was so cross he didn't know what to do. He was angry so he picked up the axe and did the same to his daughter, shot the messenger, and left to go and find his wife, to kill her too.'

'Didn't nobody call the feds?'

'Ain't no police. The mother came home, her hood over her head to cover her make-up – obviously 'cos she'd been out being a prossie – and when she saw her daughter and her lover fucked up, she . . .' Badger made a grimace at the phrase 'fucked up', raising half of her stern uni-brow. 'Sorry, miss,' Alex sneaked.

'Bloody hell, Al, this is intense,' one of the girls distracted.

'Then she ran outside with her husband's gun and shot herself in the mouth, ka-dunk, brain splattered everywhere like, erm . . . like . . . some nasty maggots. You can imagine, when the husband returned home and saw his family bus-ted, everybody dead . . . Well, except for the cat. The only innocent one in all this was the girl. So now, like, her spirit remains, searching for anybody to tell that she is innocent.' Alex's voice twirled up into an Australian twanging question mark.

'Where's her spirit now?'

'Right . . .' Alex spun the torch over the faces of the girls in the round, some lowering their heads as though playing a silent game of Duck Duck Goose, '. . . HERE!' She threw the torch onto her face where she had prepared a terrifying distorted grimace, the girls yelped, like a bunch of old nans when their numbers are called out at the bingo. Flapping.

'Enough!' Badger said. 'Five minutes. Lights out.'

'Don't you mean *torches* out, miss?'

'Stop being such a smartarse.'

The girls, like kids after chocolate with grey foggy minds, headed to bed, overanalysing, over-thinking, Alex felt uncomforted by her inventive story – how did she think of all that? She just opened her mouth and the words like colourful bunting seemed to sew themselves together. Very odd.

'The map says it's here. Look, Suzy.' Alex read the clue, '"There are hundreds of me, I am nature, but I am not alive." It must be here, under the stones.' Alex shook the treasure map in front of Suzy who was slurping the marshmallow of a Wagon Wheel.

'I didn't even know they made those anymore,' Alex commented.

'I think it's old.'

'O-kay.' Alex, frowned and kicked the stones.

'Hey, look, why don't you ask that girl there?'

'What girl?'

'That girl – there.'

Suzy pointed a chocolate-smeared finger to a nearby tree underneath which sat a girl. She was in a Girl Guide uniform and looked almost identical to the ghost that Alex had seen the night before.

'I didn't see her there before,' Alex said, her heart thumping, her knees weakening the longer she looked.

'Well, she's got a uniform on, maybe she's done this stupid hunt before.'

'Good point. Come on then.'

The two of them plodded through the morning sunshine, the springs of grass tickling against the new hairs on their legs.

'HEL-LO,' Alex called.

The next morning, the murderer rose after a sleepless night thanks to the Girl Guides clucking throughout and his cloudy conscious reminding him over and over and over about how shit he actually was. He lit a cigarette and dictated a very informative letter to his mother, who sat at her typewriter plonking the words out and sipping her miso soup.

The doorbell rang.

'Who's that?' the murderer asked, alert with fear.

'Oh, it's probably the ghost of King Henry the Second. I don't know, answer it and find out,' his mother bit back.

'Did you invite over that weird man from the greengrocers again?'

'Who? Gilbert? No, why would I do that?'

'I don't know. Why would anybody ring the bell?'

'I don't know, Gregore. Why *would* anybody ring the bell?'

'Don't you dare say my name out loud when there is a stranger ringing the doorbell. Have you got dementia, you old crooked crow?' he said, his dramatic oversized mouth whispering in hot chalky breaths.

His mother refilled the teapot. The loose tea leaves swam like tadpoles.

'I'm going to answer it,' the murderer continued, walking over to the front door. He smoothed his greying rockabilly haircut behind his ears and put his hand out to reach the latch. The bell rang a second, striking time.

'No, no, I can't. Oh, my goodness, I can't.' He shuddered under the pressure, his mother walked towards the door, propped her glasses onto her head, rolled her sleeves up, waved to her cowering son to get out of way and opened up the front door. The bell rang a third time as she opened it.

'Eager, are we?' she commented. 'Hello?'

Two girls, both in uniform, stood on the doorstep. One girl was Asian, she might have been the first Asian she had seen

– What an absolute privilege, this would be going down in her journal later, how . . . *cultured*, the murderer's mother thought. But what a face, so mean, she could have easily done as a bully in a school play. The other one was mammoth, plump, braces, lazy eye, she could have easily done as a roast hog, a stew *and* a casserole.

'Good afternoon,' the hog said. She was very polite and well practised, the murder's mother wondered if there was a Girl Guide badge available for public speaking, if so, the hog must be well on the way to receiving one. 'We are Alex and Suzy and we were out on a treasure hunt and have lost our friend,' she grunted, in short, stubby, bad sitcom sentences. Alex took over, frustrated by the bulging eyeballs of the woman in the house, had she never seen anybody that wasn't white before? Jesus Christ . . .

'Look, it was just a bit of hide and seek. It was her turn to hide and now we can't find her. It was weird, it was as though – I dunno, 'cos it sounds dumb – but like she disappeared. Have you seen her?'

'No, I haven't, I'm afraid, girls. How long has she been missing?'

'Only three quarters of an hour,' the larger one sighed, pleased with her specifics.

'Yes, well, you're right to begin asking about.'

'If you decide to go out today will you have a look for her for us?' Suzy added with a cheesy spitty-braced smile.

'Seeing as though the two of you asked so very politely, I will, in fact, make a point of doing so,' the murderer's mother smirked a greyish grin. She knew this game only too well.

'Thank you very much,' Suzy sang as she waved goodbye. She skipped off calling, 'STEL-LA, READY OR NOT, HERE WE COME!!'

Alex followed behind her. 'Racist bitch,' she scowled.

'She wasn't, she just *cares*.'

The murderer's mother tied on her hat, put on her canary-yellow gloves, picked up her basket and left before the murderer could even ask where she was going.

At the camp that night, the girls were preparing dinner. A hot pan spat sausage fat, dotting the air, mushroom smoke pluming in frumps. The atmosphere was not so steady this afternoon, waiting for a smudgy drench of barbequed grease to dollop onto each girl's plate. The evening was clear, the twitch of a bird could be heard, the chilling rattle of a leaf, and then a murmur, a calling, echoing through the air, the haunting leap of its lurching summoning voice as it preyed on the ears of the little women.

'Oh, St-ella . . .' it called, and then the alarming note rang again. 'Oh, St-ella . . .'

Scary on this lavender evening, when there was not another person in sight for miles.

'Must be somebody searching for their dog,' Badger hoofed, frazzling the sausages. It took only a single beat before Suzy began to cry and told the whole group about Stella and how she had got lost during the game. Blobby salty tears gushed from her deep-rooted tiny eyes, falling down her red cheeks, in hot heavy guilty breaths. Alex up heaved a clod of dirt with a stick. *Suzy, what a wet blanket.*

'She's calling your bluff,' Badger barked dismissively, cackling to her sheepish helper, who smiled politely and passed her eager crabby claw the tomato sauce. Alex watched in disgust and then decided she didn't really feel like eating anymore.

After dinner the girls set about washing up. Alex dried the plates, whilst a looming Suzy scrubbed beside her.

'What are we going to do?' Suzy eventually exhaled.

'I dunno.'

'Poor us, we were just two best friends, out on a task, we didn't mean for anything bad to happen.'

'Erm. We aren't best friends.'

'Well, we kind of are.'

'Not really.'

'Well, sort of . . .'

'No. Suzy. No. We are not.'

'Well, partners in crime at least.'

'No, Suzy.'

Silence fell upon the girls like a broken set of shelves, stunted and painful.

'Is she dead?' Suzy asked. 'What if she's been eaten by wolves? What if she has been mauled?!'

'Too easy Suzy, but I intend on finding out exactly what's going on.'

'Oh Stella . . .' the murderer's mother called as she wandered through the woods. 'Where are you, darling? Don't be stubborn now, darling, come out, come out wherever you are . . .'

The trees stood, pillars holding up the sky, acorns fell. The floor was a blanket of crunchy flakes and broken kindle. The murderer's mother began collecting some, she tasted a blackberry from a nearby bush, let the tart sweetness flood her mouth and stain her tongue, her eyes constantly scanning the green.

'Oh, won't you come out, you naughty little girl?' the mother said as she began to get antsy. Her perfect white bunny moustache, inquisitive, snarling. A rumble came from a thorn bush and the mother flicked her head back, each second two heartbeats.

'Oh, Stella, darling, we are very worried about you. I've set out to find you, Stella. Won't you come and have some miso soup? Have you heard of it? It's a magical soup from Japan. It makes you strong.'

The silence became numbing, as though it were sucking on a cube of ice.

The bush rattled.

'Oh, Stella, I know you're there my little one, poor child. Come on.'

'Where hab du been?'

Her son venomously threw the words at his mother, his eyes watery and red, a bottle of whisky rested in his hand, his rounded gut folding over his tracksuit waistband.

'Look at you. You're a mess.' She hoofed his legs, resting on the poof.

'Du lefft me,' he dribbled. 'Du lefft me with dose hawful Brownies, singdring and playing and remining me of the fact I can't blubby murder dem.'

'Get up and go to bed, you waste of space. And, for the final time, they are *Girl Guides*.'

'Wal eber dey are, I hate dem!' He threw the whisky bottle to the floor; the neck came right off, a trickle of gold fell from the gash. Garlic poised under a chair, eyes wide.

'You are a sorry excuse for a man, throwing a bottle at your mother like that. Get out of my sight.'

'I dibben't trow it at du, I trew it at the floor.'

The murderer tried to sober himself up, scurrying for his strings to pull him back straight again.

'Behave yourself,' his mother hissed. 'Go to your room.'

The murderer began to cry. His wails drowned out the noise of everything, a furious gush of deafening clout, his mouth gaping open, as though he were chewing an invisible doorstep, his dribble in long spidery webbish lines, like a cage of spitty elastic bands. His mother came over, took her gloves off and neatly placed them on her knees, she held him and rocked him gently, and started from the top, *The Owl And The Pussycat*. Eventually, the tears fizzled out like the dilution of an aspirin.

'I have something in my basket that just might cheer you up. Sober yourself up, wash and change and come down when you are ready.'

The murderer came down the steps in the same tracksuit.

'Still a tramp then, have you not washed?' she pierced him.

'I washed my face.' He had sobered up, slightly. 'And brushed my teeth.'

'Are you still drunk?'

'No.'

'Liar.'

'What have you got? Did you find her?'

'No, I've got something even better! Go over to my basket.'

The murderer's eyes lit up. He smiled an oh-you-shouldn't-have glint and went over to the basket. It was more of a hamper really. Heavy, it could hold a dozen rabbits at a time and had in its past carried home many a dinner: lambs, pheasants and even a pig.

The murderer went over to the basket; blood swam down the front of it – never a bad sign. He looked over to his mother for reassurance as though he were a five-year-old waiting to scurry into a mountain of presents. His mother played along and nodded.

His clean nails handled the wicker as he muddled with the strap, before . . .

EMPTY.

'I don't understand. I had that wretched thing in my hand, I watched her squirming under my grip, I could feel her tiny heart racing through my fingers. I had her.' She searched the house like a worried child exploring during a game of Blind Man's Bluff, her fragile papery hand clasping onto her chest.

'Shall I make some pie?' the murderer suggested, disinterested in the basket and now sieving flour.

'I'm not hungry.'

'Well I'm going to make some. Plum, I think.'

'Go on then.'

The murderer went over to fruit bowl, choking a plum, and began plotting pie. His mother sat on the couch, frozen, as though she had just been told to sit down by a doctor with bad news. 'How?' she announced. 'How?' she repeated with the same gush of shock.

'Maybe you left an opening in the basket?'

'But I felt her weight in the hamper the entire walk home.'

'Perhaps you mistook her for something else?'

'For what? A magical disappearing turtle?'

'Perhaps she ran out really quickly when I opened the basket up?'

'She's not some kind of sp—'

Then the murderer's mother stood, motionless, staring through the glass. Her son turned to follow her eyeline. She mouthed like she wanted to speak and then she did, 'Can you put blackberries in the pie too?'

At 4.30 a.m., the murderer's mother shot bolt upright in her sleep. The sound of a creaking door had disturbed her. She reached for her mallet. If that girl were in the house she would smack her over the head with the mallet; Gregore would have to miss out this time. Besides, he worked best with an axe. Her feet fit snug into her slippers, she opened her bedroom door. Bobbly with nervous, excited prickles, she looked either side

of her room – she didn't want to be pounced on. 'That cunning brute,' she hissed as she went to climb down the staircase, tiptoeing, clown-like.

She clenched her mallet, her grip eating the shaft of the handle up wholly. The noise was louder down here, rustling, clattering. She couldn't see a thing; blind as a bat she edged along to wall and pinged the light on.

'Gregore!' she raged.

'I was hungry.'

'Gobbledy guts, you made me think it was that damn girl!'

She plodded over, releasing her grip and threw the mallet onto the couch.

Both ample in size, the two of them bumbled about like clay jugs, their bums both sponging against each other, flabby and doughy like two sticky buns. The mother rammed her finger into the jar of homemade strawberry jam; she smiled in guilty pleasure as the gooeyness tickled her gums.

And then the noise again, the creaking door.

'Gregore!' she squealed, 'tell me you heard that.' She spun round to find her son underneath the kitchen table, shuddering, and Garlic's back on static arch, her tail swollen.

'Right!' She sprang forward, eyes darting ahead she scrambled for her mallet, and fiercely began to move, now strong with the weapon. The latch to the back door gulped, clicking itself shut. She spun round, her mallet high.

'Did you see her, Gregore? What did you see?'

'When?' he asked

'When the door just shut.'

'Nothing, I thought that was you leaving.'

'DRAT!' she spat. 'I think you'll find nothing is what you are good for.'

A search team had been organized to find the missing girl. A group of co-operative locals, who seemed quite suspicious themselves, had almost a rehearsed approach of searching, with a set of rules that they applied to the mission. Eventually Badger decided it best to take home the girls, the trip had gone, in her own words, 'tits up.'

The murderer and his mother had finally smoothed things over after a day and a half, a hot pot, four cups of miso soup, a fruit bowl, ravioli, sourdough bread, cornbread, chilli, a board of cheese and crackers, a chocolate tart, eighteen cups of tea and that faithful bear trap that the murderer always had sitting outside the kitchen door, just in case. How it raised his mother's heart in adoration and pride to see it snap that young girl's calf in two. The iron fangs piercing into her skin like a robotic piranha. Perfect. Garlic ate the contents of a tuna tin, scraping it over the floorboards. The clock clicked in its case. The doorbell rang.

'Who's that?' Gregore punched into the air, alarmed, his full belly gurgling.

'I don't know, put your tummy away, and calm down.'

'Why are people ringing our doorbell all the time? Can we get rid of it? I can't open it.'

'Nobody's asking you to. Stay where you are, I'll get it. Throw some lemons in the oven, will you? Make the house smell less . . . catty'

Fumbling, Gregore stood but kept his eyes on the door, which seemed to almost pulsate in its frame. His mother encouraged him to move. She popped her head through the window and banished the murderer to the kitchen.

'It's a pig,' she piped. 'A pig.'

'A what?'

'A pig. Good evening, Officer, how may I help?' the murderer's mother smiled, her teeth rotting and fudge-like.

'May I come in please, ma'am?'

'Why of course.' She opened the door up reluctantly, screaming behind her teeth.

'This is my son, Gregore. He will prepare some tea for us. You might recognize him, he writes for *The Dozy Sheep*, page nineteen, comfort food. Looks better in real life though – stupid photographers, eh? Never can quite grasp that shot.' She laughed automatically, awkward, rocking in her slippers.

'Indeed. I think I know of him,' the officer smiled. A youngish copper, he was slight and small, and Charlie Chaplin-like.

'Erm . . . how . . . how . . . how do you take your tea, Officer?' Gregore came over, like a waiter on his first day, bowing. His mother picked up Garlic, petting her incessantly.

'Milky, one sugar, thank you.'

Gregore returned with a rattling tray, cups ringing in their saucers, their teaspoons jangling. The murderer's mother shook her head, her lips pursed. She flapped to make a space on the coffee table.

'So I assume you know, from all the flurry with the search parties that thirteen-year-old Girl Guide Alex Venshi is missing?'

'I'm sorry, Officer, we had no idea,' the murderer's mother whistled through her teeth. Her son stood sweating in his underpants. 'She sounds . . . *Asian* . . . by her . . . erm . . . surname . . . obviously.'

'Yes, the other girls have gone home now but there was talk that she had left to find another Girl Guide from a separate camp, who went by the name of Stella. But when searching, there were no other Girl Guide camps here at this time. We could find no trace.'

'Well, of course, our Stella isn't a Girl Guide,' she said, laughing, twinkling her teaspoon in her cup.

'I'm sorry, *your* Stella?'

'Yes, that's my granddaughter, Officer. She's out playing in the forest today, red hair, you can't miss her.'

'I see . . .' He scribbled down a few notes, gulping a hard lump,

'Who are her parents?'

'Her mother . . .' the murderer's mother went into a whisper, like that of a child, 'she was a bit . . . well . . . loose, you know?' She went on to Hail Mary. 'And this is her father. He's had the real brunt of all of this, he really has, Officer. Luckily for me he takes his aggression out in the kitchen.' She chortled, winking at the policeman. 'Terrible what they've been through, this family, I'll have to tell you some time all about it.'

'Can you tell me now?'

'Well, I don't see why not, try your tea and then we'll begin.' Her gluey eyes, thick with dishonesty began to sink, fully engrossed on the teacup and anxiously awaiting the approval of her brew. The officer lifted his cup from the tray. He sipped it.

'Funny,' he smirked, 'it tastes so much like blood.'

'Oh, you'll never get to heaven
In a pink canoe
'Cos the Lord's favourite colour is Girl Guide blue.
Oh, you'll never get to heaven
In a pink canoe
'Cos the Lord's favourite colour is Girl Guide blue.
I ain't grieve, my Lord, no more.'

Tara cracked open the bag of sweet popcorn, shovelled a handful of the toffee-flavoured puffs into her mouth, crunching out the kernels. She lifted the torch to her face, 'Wanna hear a story?'

The other girls all sat round the fire, huddled, some chewing on sour cables, one blew a bubble out of purple gum, jumpy as it rebounded on her face.

'It happened here, years ago. Alex used to be a Girl Guide and came away camping, like us. She was known for her attitude. She had a real strong personality, she was relentless . . . but she had this, sort of, well, sixth sense, I guess.'

'Was she mental?'

'No, shut up. One day, Alex was doing one of them annoying tasks – you know like how we have to do – when she met this girl, Stella, her name was. Stella and Alex played hide and seek and got on really well until Stella disappeared.'

'What? Just like that?'

'Just. Like. That.'

'Alex and her mate went looking for her everywhere but had to eventually give up. They went back to their camp and told everybody that this Stella girl had gone missing, but nobody seemed to care, they just ignored it. But not Alex. That night she ran away, into the woods, to search for Stella. She went every-where, the caves, the trees, the river until . . .'

The girls became jumpy.

'Wait . . .' Tara ordered. 'Alex met an elderly lady in the woods. The lady said she was searching for her granddaughter, Stella. Alex said she too was looking for Stella, and so the elderly lady suggested the two of them search together. The lady told Alex that Stella could be a very naughty little girl and that she was very capable of running away. The two of them searched and then after a while, when they were tired, the lady said it was getting very dark, perhaps Alex should come back to the house to taste some plum cake and some miso soup. Alex said she really should be getting back, but thought, whatever, it's not Badger exactly *cared* when young girls went missing, and so she said yes – mainly to prove a point. But this wasn't any usual old lady . . . she bashed Alex over the head with a rock and then rolled her knocked out body into her picnic basket and took her back to her cottage where she lived with her maniac son who happened to be . . .'

'Jay-Z?'

'No, you twat, a notorious murderer.'

The group gasped in fear, each grabbing another girl's hand, sticking together in a slippery grasp.

'She never tasted the plum cake; she never tasted the soup either. She was murdered!'

'How did he do it?' Helen asked.

'I'm not sure I should tell you, because it's pretty gross,' Tara said, knowing full well she was going to spill the juice anyway.

'Go on!' Caroline encouraged.

'Well, first of all, Alex managed to escape. She climbed out of the basket and went snooping round the house, only to her horror to find herself in the bedroom of a young girl. It was a cobwebby mess of toys and dresses – completely untouched as though nobody had gone in it for years . . .'

The group gasped. 'Was it the bedroom of Stella?'

The stuffy leader, Squirrel, came over. 'Girls, come on, that's enough. Time to be going to bed now. Torches off, into your tents.'

'Can't Tara just finish off her story?'

'Fine. Two minutes.' She folded her arms and walked off; she could do with a fag anyway.

'And then she saw newspaper after newspaper report of a story where an angry jealous hunter killed his wife and daughter in a raged attack of jealousy! The daughter, none other than Stella herself!'

'So she was a ghost all along?'

'Uh-huh.'

'Well, why wasn't this dad put in prison?'

'His mother! She smothered him and she was a bloody good talker, and she persuaded the court that he was crazed with jealousy and spite and wasn't acting, himself so they gave him a short sentence in an institution and that was that. The mother encouraged her son to cook and to write down his recipes, it wasn't long before he was quite a prestigious chef.'

'And Alex?'

'She tried to escape as soon as she found out that the grandmother was crazy and a liar, and she nearly got away, but there was a bear trap by the kitchen door that she tripped on, and she was hauled into the house and cooked up into a variety of different foods – the son was a chef, after all.'

'Oh my God.'

'Anyway, it's said that Stella haunts the forest. She likes to show up as a ghost, but she looks real. She plays hide and seek with the Girl Guides and every year she loses herself in the trees, hoping that that mad man father of hers and her twisted grandmother will come looking for her so she can get her revenge. But . . . it gets worse. Every year, when Stella comes to haunt, she will compel one girl from the camp so much – *so much* – that the girl has *got* to find her, and this girl . . . this girl, will be murdered too.'

'That's horrid.'

'What if she comes to one of us?'

'Then, whatever you do, stay as far away as you can from that cottage there!' Tara threw a salty savoury finger to a hollow gutted house.

The girls wiggled, jelly-like. 'They live so close!' Caroline warbled.

'Exactly,' Tara raised her eyebrow.

'Come on, girls, bed now,' Squirrel came back, a haunting smell of tobacco dragging after her like a foggy sheet.

The girls did as they were told, parting, laughing, gossiping all the way back to their tents, some excitedly hopping, too afraid to even clamber out of their sleeping bags.

From her tent, Tara folded back the front flap and watched the house, the boarded up windows, the garden a heap of thorns and ivy. She imagined the neglect inside, the coffee table, the tray on top with the cups and saucers, silent and forgotten, rotten teaspoons and mould-ridden sugar cubes. The lemons as dumb and as dead as silver, cold, and still in the oven. The bones of Alex under the stairs, Stella in the echoes.

A charity ball. A hopeless bundle of scatty tailcoats came
for the jolly, drinking the booze, catching up on some
twatty conversation. Cameron left to go and find his
boss. Ella helped herself to a glass of champagne. It had been a
while since Ella had tuned in to some serious people watching
and it never failed to amuse her. The trouble was, trying to look
as though you were 'cool' with being alone wasn't always easy.
People were disgusting, weren't they? The way they flashed busi-
ness cards as though they were feathers on a peacock, their grey,
red wine-stained mouths, cavernous and wicked and laughing.

A waiter came over with a platter of canapés.

'I'm sorry, what is this?' Ella asked the waiter in her poshest
voice.

'Roast bear,' he replied, snooty, in a strong French accent.

'Roast *bear*?' Ella asked, surprised.

'Bear,' the waiter repeated and then looked over her shoulder
for fatter, richer people.

'Bear? As in RAH . . . as in *grizzly* bear?' Ella put her hands
into claws.

'No, darling. P-ear as in *pear*.'

'Oh, sorry, I thought . . .' Ella began to laugh, embarrassed, red blotches crept up her pearled neck.

'Indeed.'

The waiter left before Ella could help herself to a canapé. She sipped her champagne.

Two more glasses of champagne later and Cameron still wasn't back. Ella hadn't eaten much of her dinner of overcooked bolognaise before she came out and was now feeling the alcoholic poison swirling in her brain and kneecaps. Pink balloons hovered in the air and guests smooched and swooned and showed off. Ella fondled her pearls. This was a bit un-gentleman-like of Cameron; what kind of man leaves his date waiting for him for almost an hour? *Dick. Idiot,* she thought as she drained what was left of her glass and headed for the Ladies'. On her walk over she hoped he'd be looking for her. Annoyed with herself for having that thought, she plucked another full glass of fizz.

The lights were overwhelmingly bright, neon almost. There was a small queue for the toilets and Ella was suddenly desperate to go.

A lady in front of her in the queue spun round to Ella and said, 'Excuse me, is my bra showing?' and then spun back round to show Ella her back. It was the back of a well-looked-after fifty-year-old woman.

'Yes, just a little bit.' Ella said, slightly embarrassed for her.

'Excellent.' The woman chuckled and headed into the next available cubicle.

Ella waited, leaning against the cool tiles; she downed her glass of champagne. When the next toilet became free she locked the door and wriggled her tights down. She made two attempts to sit directly on the toilet, her balance was rather off.

'Fuck you, Cameron,' she mumbled to herself. 'Fuck you.'

The bra lady was already by the mirror re-applying her lipstick when Ella emerged from her cubicle. Ella went over to the same mirror and began fixing her own hair. The lady stared at Ella.

'Are you having a nice evening?' she asked.

'Yeah, it's okay.'

'What's the matter?' she demanded.

'I just don't know anybody. I came here with this guy and now . . . well . . . he's sort of left me and—'

'You're thinking, who the hell can I shag now?'

'Well no, not exactly. I just don't want to be standing around like a lemon.'

'BAH!' the lady cackled. 'You're better off without him. When the man wanders off that's your time to *show* off. I was left fifteen years ago and I've been showing off ever since.'

She had red curls held reasonably close to her head, her curvaceous body filled her dress; she was all woman. She looked like a kind person, her face was beautiful and striking, yet easy on the eye and not the slightest bit intimidating.

'Are you checking me out?' she asked.

'No . . . no!' Ella stuttered.

'You know what they say, baby: if you can't hide it, decorate it!' she gargled, stroking her rounded hips as though they belonged to somebody else. Ella giggled.

'Tell me,' she said, 'do you smoke?'

'No,' Ella said.

'How about cannabis?'

'No.'

'Shame.'

She rubbed her huge lips together, they were like two orange segments, plump and juicy. 'Orange, darling, it's my colour. Know why?' she asked, aiming the orange lipstick at Ella. 'It's always in stock. How many women do you know who wear orange lipstick? Exactly,' she answered her own question. 'You know what? When you can pull it off, you can wear anything.' She popped the lipstick back into her handbag and made her way to the exit.

'Would you rather stay there then?' she warned Ella who was so transfixed on this wild stranger that she missed her milky moon-like hand holding out towards her.

'Oh no, no, sorry,' Ella said and followed eagerly after her.

Ella looked around over people's heads to look for Cameron. Suddenly everyone looked like him, and faces transformed into his and then disappeared. Where had he gone?

'You're not still looking for him are you?'

'Well . . . sort of,' Ella replied gingerly.

'Listen, my little dove, he is so last Tuesday.'

Ella smiled politely at the older woman's attempts at being 'down with it' but she still wanted to find Cameron. Ella decided that this lady was clearly one of those women whose relationship had broken down a while ago and now she was all feminist, alcoholic, I-do-what-I-like-ist. Inspiring, but sort of annoying; a little bit try-hard.

'Electra,' she pounced her paw onto Ella's tiny hand as though it were glass she wanted to smash.

'Pleased to meet you. I'm Ella.'

'You're still not over him. Look, shall I get somebody to search the men's loos for you, darling?' Electra asked. 'I know all the boys here!'

'Maybe.'

'Right, come on then.'

She headed for a round table where a couple laughed in the corner. A small mouse of a man sat alone with a scrunched-up napkin in his hand. He looked up as he saw the ladies coming over.

'No good,' Electra snickered and walked off to find some-body else. She headed straight into the middle of the dance floor and found an odd, curly-haired surfer-type guy.

'Excuse me,' she inserted her arm into the dance floor and like an octopus hauled him out and produced him in front of Ella. 'Describe your man to him, honey.'

The guy returned from the men's toilets shaking his head.

'Weird,' Ella said, staring at her mobile phone, 'I've no reception here either.'

'No, none of us do,' Electra laughed. 'Fabulous isn't it, darling?'

'Well . . . I guess, if everybody is enjoying themselves.'

'Look at them!' Electra flung her arm out, inviting Ella to watch the guests. Electra was spot on: clusters of people danced harder, with more dedication, than she had ever seen, it was as though they were on drugs, sweating, eyes closed, deliriously throwing themselves about. This was a charity ball not a drum and bass night. Groups of people huddled in conversation, like lily pads on a Perspex pond scattered about in circles – their shoulders shaking, laughing as though they were indulging in the funniest snippet of conversation they had ever heard. The more she looked, the harder they laughed, all teeth and watery eyes; some of them even had their hands on their knees, laughing so hard it was painful. Occasionally, the revolving door would whiz round and more guests would arrive, but instead of sheepishly waiting in the corner to mingle, they too ran straight for the dance floor, where within moments they were in a trance, hands up, eyes closed, engrossed. Some of the other dancers, the ones that had been on the floor longer, had these strange looks on their faces, tired but driven, dilated pupils but with brown rings under them. Very odd.

'Well, I think I'm going to go home now. I can call Cameron from there.' Ella decided she had seen enough.

'No, you mustn't let him spoil your evening,' Electra insisted.

'No, really, I'm very drunk anyway, I just want to go to bed,' Ella grumbled, disturbed by the oddityof the evening.

'Well, let's put you in a taxi.'

Electra headed for the revolving door and flagged her arm at the long line of black cabs to encourage one to come forward. 'Marvellous,' she grinned, as the taxi got close.

Thank goodness, Ella thought. But then they both piled into the back seat. Ella was confused as to why her new companion was getting into the cab too but didn't want to be rude. *Perhaps,* she thought, *they would make a stop off.*

'Hello, handsome. Kensington please, darling,' Electra instructed the driver.

'Kensington? No, I live in Balham,' Ella argued.

'Oh, no, you don't want to go to Balham, my little dove, Balham's not a very nice place.' Electra turned down her orange lips in disgust.

'That's where I live.'

'Yes, but I live in Kensington, darling.'

'Kensington or Balham? Where we going, ladies?' the driver asked.

'Kensington, darling, obviously. Wouldn't catch a fish like this in a puddle such as that. Balham, never.'

Ella shook her head, 'Listen, I appreciate your help but I must go home. I have a cat to feed and Cameron will be worried about me.'

'Really, darling? That's why he deserted you is it, darling? Because he cared oh-so-much about you? Poor dove,' Electra frowned sarcastically.

'True, he's an idiot,' Ella huffed. Maybe Electra was right, women need to stick together, men can be such wankers. Whatever.

'Now, driver, turn the heating up, will you? I have on very small underwear this evening,' Electra instructed.

Ella leaned her head back into the seat and closed her heavy eyes. The taxi passed the city at night; drunken yobs fought in the road, queues snaked out of chicken shops and mismatched strangers shared kisses at traffic lights. But it was as though she was watching a world that she understood and as though, as lovely as Electra was, she felt far more vulnerable in the taxi with her. However, nothing had seemed to really make sense this evening, as least she was safe.

'We are here, darling!' Electra stroked Ella's arm. 'Wakey wakey!'

'Sorry, I must have fallen asleep. Have you heard from Cameron?' Ella asked, foggily.

'No, darling. Who's Cameron?'

'Cameron – my date.' Ella was so drowsy she could barely stand.

'No, dove. Sorry, can't say I have.'

The lady helped Ella get her balance and then led the way to a huge, heavy wooden door. Beautiful pink roses crept up the building and all over the door. The lady stood Ella against the wall as though she were an ironing board waiting to be delivered. 'Stay there, dove,' she reassured as she rooted through her handbag for her key. 'Voila!' she beamed as she put the key in the lock. Clunk, clack – the door released and opened up.

'And then there was light!' The lady opened up her arms up to an enormous elaborate chandelier dominating the hallway, as though she wanted to cuddle the sky. Her velvet shawl slipped off her shoulders.

'I live on the fourth floor, we must get the lift.' The lift was one of those old open lifts with the sliding caged door.

Ella was reluctant. 'I really should go home,' she said.

'Absolutely, if you want to. Call a cab from my flat, darling; we're almost there.'

The two of them bustled into the caged box, the metal bars slid across them. Ella felt trapped, she held her breath as though she had to cling onto every bit inside of her, she didn't want another hush of air to sneak out of her lips. The lift rattled up to the fourth floor, the noise it made was as though it had been constructed from chicken wire and tin cans – not that reassuring

– and it seemed as though for every moment it went upwards, it would suddenly jolt down a few pegs too.

Electra led Ella out. She put her key into the front door and let the two of them in. For a moment, they bustled about in the darkness, trying to find their bearings, Then Electra flicked the switch and a mystery unfolded – the flat was nothing short of a masterpiece. A wooden waxy floor of dark wood flooded the entire place. The apartment was filled with furniture of such elaborate design, heavy, creamy rugs sprawled the floor and marble tiles shone under the light, and artwork on canvas hung like huge, exciting abstract paint boxes, making Ella's eyes dance.

'Drink?' Electra asked.

'Tea would be lovely.'

'No, you must have a proper drink,' Electra instructed, disappointed.

'Really? Okay . . . well, what do you have?' Ella asked, beginning to feel a little more relaxed.

'What would you like? It's easier that way.'

'Sailor Jerry's and lemonade?' Ella asked.

'Excellent choice.'

Ella heard the ice cubes clank against the glass; she could really do with something to eat. She felt vomit swishing about in her stomach and throat. She didn't eat as much of that spaghetti as she should have because that bastard Cameron was there, making her feel all self-conscious about how much she ate. Idiot. She lifted her hand up to her eyes and pulled out clumps of dry mascara, letting them sit on her fingertips like squashed flies.

'Here we are, dove.' Electra put down the drink as well as a board laden with bread, meats and cheeses. 'Everybody gets hungry after a little drinky-winky, don't they?' She winked at Ella. Ella's eyes lit up and she tore at the bread and stuffed it with the soft brie, she then ripped at the sheets of Parma ham, dunked it in olive oil and sliced the chorizo with the antique knife.

'You are a hungry pretty lamb, aren't you?' Electra smiled as she stroked Ella's hair, 'Such a silly man to desert such a pretty, pretty lamb.' Ella munched down on her mammoth slice of cheddar, like a small mouse that had rescued a morsel. 'Port! We should have had port. Do you drink it?' Electra gargled like a bubbling drain. Ella shook her head.

'Can I order my taxi now?' Ella asked.

'They won't come at this time, darling. Let's dance instead. Do you like music? I just love it; Brazilian music mainly, you know, music that takes you on holiday. Listen to this.' She began rummaging through her records, the card sleeves flapping against each other and Electra shouting in sporadic, dramatic bursts: 'Glorious!', 'Extravagant!', 'Seductive!' as she titled each of her records. She wrapped her red nails around the one she was looking for and began to wail. 'Oh fabulous, just fabulous!' she cried to the sky as she kissed the cover of the sleeve and took out the record as though it was a fragile ornament. The music began to spin around the turntable and like a trance it sent the lady wild. She flung off her heels and took both her hands to her head, lifted up her curls and closed her eyes. Her orange mouth stretched into a slice of honeydew melon. 'Can you hear it, lamb? Can you?' She swirled in circles round and round, making shapes with her vase-like body. Ella sipped her drink and gulped the fluid down. This was okay, she thought, not ideal, but it was okay. Electra was nice, she was.

'Whoa!' Electra threw herself onto the couch next to Ella. 'That was fun,' she laughed, panting, breathless. Her cheeks had rouged and her pulse: fluttering. Ella watched a vein in her neck pulsating.

'I'm an artist, I'm very, very good at art, did you know that? Sometimes I blow even myself away. Could you imagine that, princess? Blowing your own self away? I don't suppose you have even considered what it takes to do something so . . . so . . . Oh, you're tired aren't you, pretty lamb? Shall I put you to bed? You can get a taxi home in the morning.'

'No, I'm fine. I'll wait up,' Ella insisted.

'I used to be an actress, you know. I married this man here,' she pointed to a frame next to the sofa.

'His head's been cut out of the photograph,' Ella acknowledged.

'Yes. His face gives me goose bumps – he had an affair you see, the swine.'

'I'm sorry,' Ella sighed.

'It wasn't with you, darling, was it?' she teased.

'No!' Ella corrected herself.

'I'm just playing with you, darling. He had an affair with my best friend. My greatest friend in the whole world. I don't blame him for it, she was a wonderful woman.'

'That's terrible,' Ella said.

'That's people for you.' Electra knocked back her drink. Ella focussed on the photograph, which was of the lady, when she was younger, and a headless gentleman in a mauve suit. 'It gets lonely,' Electra said after a long, reflective, pause. 'Anyway, enough of that; let's put you to bed.'

She showed Ella to the spare room which was just as marvellous as the living room. The walls were a calming violet and on the dresser were lavender sprigs in vases. Lilac bed sheets and a plum velvet throw sank either side of the gigantic bed and enticed Ella to plunge straight into it. Ella noticed a folded nightie lying on the foot of the bed.

'Oh, a nightdress, thank you. Do you always have such spontaneous guests, then?' Ella asked the lady.

'Hardly, darling. Put it on, I'll fetch you some water.'

The lady left the room and Ella slipped off her black halterneck self-consciously; it felt as though even the lavender had eyes. She took off her opaque tights and rolled them into a ball, stuffing them childishly into her heels. She unclipped her bra, her breasts hung looser and she stretched her back before quickly slipping the nightie on. She then made her way to the en-suite bathroom, feeling much comfier in the nightdress; more vulnerable, but certainly more comfortable – she could breathe at least. In the bathroom she went to the mirror and pulled her hair off her face and that is when she saw it: 'ELLA' written in pink-looped, embroidered writing on the left pocket of the nightdress. E. L. L. A. ELLA. ELLA.

Ella was so confused, how odd, why was her name on the nightdress? How did the lady know she was going to stay? How on earth did this happen. 'Be rational,' Ella said to herself, 'there must be a perfectly good explanation for this.' The lady must have a maid, a maid that she must have called at the party to let her know Ella was coming back. But there was no phone signal at the party, she remembered. There must be another explanation, she must have a relative called Ella. This was nothing but a coincidence, she would simply forget about it. Ella opened the bathroom door and Electra was right at the door, leaning on the doorframe, holding a glass of water. For some bizarre reason, she was naked. Naked as the day she was born.

'Excuse me,' Ella said. 'Sorry, I didn't know you . . . wanted . . . to use the bathroom.' Ella excused herself and tried to get past the naked lady.

'Where are you going, darling?' Electra now spoke in a deep, powerful voice.

'Please may I get past. I think I should go.' Ella hugged her hips.

'I think you think too much.' Electra spoke slowly and sternly.

Ella looked at Electra's body; plump and cloud-like, it came down it vast white folds like rolls of marshmallow. Her hips were wide but smooth and her legs looked creamed, shiny, and framed her dignity which was pruned like a well-kept ginger hedge. As Ella tried to squeeze away from her, Electra put her hands round her pretty, teary-eyed head and kissed her full on the lips. Those slippery orange lips of hers and her closed eyes embraced Ella with such passion as she brought her china white arms round over Ella's waist and breathed her in whole. Ella felt as though her life was rushing before her.

As soon as she realized what was happening, she battled with Electra violently and used her small wrists to try to force the lady off her. But by then it was too late; Ella collapsed into the bra lady's arms like a defeated damsel. Electra lifted Ella onto her shoulders like a magnificent feather boa and slammed her onto the bed.

Ella came to after an hour or so. She was delusional; she looked about the violet room, lights from the city tiptoed over the walls. Ella heard a strange noise, the same noise as when a dog cleans his fur and then a separate noise, like ringing out a wet tea towel. Ella tried to lean up and then realized she had been tied to the bed. She recognized the nightdress with her own name upon it, she saw her shoes, tights and dress pegged up on a makeshift washing line that was strewn across the bedroom ceiling. She wanted to scream.

'Ella . . . little lamb,' a voice called. It was Electra, she was making her way towards the room, her haunting voice warbled down the hallway. Ella's eyes bled with terror. The doorknob twisted and Ella wriggled and stretched and panicked, trying to escape. The doorknob twisted further until the door eventually opened and a very large, soaking wet, textured tentacle slammed into the room. Ella tried to scream as two more tentacles fell onto the carpet. They gripped onto the floor and sucked up the air like a vacuum, dragging a slimy green body into the light. The lady had turned into a giant octopus.

'Did you sleep well, pretty lamb?' the octopus asked.

Ella couldn't quite believe the voice was coming from the strange monster, and she whimpered as one of the larger tentacles swam up her calf and into her inner thigh. Ella wriggled and clamped her legs together.

'I made you breakfast.' The octopus seemed to grin as it slid over to a tray in the corner of the room and brought forward a stainless-steel dish heaped in a mountain of sardines, all infested with hundreds of maggots. 'Your favourite!' the octopus cackled with delight as it picked up a set of steel tongs and began serving the maggots to Ella. They fell clumsily over her hair and eyes, in her nostrils and slid over her pursed lips.

'Ella!' a voice came from outside the bedroom. The octopus froze and then it wiped away the maggots and sardines from Ella's face in a huge slimy wipe. The octopus then hid the tray in the en-suite bathroom and went to meet the voice in the hallway.

'Where is she?' the voice approached.

'In the spare room,' the octopus answered.

Ella strained her wrists and ankles, her veins began bulging out of her slender neck, sweat sliding down in beads, her eyelashes bent like the leaves of plants, teardrops waiting to fall.

'Ella . . .' The voice became familiar.

'Cameron?' Ella whispered, hardly daring to hope it was him. 'Cameron, I'm in here. Cameron, help me . . . help me, I'm in here.' Her voice screeched, dry and husky and then she became berserk with the idea of being saved as she thrashed manically about.

Cameron appeared in the room and ran to the bed.

'Look at the state of you . . .' he spat. 'What have you done to her?' he growled at the octopus. 'I asked you to take care of her, Mother, not to abuse her.'

'I don't know in what world you call *feeding* somebody abuse, but whatever . . .'

Mother? *Mother*? Ella could not believe her ears and eyes.

Cameron came closer to her face. 'I'm sorry if we startled you,' he said.

Ella's eyebrows frowned; she gathered her words. 'What is going on? Get me out of here. Now.' She began to cry, tears fell from her eyes in fast tracks, they shone like snail trails.

'I can't, I'm afraid. I can't. I need you.'

'Is this a sick joke? Let me go.'

'You're a part of it, Ella. Didn't you realize? Ella, I need a wife. A beautiful, clever, interesting wife; a wife just like you. Now, I need to give you an injection, Ella, just a small injection.' Cameron rolled up his sleeves and opened up a small case, fiddling about with bottles and contraptions, the rustling of equipment seemed deafening.

'No . . . no . . . Cameron, please . . . Don't do this to me,' Ella begged. Unsure of how to be, she panicked, then gripped him firmly with whatever force she could find and put all of her energy into her voice to allow her to speak clearly and firmly. 'Please . . . we can make it work another way. Please?'

'Listen, Ella, it's just a scratch, you won't feel anything, honestly.' Cameron seemed unfazed and pointed the needle to the sky and flicked the liquid with his index finger.

'You look so beautiful.' He leaned in for a kiss and plunged the needle into Ella's leg. It sank in deep. Ella tried to bite Cameron's tongue, but he was too quick. He held her close, folded her into his arms as though she were a jack-in-a-box, hushed her and stroked her sweating head, kissing it. Rocking her gently, easing the worry and then moving his arms to her stomach, he stroked and smiled. 'We are a family now.'

'A family? A family? No, I am not your family,' Ella squealed, drowsy from the injection. Cameron ignored her reluctance, hushing her, swaying her, moving her backwards and forwards and backwards and forwards and combing her hair with subtle concentrated brushes. 'You are not my family. You are not my family,' Ella repeatedly chanted until her voice become slower and slower and quieter and quieter and drowsier and drowsier and off, like a television set clicked onto standby.

The carving happened right there, in front of the wardrobe which was already full of the body contents for the perfect wife. Legs from a lady the pair met in Morocco, arms from Japan, the hips and waist from the most beautiful Parisian; all complete but a face. It was surprisingly easy to peel away, as simple as taking a sticker off a sticker sheet and it fit as right as the perfect word at the right moment. When Electra saw the finished masterpiece she slapped her tentacles in fierce appreciation, marvelling at the work, the detail, each piece had been sought from the finest of places and how it fit!

'Oh Cameron!' she cried. 'You will never be alone again.'

Ella cannot feed herself as she has no mouth.

Cannot smell the scent of home and house.

Cannot sleep as she has no lids to shut over disturbed eyes.

Cannot feel sadness, only guts can cry.

Cannot itch the itch that never rids as she has no place to scratch,

Only in her mouth, maggots hatch.

And, twitching in her lonely bloodstained quilt,

Still after this, is only riddled with guilt.

The end

The Dove

In the dovo,
'ive gone off cream,'
I say.
'I had a pretty creamy childhood,
Lots
of milk
and
eggs.
It makes me sick just thinking about it.'
Curdling
the way the butter
sat
like glass on
marble.
it's hardly a hand
to the handle
but it's conversation that gets me through.

I see a woman on the other side of the bank
through the bushes
I make her out.
Draw a line around her silhouette with my finger
And point
her ankles bare and ordering the sky to help.
knees lifted tall and bony blue
like arms to the bow.

And next to her men set out to canoe
And then I see she has laid down a perfect picnic
blanket
for the Occasion
of giving birth
or agony
but I'm assuming it's both of these or
a slice of hilarity
that she is indulging on.
A pack of duck around her
quack.

And the more she trembles,
Her body like a Volcano
ready to go
hissing down the Villages
her throat squawks
a deathly groan,
the pitch of a dog whistle
and hips bearing blood...
and then she lunges ~~forward~~ forward
and her gums

are raw where
She's scratched
for her love
and I see her look above
and watch in the sky
a dove.
Her toes, the veins
leaking
And then I don't know how
but she breathed in deeply
and the baby's ♥
head popped
out of her mouth!
The bloody embryo-
Sickly-
the cord blue,
Chilly and
the cable twisted
sweet iron,
leaves a rusty
residue.
She is SCREAMING
and fists punching into the earth,

As her lips
are tearing Open,
As her mouth
is giving birth!
And the baby
begins to cry too now,
a raw squabble
grate,
and the mother is
shrieking through the nostrils,
which are now halfway up her face.
The shoulders
And the elbows
of the child
are new
and fat
and white
and the mother's head like a
reveal after a Halloween mask
are behind her and Out of sight.

One creak and the jaw
of her is hanging off and
her fillings on the grass—
The baby's legs, thighs, kneecaps and calves
swoop out the bloody loop
and flop onto the blanket at last.
A bunch of canoeists spot the wreckage,
Take the baby in hand
and get a shovel, and then a couple
of the canoeists
bury the woman in the sand.
My eyes pop out my mind I say.....

         "I cannot believe this is true."
My company looks at me and says,

        "That's what nine pints does to you."

Once upon a fairy tale there was an enchanted kingdom where the sun was always at the top of the sky and when it wasn't a perfect crescent moon would take over, glowing the land, warming the faces of the people. Today was the greatest occasion the kingdom had celebrated for years, the birth of the long-awaited princess.

The palace gates were visible from all surrounding houses, the road echoed the brass band celebrating the birth of the King and Queen's first child. The road towards the palace was jammed with traffic; taxis, unicorns, dragons, pumpkin carriages, silver carriages, horse and carriages . . . so basically loads of carriages.

The parade was in full hog: acrobats, fire-eaters and magicians filled the front lawn. A hula hooper and trapeze artist teased guests by the palace lake and a contortionist put a lot of guests off of their bellinis. Yvonne rolled her eyes as she made her way to the heavy golden doors.

Inside, the place was alive. Half-naked mermaids flirted with clichéd lords from neighbouring kingdoms from behind a bar, perving on them as they tossed cocktail shakers into the air and pulsated lemons in their palms like acidic hearts. Yvonne recounted many eventful evenings at this place, it was where she had met April's father. Fuckhead.

'Sex on the beach?' a barmaid asked.

'Sex on the beach, too bloody right.' Yvonne nudged a goblin standing next to her. A pretty blue-haired mermaid poured Yvonne a strong exotic cocktail complete with a hummingbird. The goblin was stunned by the mermaid's beauty. 'Stop that,' Yvonne instructed. 'You'll be amazed by what a bit of magic surgery can do.'

A fierce dragon was in charge of the grill, he had on a tall chef's hat and was charming everybody with his jokes and stories, he served up mean mini-burgers and lamb kebabs. Then a chaperone ushered Yvonne to a round table with thirteen silver plates and thirteen chairs, thirteen knifes and forks and thirteen wine glasses. Within moments all seats were filled bar one.

A triumphant feast of pork jelly cake, apple and gooseberry pie and hog's head stuffed with orange and cranberries followed and the party flocked around a chocolate fondue and carved wedges of raspberry forest cake and coffee truffles. A cheeseboard perched on a heavy wooden slab and a bowl of grapes, dragon fruit and pomegranate stood like a tumbling avalanche in the centre of the feast.

A spoon tinkered on a glass.

A fat stubby man with a bald head and a bright red face took out a dirty handkerchief from the top pocket of his glittery jacket and dabbed it across his forehead before he went to the microphone. It was then Yvonne saw he had hoofs. 'I thought he was human for a second,' she whispered to Tina, her neighbour at dinner.

'Today is a very special day for the King and Queen. They have, after many, many, many attempts . . .' he joked and the guests laughed with warmth. The satyr relaxed, his natural Greek voice hummed into a sweet drone. He sipped his red wine, chuckled and continued, '. . . have had the most beautiful baby, I mean, I've seen her, she's gorgeous. So, would you all please join me in a toast to welcome to the stage, His Majesty the King, his sensational wife, Her Majesty the Queen . . . and their beautiful daughter, Princess Belle.'

The crowd leapt up in symphony, some cried, some laughed, some muttered to each other about the name choice and commented on the atmosphere.

The King charged forward, proud. He bowed and then heroically welcomed the Queen, Nina, looking more glamorous than ever. Curvaceous and calm she trotted up on the stage and linked arms with her husband. Her curly brown locks bouncing with her amble hips in time and in her other arm, in the very crease on her elbow, sat Belle.

The crowed cooed in unison.

'Thank you everybody for joining us here,' the King began. 'Both my wife and I have waited, as many of you know, an achingly long time to be gifted with a child and we would both like to thank you for all your gifts. However, it has now come to that time when Belle shall be granted her thirteen characteristics from the thirteen fairies from the circle. So I would like to invite the fairies up to begin the ceremony.'

The guests did not applaud the fairies as most of them knew how difficult the task of awarding characteristics was and it was a ritual that was taken extremely seriously throughout the kingdom. However, far more solemn than any of this was the fact one of the thirteen chairs around the table was empty, like a lost face of a guilty person.

The first fairy was the eldest, Agatha, She was kind, fair and just.

'Belle, your future I cannot tell,
But one thing I know is this:
You cannot go through life without moral soundness,
And so integrity is my gift.'

Rapture from the guests. Agatha smiled and kissed Belle in her cradle; two imps assisted her as she sat her back in her chair.

The second fairy, Salena, chaotic, extreme, enchanting gave Belle the gift of adventure.

The third fairy, Mocko, was fiery and driven; she was the most beautiful of all the fairies because of her self-confidence and elegance. She spoke in a heavy Nigerian accent that drew ogres, lords, cats, elves – any male creature for that fact – to her feet like a sea kissing the shore. She granted the baby the gift of honesty.

The fourth fairy, Vex, the first boy to ever join the circle, came forward and gave Belle knowledge. Yvonne clapped his sweet little speech vigorously and winked at him as he lunged back to his seat, his long legs frolicking under the chair.

The fifth fairy, Rita, granted gratitude.

The sixth, independence, which made sense because nobody ever saw or heard from the sixth fairy, ever. 'Trust her,' Yvonne bitched to Tina, moody that the sixth fairy had not replied to her last couple of text messages.

Strength, from the seventh.

Joy, from the eighth, who was pissed and changed hers from loyalty on the way to the microphone.

Next was Tina. Flushed, she weaved her way to the baby in small, abrupt glances and padded, soft-footed to the microphone. She took a long breath and announced her gift: good taste. The crowd's response was, of course, as always for good old Tina, hugely, electrifyingly positive.

Wealth, granted the tenth.

Love, the eleventh.

And then Yvonne stood up, humble and strong, and eased her chair back . . .

But before she could speak, the palace doors heaved open, scraping the tiled floors and cutting through ears like arrows. Everybody turned, like a bobbing sea of anxiety, in horror. A pale veiny hand gobbled up the handle and clawed at it, strong as an anchor and in she launched. The wreck. Her hair a peroxide, weedy, knotted scrag. She was wearing a leopard-print mini dress and a ripped denim jacket, her wings were covered in mothballs and cigarette burns, jiggered and haggard. Her face, haunting, lipstick strewn across it as though a child had been asked to draw what they believed a terrifying ghoul should look like, mascara in clumps, obviously applied at the beginning of the week and drizzled down her face in leaky roads and rivers.

Her knees were worn and bruised, a heel was missing from one of her red shoes and her handbag poured open, a gash spilling tissues, money, receipts, sunglasses, make-up, Valium. She rubbed her hand over her face. 'I'm here . . . I'm here,' she interrupted, drunk as a walrus.

Yvonne remained standing and looked ready to tackle Elixir who was swaying and then watched as she fell, like a domino, down. The room shared a gasp, some ran to catch her; a loyal footman helped her up to her feet.

'Thank you,' she whispered to him, dirtily and giggled, stealing a bottle of nectar from a waiter and throwing it into the air, a spray of foaming bubbles. 'WOO-HOO! Let's fucking celebrate!' she curdles, the room cringes. Some are annoyed by now, some laugh out of awkwardness. 'Don't fucking laugh at me, you pixie bitch twats. I'll fucking shimmershowpigeonstablkgdyu you . . .' she threatens, her eyes sleepily droop. She can't remember what she is here for. 'Where the fuck are those fairy bitches?' she grumbles.

The King is furious; he looks nervously at his wife. The footman shrugs her arms around his neck and directs her to the round table. People look on in disappointment and crumple with sadness and shame when she passes them, some look her up and down in shock, stripping her with their taunting eyes.

She collapsed through chairs, like a wobbling newborn deer, cowering. 'What the fuck is everybody fucking staring at, you fucking bunch of losers?!'

The guards came to attention, honed in on her as though she were a dodgy bag at an airport. Contaminated, evil, against everybody.

'Get the fuck off me. I'm a fairy, I can fucking . . . *do* shit.'
She prodded the air and continued to curse. The King halted the
guards as Agatha put her hand into the air as a signal to speak, as
she was the eldest of all the fairies, she was admitted.

'Elixir!' Agatha warned. 'You are making a complete and
utter monstrosity of yourself, sit down and have a glass of water
or *leave!*'

'OOOOOOOOOOOH . . . get a grip, Aggie. Fucking
ancient bitch, go fuck yourself with your fucking cane, you
fucking goose.'

The guards moved in on Elixir who shrugged her shoulders
in acceptance. 'No, I'll sit, I'll sit, when the old lady speaks, she
speaks, don't ya, grandma . . .?' She sat and then dramatically
tucked a napkin into her dress like a child before picking up a
knife and fork and standing them on their ends.

Agatha slashed her cane across the table and spoke, her lips
twitching, her eyes filled with glassy tears, 'Elixir, you have
been warned, give your gift to Princess Belle and then say your
goodbyes.'

'Who the fuck is Princess Belle, Agatha?'

The baby cried.

'Oh . . . a baby. Is that what you're all licking the King's cock
over? A stupid baby? What we doing? *Celebrating*? *Celebrating*
her birth so she can grow up into somebody as fucked up and as
miserable as you lot? So she can drink and smoke and bitch and
gripe and bully and mock and fucjnnrmevkfkw . . . I don't fuck-
ing know what . . . bullshit . . . so she can be a fucking *outcast*
and live her shitty little life in gaga land? I'll tell you what, I *will*
give her a fucking gift . . .'

The guests hopped to their feet, some of the braver moved Elixir towards the door.

'I'm going, so don't worry about it . . .' she reached the door, falling, closed her eyes, pointed to the cradle, opened her eyes up again and said, 'When you are – what age does stuff start going to shit? I mean like . . . *real bad shit*? Sixteen? No, fifteen – when you, my love, reach the age of fifteen . . . now, I'm helping you here, you won't see it at the time, but believe me, I wish somebody had done this for me . . .' She took a cigarette out of her bra and propped it in her mouth. 'When you reach the age of

fifteen, you will be pricked by a spindle, and you will *bleed* and then you will die and then . . . well that's it. FUCK YOU ALL!' she wails, rolled out of the doors and left.

Some of the guests chased Elixir out of the palace; some ran to the King, some to the Queen. Some were frozen in shock, some sobbed in misery, as everybody knew that once a fairy made a wish it was there to stay and nobody, not even the very fairy who conjured it up, could remove it.

The King and Queen cried into each other's arms, sobbing outrageously, desperate for a solution. The guests tried to stay calm, discussing possible potions that could reverse the spell, everybody using their powers and knowledge to combine a barrier against Elixir's evil stroke, and then Yvonne took to the microphone. Everybody froze, not forgetting Yvonne had not yet given the baby her characteristic,

'Hi everyone . . . I don't know where to start. I mean . . . Elixir . . . she's a . . .' She caught her swearword, trapped it in like a balloon full of air. 'Look, I'm not good at speaking, so I'll get on with it. I can't reverse what Elixir has done, but I can lighten it. Your Royal Majesty, please accept my gift of a sleep, a sleep that will last well, let's see, one hundred years. This will mean once Belle has been pricked, instead of her heart stopping, it will reduce and she will wake again, but only by a kiss from her true love. I'm sorry, I can do no more.' She gulped, clenched her jaw and returned to her seat. Tina squeezed Yvonne's leg under the table and Yvonne gripped her hands.

The Queen ripped a deafening scream into the sky.

Fifteen Years Later ...

All the spindles were banned, were cast out, were banished and burnt, yet still one remained. It sat in the tower, spinning wickedly by the handle of an unknown lady. Belle had never seen anything so wonderful, the way the cloth wove into itself, and so tempting to just ... touch ...

As intended, as suspected, and no matter how they knew it would happen, it didn't cushion the shock of the prick to Belle's finger any less and down she fell ...

Yvonne fell silent, asleep, as did the house next door, and the one after and the one after. Not a mouse did squeak, nor a bird cheep, not a thief did sneak, or a child creep, no word on no lips, nobody awake to speak, just silence, and pleasure, heavy breaths forever, under the beautiful umbrella of sleep. The Queen at the mirror asleep on the dresser, the King was watching *Match of The Day*, the cook, the cleaners, the gardener, the P.A. all fast asleep where they lay. Wolves snoring steady and fast, the carriages in the road came to a halt, all giants, all dragons, all ogres did fall, how they all now seem so small. All beasts now raged free and dopey, all fairies now out-gossiped and quiet, all worry and horror left to the corridor in their head, activity in between the pillow and the bed, not able to stir, no word left to be said, just glee in nature's slumber, hibernating and let be.

The ground soon took over, grew tall trees and nettles fast, roses grew over the palace like a cage over a dead heart, the willow slumped to the ground, the apples fell to the floor and were left, the vines grew spines and legs and led, creeping ivy after it.

The ocean overheard the snoring and whispered it all to the fishes. The fishes were gossips and sold it to the old whale for free rides whenever they wished it. The whale blew it out through the hole in his head – he said, that hole can't keep a single thing in – and a ship heard it as it went past and horned it to men who were swimming. The men walked onto the beach, they were locals, poor but fun, they took the story of the sleeping land to the pub and how the news went round. The prince was painting fruit in the garden, he couldn't quite get the angle of the pear, he soon stood to his feet in attention, and ordered his pilot to fly him there. The pilot was pleased for the mission, he sailed over land and sea, and when they got to the sleeping kingdom, what a tangle they did see. A nest of a world of nature, a twisted knot of oddity and bewilderment, a bed of leaves, of land and green and the habitants sewn into it. They landed the plane by the palace, the valiant prince took his sword (gun, iPhone and Twix in case he got lost and got hungry) then he saw to the brittle and mess. He fought the strangling vines, like Tarzan he navigated his way to the palace doors and then he let himself inside.

He saw the King snoozing on the sofa, untouched exactly as he'd been. He saw the ladies-in-waiting in the parlour and by the mirror the mesmerizing Queen. He climbed up into the tower, found a small door and the fingertip of a winding set of steps. He creaked the door and it fell open and he saw Princess Belle asleep on the bed, her hair long, blonde and in waves, her simple, effortless breath. He couldn't take his eyes from her most remarkable face, so he put his hand underneath her head. How peaceful and dreamy she seemed, indulging in another world in her head. He saw the blood drop fresh again from her finger, the iron smell ignited him and he said,

'Fair princess, your story has travelled the sea
Through fishes, and whales, and ships to get to me
I shall make up all those years that you have missed
As I break that cruel spell with a kiss.'

And then he softly stroked her hair, and held her sweet head in his palms, and kissed his princess on the cherry heart of her lips. The trees outstretched their branches and untangled themselves from each other, the overgrown plants, de-looping, broke free their arms from the palace gates so that would open once again. As did the eyes of Belle; her eyes they opened and closed, and opened and closed and opened.

F oyer and Son, a small funeral directors, was Patrick's empire (the real Foyer, Stanley, had died years before). Patrick's son was training to be a bullfighter in Portugal so wasn't around to help his father with the business. That left the youngest child, Etienne. Etienne had, apart from attempting suicide eight times in her nineteen years on the planet, spent most of her time avoiding her father's funeral directors, particularly as a member of staff.

'Are you sitting comfortably?' Patrick began.

'Yes,' said Etienne.

'Margaret's dead.'

'Why are you telling me?'

'I need you to work.'

'Not again,' she grumbled.

'Before you begin to whinge, you won't be doing any cleaning this time.'

'What then?'

'Front desk.'

'Front desk?'

'That's even worse. People will have to see me.'
'Yes, well, you're probably the most alive of all of us. Please?'
'Starting when?'
'We open in five.'

Margaret had been the receptionist. She was employed way back when Stanley was still around, and she was older than the brick-work. It would be wrong to say that Patrick had been glad to see her go, but working with Margaret was like going to the hairdressers, only to find the hairdresser needed a hairbrush more than you.

So Etienne, against her own will, had fit snug into that title of 'Son' and her father was rather pleased with himself in his efforts to reinstate the missing piece of the family puzzle.

No. 8. AGE 19. Overdose, 27 Nurofen.

The phone rang.
  'Hello Bumblebee.'
  'Hi Mum.'
  'How's it there?'
  'Dead.'
  'Are you working hard?'
  'Yes.'
  'What are you doing?'
  'Talking to you.' Etienne itched her scarred arm, irritated. 'Look, is this important because I kind of just want to go and slit my wrists.'

'Oh, you spoily sport, I was only having fun. I'm proud of you, working, earning money, now you can save up for that car you've always wanted.'

'Yeah, if they actually still make cars.'

'What do you mean by that? Look, I told you we don't have the money to buy you a car, we didn't have it before, we don't now. Why do you always have to take, take, take? Why is nothing enough for you? Surely your friends aren't still living with their parents, their fathers getting them jobs! I'm sure they don't . . .'

No. 7. AGE 19. Self-strangle with tie.

Etienne slammed the receiver into the cradle. She knew she would suffer later for hanging up on her mum. *Why did you have to go and die on me, Margaret?* she thought. Procrastinating, Etienne read through a few parlour catalogues to pick, like a bride choosing a wedding dress, a coffin. Her death had to be perfect. Sometimes she visualized it, the people in her life that had dicked her over, how stupid they would feel when she was gone. Then they would be crying, wouldn't they? They would be the sorry ones.

There it was, *The Nightingale*, by far the best coffin in the catalogue. Maple woodturnings, a hand-carved design of flowers and birds, and inside, the detail. Lined with a 1500-thread Egyptian cotton sheet. 'The base is the latest technology of comfort and design. Unlike your loved ones, the memory foam will never forget you. *The Nightingale* includes a free iPod and with the luxury of the inserted speakers you can allow your loved ones to create you a personalized playlist to make sure you are sent off not only in comfort, but in style too.'

'ET-I-ENNE!' a shout came from her father's basement. 'I need you to go out and get me a something to eat, I'm starving down here.'

'What do you want?'

'What are you going to have?'

'A bottle of vodka,' Etienne griped.

'Ha! You wish, my girl. Go to Mario's, they do good pizzas, get me one and whatever you want for yourself, take money from the float.'

'Take money from the float,' she imitated in a mocking tweet.

She went to the drawer and took out £20; £5 would be her pay for being her father's slave, she decided, although he would never know that. That was £5 closer to *The Nightingale*, £5 closer to hell.

Etienne sprawled out on the counter of Mario's waiting for the pizzas; her arched back crooning like a long scruffy stray cat, her Converses splitting at the rubber like hinges. Her jeans were ratty and tattered at the bottom and carried a constant trench of road sludge with them. The coat she wore had been shop-lifted from New Look, she hated it there and wouldn't normally bother going in except her next-door neighbour, Marianna, was the store manager and was a total knob-end so that made it seem a good idea. Etienne could be a pretty girl if she tried, she was when she was younger, but she had since given up. She had dark circles under both eyes and her skin was spotty and scattered in scars from attacking the spots at any given moment. She had two nose piercings, which started off reasonably attractive but were now groggy and infected, the studs grew out of her plant pot of a nose as mossy and as green as a weed.

No. 6. AGE 18. Threw self down set of stone stairs.

'Good afternoon-a Hibiki,' Mario said. Mario is fat and old, but he makes a good pizza.

Etienne stood up to peek at who had just walked in.

'Hello Mario,' Hibiki smiled, straight teeth, as square and as flat as a set of bathroom tiles, they radiated round the pizza place like a newly fitted chrome kitchen. As he settled, he pulled a tiny speck of fluff off his suit jacket and placed one superb hand onto the counter.

'I hav-a for you-a, one-a moment-a please-a,' Mario bagged up Etienne's pizzas and handed her a chubby fistful of toothpicks.

'Seize-yoo later,' he called and Etienne begrudgingly left the shop, her head peering back as stiff and as distorted as a hairpin.

He was beautiful; absolutely mind boggling hot hot hot. How were people born like that? To look that good? The way he made her hairs static, stand on end, sparking. Her body fizzing up like she was bottled water about to blow: pssssssssshhhhhh-hhhhhhhhhhhhh. How had she not seen him before? How had she just let him slip through her fingers like sand?

Hibiki, she whispered to herself back at the parlour whilst pulling apart the slices of pizza. *Hibiki,* she said again. *Hibiki, Hibiki, Hibiki.* She laughed, crimpling flabby folds of pizza into her happy face. Amazed at the incredible man she had set her eyes upon, she had become fascinated by his enchanting aura. She imagined him being born in a special place, a mountain maybe? Or by a waterfall in an enchanted Japanese garden? His father a philosopher, his mother an artist? She typed his name into Google:

> Hibiki: green tea . . .
> Hibiki: sushi restaurant . . .
> Hibiki: character in Capcom's *Street Fighter* . . .

No. 5. AGE 17. Consumption of homemade poison.

At 5.25 p.m., Mrs Foyer beeped her horn dramatically outside the front. Within moments, a disgruntled Etienne flopped out of the shop and into the back seat. Patrick followed her, locking the door behind him.

'So, moody bee, how was your first day as a working gal?' her mother asked, peering at her daughter through the letterbox of the rear-view mirror above her. Etienne poked her tongue out at her mum, folded her arms, looked out at the grey streets before groaning, 'Fine.'

And that was when she saw him, Hibiki, walking down the road, finer than the best ending to any ending of any excellent play, the ones where the audience stand up, some cry, probably. So beautiful. His walk was long effortless strides, smooth and rolling and seeming to go on forever. His arms, perfect for scooping up puppies, bunny rabbits, friend's babies – maybe even a baby of their own one day? She was getting carried away, but who fucking cared?

'That's him!' Etienne shouted, jabbing the window.

'That's who?' her mother barked.

'Hibiki!' Etienne squealed with excitement, as the car rushed past leaving Hibiki behind.

'You're not on stage, Bumblebee!' her mum mentioned as the three of them piled into the car the next morning.

'What do you mean?' Etienne asked, she felt more attractive than ever.

'All that eye gear you've got on, that's obviously what you were working on when I called you for breakfast.'

At the desk Etienne researched Japan on the Internet. According to Wikipedia it is located in the Pacific Ocean and has a nickname, 'Land of the rising sun.' How fabulous, Etienne exhaled before sucking in all of the luxury again.

'Dad!' she blurted down the staircase, 'I'll go and get the pizzas now!' She reached for the float.

'No, I don't want any junk food today darling. Your mum says I'm getting a tum, says it's driving her nuts, why not get us a salad from the café?' Etienne felt the way a potato feels when it is forked all over its tired starchy body before being roasted in a hot oven for ninety minutes, a tank of salt rubbed in each of its wounds. Hurt, disappointed and regretful that things had had to turn out this way.

'I'm getting pizza,' she spat. But she wasn't, Patrick already had his coat on and was halfway out of the door.

'Need a bit of fresh air,' he giggled.

Etienne swallowed. Hard. Played air drumsticks with two biros for a bit. Then the door opened.

'Hibiki,' she mouthed, her jaw ajar, swooping, dysfunctional.

'Hello, is this a beauty parlour?' he asked in the most elegant, softest Japanese accent. His eyes hit hers, drugging her into a robotic lull, his bottom lip quivering as though even he was afraid of his own attractiveness, as though it was too much for even him to handle.

'Err . . . no,' Etienne snorted, clumsily. 'Why?'

'I just assumed it must be, seeing as you are such a beauty.'

Etienne knew that was the cheesiest line she had ever heard in the history of cheesy lines, but it was Hibiki. *Hibiki.* She tried to focus, but her mind was straying, *The Nightingale comes in a range of colours, or why not get your loved ones to illustrate your coffin to make it special for you?*

'What is your name, Bumblebee?' Hibiki asked, popping her bubble of escapism, his eyes as persuasive as the cheeky village larrikin.

'What?'

'"What"? That's an unusual name,' he charmed.

'No, sorry, Bumblebee, it's just my mum, she calls me . . . whatever. Etienne.'

'French. Classic. It is astonishing.' He kissed Etienne's hand and then, as peculiar and as outrageous as it was, right there, in the reception of Foyer and Son, Hibiki leaned in and kissed Etienne fully on her stunned lips. Somewhere in the world a sack of sugar was split, the grains ran free.

As their relationship grew, Etienne became clingy, ugly, and grotesque. She knew her behaviour was clingy, ugly and grotesque but the more she knew, the worse she became. Hibiki was disappointed with Etienne for attempting to take her own life; he found it to be selfish and upsetting. He was even more frustrated when he discovered her obsession with *The Nightingale* coffin. This perverse nature made him feel awkward and uncomfortable, but Etienne promised she would pack her habit in. Besides, as depressed as she was, she felt she had something to concentrate on now. She had something to love.

She lost a lot of weight during her desperation and would sink into self-indulgent, self-loathing pitiful pits any time Hibiki left her side. She drained him, mugged his energy. Like an addict she wanted, needed, him constantly. His night shifts didn't help either, she would cry for him when he left her, ring his mobile sometimes twenty or thirty times until she got an answer. With her family she was difficult and cagey, answering questions with short stubby words that sat like carrot tops on a chopping board. Useless, throwaway. At work she was grumpy

and blue. Neglectful of her responsibility she shadowed at a
window, hopeful and hopeless.

'I'm worried about you Bumblebee,' her mother mentioned,
concerned. 'This Hibiki, he's awfully lovely, a true gentleman,
however . . . perhaps he isn't good for you.'

As odd as it was, and as surprisingly as it came, Etienne
agreed. 'You're right,' she said. 'He is not.'

And the next time she saw him she told him so and as odd
and as surprising as it came, he agreed also.

The break was just as difficult as their relationship. Achingly
long conversations were had over the telephone. It was depress-
ing for everybody involved. Etienne and Hibiki decided to not
see each other again.

No. 4. AGE 16. Consumption of rat poison.

What with all the shifts she had begun to work, there was plenty
of money to be earned, and plenty of money to be stolen from
the float. She knew it was wrong, that it was selfish, but it was
a small price to pay really, wasn't it? Once her father realized
that she had gone the way she had wanted to, in style, he would
understand, how could he not? And Hibiki, how he would rot
with sadness and guilt when he knew she was finally gone; and
it wasn't long without him around before a delivery came. *The
Nightingale* arrived in a wooden trunk, like a beast arriving at
a zoo.

Patrick peeped his head round. 'Ooh, expensive. That must be *The Nightingale*,' he acknowledged. 'Must have hit a gold-mine, eh?' he winked at Etienne, oblivious that he had just spent £9,000 of his own money on a coffin for his only daughter. The horn beeped outside the front and the two of them lugged the coffin into the car.

No. 3. AGE 16. Bath with television.

No. 2. AGE 15. Hit by car.

After dinner, Etienne's parents curled up on the sofa and watched Jamie Oliver, Patrick called him 'Joliver' for short, which always made his wife happy. Etienne came down the stairs. Tonight was the night, it had finally arrived.

'I'm going out,' she said softly.

'Okay, it's late though, Bumblebee.'

'Yes, I know.'

'It's not to see that bloody Hibiki is it?' her mother feared.

'No! No, he's well out of the picture. I'm going to meet an old school friend,' Etienne insisted and headed for the door. As she cupped her hand around the latch she retraced her steps. Her eyes began to leak and the lump in her throat sat fat like the egg of an ostrich. As difficult as it is to swallow when you want to cry is how it felt to speak.

'Bye,' she managed. And left for real this time.

The rush of relief she felt when her copied key sank into the lock was unforgettable. And an overwhelming wash of uncertainty swamped her when she fumbled about the shop, at night, in the dark, alone.

No. 1. Slit wrists in bath. Ambulance came too quick. Fuck this.

She didn't want to switch the window lights on; she didn't want to be disturbed. With trepidation she made her way down to the basement. Her father's certificate framed on the wall made her want to sob her heart out. Here she felt safe enough to bring in some light, she ran her hand up the wall, found and felt the switch and then . . .

A noise. She froze. Her heart stopped.

Irrational. *Work it out, Etienne,* she thought. *For once, be logical.* This noise, it wasn't a water pump, a furnace, a heater, a pipe. This noise. Of all the noises. What was this noise? This grunting, gurgling, swishing, sopping, soaking sound of nastiness. It sounded at times like a mop rinsing in a fudgy bucket, at times like a collection of crunchy celery sticks being snapped and throughout like a toothless lummox gorging himself on something sloppy.

How ridiculous, that when you are about to kill yourself you can still feel fear, surely nothing matters now?

She flicked, in one touch, the light on.

The sight, this sight, is a rarity and not easy to describe in a clear and understandable way so let me tell you, slowly and digestible.

His feet, long and corny, easing out of his shoes like a flopping oversized sandwich filling. Pointing outwards, sloppy. Then his long legs stretched up and blue, rotting in places, and patches of dog hair in clumps. He was naked from the bottom down but his manhood, not that it mattered at this point, was covered by a tear-shaped bulging stomach that sat spotty and speckled, the skin over taut and throbbing like a bruised bloated testicle with a bellybutton of a cashew. And the base of his spine, protruding in jolting knobbles, like the ridge of a fat-toothed comb. All over purple and blue, a shirt over his torso was roughly done up, there is always something so unattractive and goofed about wearing clothes on top and nothing on the bottom, unlike the other way round. This shirt he was wearing was dirty and tainted and drenched in a deep red mess. The most noticeable thing about this creature was this long pokey neck, as though he had been tortured, stretched like an elastic band and so skinny. Whip-like, eelish, long and spindly, sprouting hairs and warts decorated it.

And finally the face.

In agony, it cried, eyes the size of mug bases and haunting. Needy and empty they sat. White and hollow. Sucked-in cheeks, shady, skeletal and ridged and overall terrifying. Then came together these lips, old lady, smokers' lips, stitched together, purse-ish lips and then presenting the tiniest mouth you ever did see. As small as the head of a pin and as much use as one too. But above this, above all of this, the long legs, the big belly, the cringing mistake of clothes on top and nothing on the bottom, was what was going on. Wrapped inside this monster's claws, were chunks of dead flesh. Then stringy blood snaked the flesh that in areas was porridge in substance and like a damp cake it fell apart in the clutched clasp of its eater.

And blood in each nail and all over its teeth thickened the plot. Etienne looked the monster right in its eye and before she could even scream, she saw somewhere in that most horrible face in the world, attributes of Hibiki and before she could even say his name, he then began to scream himself. It was an awful moan, so heinous and disturbing it could have flooded us all into darkness, even you reader, yes you, it could jump out of this story and troubled even the likes of you.

'HIBIKI?'

He stood dumb and nodded. Etienne ran over to see what Hibiki was ravishing at only to find a platter of what was left of a bloody, deceased body.

'Margaret,' the word tumbled out of Etienne.

Hibiki's body shifted into a slightly more presentable version of himself, he evolved, scooping together his destroyed monstrous self and cried. Smashing the basement, he punched whatever he could, threw whatever he could find, kicked whatever was there and screamed.

The Nightingale, the elephant, watched, silent, amazing; she wanted to bathe in it.

Finally, after a slip of silence, empty air floated and whispered up and out of the basement and Etienne began to speak.

'What are you?' she grasped at him with her eyes.

'I'm trapped. I've been cursed.'

'Cursed, why?'

'It's complicated...' Hibiki threw off the question like it was a hair on a jacket.

'More complicated than this?' she asked. Focusing in on the line of bones, teeth and bloody hairs strewn across the work surface.

'I'm not who I said I was.'

'You don't say...' Etienne mocked.

Hibiki now looked closer to his former self. How wonderful he was, his Adam's apple slotted back into its terrific position, his chiselled jaw blade-like, cutting and so mesmerising it hurt.

'I'm dead.'

'I am too,' Etienne said, pleased. 'I'm dead too.' She put her arms onto his blood-stained forearms.

'No,' he replied sternly, shaking her by the shoulders.

'I really am dead.' And he lost his eyes into his skull and replaced the kind sparkly eyes with those hollow haunting puddles.

'This is my hell. I have to pay for my abuse, for the stupid things I did as a kid.'

'What? Stupid things? What do you mean?'

'Drugs, stealing, laziness. I didn't appreciate life. I was a waste. Never satisfied, like you, difficult. Hard work... so when I died from an overdose thirty-three years ago, I was made into this, so I'd never be satisfied again.'

'So that means you can eat corpses,' Etienne breathed in the stifling sticky sweetness of the blood and vomit rose in her throat.

'It is one of the many vile characteristics of a hungry ghost.'

'Hungry ghost?' Etienne choked, pushing the vomit down, trying to understand.

'Look it up on Wikipedia like you do everything else,' Hikiki snubbed and began clearing himself up. 'Look, I hate this, okay. I hate my life, this is not an easy form of upkeep. I am desperate, I eat what I can, when I can, road kill, old food from anywhere . . .'

'Mario? He helps you, doesn't he?'

'He gives me old food . . . don't be like that, I saw the way you looked at me, and Mario, he knew where you worked and I thought . . .'

'You thought, "Oooh, she must have access to a few dead bodies. She's like a McDonald's, only with dead people, I'll make her fall in love with me."'

'No. *I* fell in love with *you*!' he snapped.

Etienne felt homesick, how she longed to crawl inside her coffin and lie, like a foetus, safe, like a snail, she wanted to immerse herself wholly in the memory foam, allow the selected music to fall on deaf dead ears and die and die and die.

Into a heap he fell, broken and eaten from the inside out, suffering.

Etienne bent down to him. Plucked the jaw of Margaret up off the basement floor, smiled and said, 'I see you left the hard bits.'

Etienne, weak and exhausted with disgust, dragged her feet slow, the tears in her eyes dried up, her head heavy. She climbed up into the coffin. Hibiki watched her, heartbroken. She crossed her arms over her chest and closed her eyes. 'I've never felt so at home,' she laughed, hysteric with satisfaction.

Hibiki came over to the death bed and peered into the coffin.

'I want you to be the last thing I see,' she added and allowed Hibiki to put his long, wonderful hand over her nose and mouth and hold hard and push. Etienne struggled, kicking, fighting, elbowing, her eyes sinking into Hibiki's in long, hard deep stretches, the green of her eyes focusing and harsh, so harsh it ached and everything she had known and loved and lost seemed to hurt so much and remain.

Until nothing. Stillness, and as though she had been stroked by a brush of tranquillity, she was placid and at last it was over. The green in her eyes faded, like the splatter of champagne when the bubbles had stopped working.

Etienne visited Foyer and Son now only in her parents' horror dreams. She came, appeared in the faces of strangers and was gone, fluttering away, always ungraspable. Sometimes she came as a child, calling them, inviting them to play, but they never met her, never could quite catch up with her little springy legs.

Once, a noise was heard, a funny rustling downstairs in the basement, followed by a whimper. Patrick, led by his torch, went to investigate and found the remains of a deceased customer lying mangled on the work surface, ribcage open like a castanet. Foxes were common in the area, more so since their little girl had gone, and a couple of them could well have snuck in through the rubbish chute. He must get that seen to.

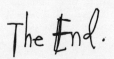

The End.

art was born onto a heap of onions, in an allotment.

His mother was a nosy parker and was spying on an affair at the time (because people often go to allotments to have affairs, if you didn't already know that).

His mother died directly after the birth and, with the help of his father, two maids, a cook, two homeschooling tutors and a gardener, Bart grew into a handsome and intelligent young man.

His father died of old age and left Bart the estate.

At seventeen, he owned the prestigious mansion at the peak of the tallest hill in the town, the land surrounding, and his parents' fortune.

Bart got cocky.

Fired the staff at the mansion and spent his wealth on alcohol and parties, he lived a lavish life-style, splurging out on expensive bottle after expensive bottle – but nobody ever outstayed his company; when the bar was closed, or the last drop of liqueur ran dry – everybody would say goodbye to arrogant, cocky Bartholomew.

Loneliness only made him drink more.

People in his town would say, 'It's terrible the way that boy lives, blowing away his inheritance like that – he should be ashamed.'

The mayor of the town would pop over, 'Bartholomew, we know you're depressed but . . .'

'No, Mayor, no, I'm not,' Bart would just argue back and turn to the bottle again.

One evening he was on his way home from a night out, lonely and drunk.

He was stumbling home clutching his empty bottle of gin when he saw a babushka on the pavement selling spring onions.

He ignored the lady and walked on by, wobbly and heavy-footed.

'Onion boy!' the lady screeched and pointed her scraggy finger towards Bart.

Bart turned round, 'You talking to me?'

''Tis you, is it not?

The boy borned unto a heap of onions?' the babushka asked.

Her hair was off her open face, which was framed perfectly by her shawl – it sat as round and as exciting as the moon.

'I don't know what you mean, you silly old bag . . .

Now if you don't mind, I'm trying to get home.'

And Bart walked off in the direction of his mansion that sat on top of the steep hill.

'I knew your mother!' the babushka shouted after Bart, and he flicked round and faced the lady.

'Before she died she told me to give you this.'

The babushka lady gave Bart a doll, a wooden, painted lady in red, with opal eyes and bright rouged cheeks.

'If you hadn't noticed, you old biddy,

I'm not a six-year-old girl.

I don't need a *dolly*.

I also don't need your sick wizardry, thank you very much.'

Bart pushed the doll away dismissively and went on towards his house, shaking his head and doing that thing people do when they want to show somebody is crazy by winding up the air with their finger.

'It is a gift. From your mother.'

The lady chased after him.

'Go away, are you deaf as well as mad?'

And he pushed the babushka by the shoulders and didn't even calculate his own strength as she fell to the ground. The spring onions fell about the floor.

The babushka's eyes filled with black, her fists clenched, she was so angry that her nails dug into her palms so much that her palms began to bleed, the nails began to tear from the quick.

'You'll be sorry, you wretched boy' she spoke with a deep, strong voice, as she slowly began to pull herself from the floor.

'Sorry as the day is long

As the sea is wide,

And the sky is thick.

Sorry as the ground is forever,

And the trees are tall

And the globe is round.

You will be sorry Bartholomew –

On your face – a frown.'

Bart turned around and stuck a finger up at the babushka and carried on home.

The walk up the hill towards the house was steep and treacherous,

And the wind blew harder than ever before

And howled and flicked at the tatty leaves surrounding it.

Bart gritted his teeth, tears ran down his face from the sharp icy current, his ears rang with cloud and pain, deafening blows to his ears made the walk almost impossible.

He approached the top of the hill – all he could see was vast fog.

Vast fog for miles.

Bart was confused as he surveyed the weather: wind and fog? Together?

Still, he laid out his hands in front of him like a blind man and tried to touch the brick of his mansion.

The fog rolled onwards like a temptress ocean.

Bart at last managed to grasp hold of the gate to his home, he gripped onto the latch in his drunken stupor and with all of his weight pushed the gate. It swung open and then hit back again, trapping Bart's finger as it launched backwards. The cold of the metal made it hurt even more. Bart growled in agony and began to run towards his front door, blind, he fell into bushes and oak trees, into strawberry plants and nettles. His jacket clung onto acorns as he finally could just about make out the big brass knocker on his front door.

Bart, still intoxicated, and hugely paranoid, scanned his body desperately for his set of door keys. When he at last found them,

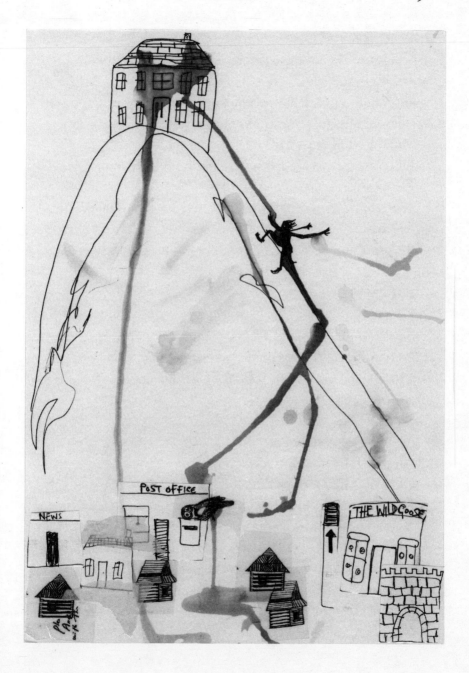

dropped them, picked them back up, felt with his index finger the ridges of the key itself, forced it into the door, missed the key hole, scratched the door, dropped the keys, picked them up again, found the key, missed the key hole, scratched the door – harder this time, tried again, found the key hole, wrong key

'FOR FUCK'S SAKE!'

Different key, in the keyhole, click-boom, the door released, clunk, yaaaaaaaaaaa . . .

The wind spread into the house – screamed as it invited itself in.

Bart, with his back, forced the door closed as if he were fighting a ghoul.

The door shut.

Silence.

At this point it would seem obvious that something wasn't right, that the battle of obscure weather wasn't quite ordinary. Still Bart made his way to bed. Took off his boots and plunged into the mattress.

CURRRRIIINNNNNGGGGG.

CURRRRRIIINNNNNGGGG.

Bart had an old brass alarm clock; he set it on days after a night out on the razz, as he was known, in the past, to sleep through an entire day. Which meant he often felt one step behind the rest of the world – especially as he pottered around in that huge empty house – only spiders knew him well.

He smacked the top of the clock and opened up his bloodshot eyes and there it was.

Sitting right next to his alarm clock, perfectly perched, grinning with her

painted face was the doll the babushka lady had tried to give him.

'What on earth?' he mumbled as he sat up. He was certain he had refused the doll, in fact, as far as he could think back, his behaviour towards the lady the evening before was actually verging on rude.

Still, he knew he had been slightly out of his box that night previous and wasn't entirely fluent on his drunken activities.

Bart decided after his crumpets, coffee and nursing his finger, to throw the doll in the bin. It was just too freaky to have the thing in the house.

Over.

It was awfully lonely in that big old house and Bart's drinking meant that the house's upkeep began to wilt.

Paint around windows and doors cracked, antique furniture became infested by termites.

The once marvellously painted ceilings were circled in grey damp marks.

Tiles fell from the bathroom as the walls were increasingly covering themselves in fungus-spawned black spots.

Inherited kettles, pots and pans that had passed through the family for years soon were frosted in limescale and chalky residue.

The once grand entrance to the mansion was now nothing more than an overgrown mess of nettles and thorn bushes, poisonous plants, inedible blackcurrants and a sea of dead holly bush and leaves.

The garden shed was like a cobwebbed house of fur and dirt, home now to wildlife and rusty gardening tools; the green grass, where Bart and his family shared many picnics and parties, was littered in empty spirit flasks, cigarette butts and rubbish bags that the foxes had torn up and scattered the contents.

The wind came back every night, making it particularly difficult for Bart to leave the house. These extreme winds meant that the telephone lines were down so it was impossible to reach anybody. Bart would spend the evenings drinking gin and reading newspapers, but once they were read and read and re-read, he at last made his way up the stairs to his father's office – his father always had a good book.

The room hadn't been used properly since his father had past away, it wasn't retained like a shrine or anything, it just wasn't necessary to go in there. Bart twisted the brass doorknob and realized it was locked.

'That's weird.'

Bart was certain the room wasn't locked – he remembered the one time when he went in to feel the leather chairs, the way the pen felt against his fingers, the rim of his father's spirit glass as he ran his finger over the carved letters of his whisky flask.

Still, Bart *did* make obscure choices when he was under the influence.

He went down the stairs and to the cellar door where he searched the keys:

Garden patio
Rear shed

Piano

Blah blah . . .

Office

But no key.

'How odd.'

Bart scratched his head and poured himself a drink.

DUNG.

DUNG.

DUNG.

'I hate that bloody clock.'

It was twelve. Bart had fallen asleep on the sofa. Another wasted evening. It was reasonably chilly, the fire had burnt out. He leant over the armchair to reach for a blanket, the wind still barking at the window, and out rolled the doll.

'Good grief!'

Bart stood bolt upright like a cat against a burst water pipe. The babushka doll rolled off the armchair and onto the carpet where she knocked from side to side until finding her balance. The eyes fixated on Bart, the painted hands and dress.

Bart picked up the doll and cupped his hands around the wooden casing and saw that she was in two halves. He pulled and twisted at the shell until she cracked like a neat egg, into two perfect halves. Inside she was hollow.

'What a strange toy.'

He inspected the doll.

'Why would my mother have wanted me to have this?'

He had another drink and it went down easy.

That night he allowed the doll to stay overnight in his room.

The next morning the alarm sang.

The doll sat where she was put, by the clock, happily smiling at Bart.

'You're not on walkabout today then, madam?'

He picked her up again as he lay in bed, twisted her in half and out fell a brass key.

The key fell onto Bart's bare chest. Sat like a hot rod against his naked skin.

'HUH!! My father's office key . . .' Bart threw the key against the wall and got out of the bed; he marched down the stairs in his underpants and took a shovel from the cupboard under the stairs. He walked right out onto the hill and all the way down – he was so driven, the cold did not interfere with his intentions. He dug and dug and dug as fast and as deep as he could until his shovel went 'plunk' as it hit a pipe.

Then he threw the doll into the hole and re-covered the grave. Cursing and spitting at the hidden toy, he cursed and he spat so much that he began to cry; he began to cry so much that he couldn't see anything except thick blobs of tears.

That very day he put the mansion on the market.

It was sold within the week to the local government to become a music school.

Bart decided to move to London. The city, he decided, was for him.

He brought a flat off of the King's Road that was terribly expensive but beautifully charming. He hired a gardener to make up his window boxes and hired a small Irish lady called Ivy to be his maid.

Bart decided the best way for him to keep on the straight and narrow would be to get work. Because of his father's title, this proved to not be difficult and within weeks he had an office on Baker Street and was given a receptionist called Alison.

Alison had long red hair and lips as through a punnet of raspberries had been squashed upon them. Her eyes were as blue as the paintings of oceans he had seen only in his dreams.

Alison and Bart worked together for just four months before they began courting. They loved the theatre, long walks and eating expensive cheese. Now that he had a girlfriend he thought it best to let Ivy go.

After six months Alison told Bart that she loved him and Bart was pleased because he was almost entirely certain that nobody could ever fall in love with somebody as vile as he – and she had.

He said it back, not only because he was pleased but because he meant it.

Bart's outlook on life had changed quite severely after meeting Alison; he saw the better things in life rather than the boring, the dull, the annoying, the dreadful. Rain clouds became hearts, a missed train was simply a blessing – gave him time to buy a paper and a bar of chocolate, lost money was seen as bad debt and happened to protect him – extra money only meant extra trouble. And Bart kept off the bottle, for he was simply pissed on Alison, drinking her in like a tall cocktail that was impossible to see the bottom of. She gave him exciting jellyfish kneecaps followed by brain freeze. He was in love.

Alison and Bart got married on a boat in Chelsea, they drank champagne until the stars came out and then went to sleep again. In the evenings they slept with every part of their bodies touching, as though they all had their own personality and individual neediness – it was quite spectacular.

Alison encouraged Bart to go to his parents' graves, where he went and wept and gave flowers, and swept away the dust and soil and cleaned the stones.

Shortly after, Alison got pregnant.

Bart never liked the idea of being a father but the more real it became the more excited he got. He talked to Alison's belly, he talked to Alison's belly so much he made himself a walkie talkie out of plum tomato tins and string and he talked and listened as much as he could. In the bath he would soap up Alison's belly and kiss it and cuddle it and moisturize it and even did it right up to the point when she lost the baby and did it even when there was no baby inside anymore.

'It's okay,' he said, 'we can try again.'

And by all means it was fun trying, they loved trying. They tried in bed, in the bath, at the train station, in the car, in the park, at the pub, almost in the cinema – and eventually it happened all over again.

Alison went into labour on the 29th of November, a storm stirred the sky and trees de-rooted and came plunging to the ground. That same day, in some places over the island, a flood drowned cats and dogs and families floated on rafts.

Bart went back to the flat to get more clothes for Alison, a shawl, a jumper, perhaps – slippers? He opened up the wardrobe and began filling an empty night bag and there she sat, on the window sill – the doll.

Bart froze.

Dropped the bag.

Went over to the doll.

He felt her body in detail, the raised paint blob on the flower on the front of her dress.

He untwisted the casing and inside, this time, out fell a second doll. Bart threw the doll out of the window and in haste packed the bag and drove away in the car.

A baby girl was born, Heather.

Heather was like an angel, blue eyes, blonde hair, chubby elbows and knuckles –

but she took Alison's place.

Alison was buried with her grandfather on the coast; she had always liked the sea.

Bart cried and sobbed till he was ill and Heather cried because babies do cry, don't they?

Bart re-employed Ivy to wash and clean and take care of Heather.

When Heather was three she was adventurous and boy-ish, she loved food and falling over and playing hide and seek. Ivy needed a word with Bart.

'Heather needs some new toys.'

'Yes, good idea. Here's some money.' Bart pushed over an envelope thick with notes.

'Very well, sir.'

And off she went.

The following week Ivy returned.

'Sir, it's Heather. She doesn't like her new toys.'

'Well, why ever not? She picked them, didn't she?'

'Yes, sir, it's just she always carries this one particular doll with her, and it's not as though I don't like it – it just makes her go a bit . . . well . . . wild.'

Bart fronted, twitched the new moustache he had been grow-ing and asked to see the doll. Under the desk, his fingers crossed, his toes crossed, his mind repeating,

'Please God – no.'

Ivy re-entered with a screaming Heather.

'Give it back! Give it back!' she screeched, her pretty face was distorted and distressed.

'This is it.'

And so it was, the babushka doll, all smart and smug and pleased with herself.

'WHAT ON HELL'S EARTH??!!'

Bart swept the desk and pushed the doll onto the floor. It came apart and produced the mini doll from before. Ivy picked up the little one, 'I didn't know there was another one.' She fon-dled the small one and opened up that one, ' Sir, there's another one!' and there was – inside the smaller doll was an even smaller one.

Bart's eyes widened.

'NO!'

He scooped Heather up.

'Listen lovie, you are to have anything, anything you want, but you must not, not ever, play with this doll. Do you understand?'

Heather was too worked up to answer.

Ivy suggested a pot of tea.

Bart made a fire that evening and the babushka doll was the Guy Fawkes.

Bart sat with the fire until it burnt out, the ashes flew like lit moths into the dead night. He went to bed with Heather curled up in his arms.

Heather went to school. She was extraordinary at art, sculptures in particular and was awarded a scholarship to an art school in New York.

She came back to visit her father at birthdays and Christmases. Bart had plenty to do whilst his daughter was away.

He worked and wrote and went to the pictures, he tendered the flowers in his window box and even took Ivy to dinner.

One evening whilst enjoying his nightcap he got a telephone call from the mayor of his hometown inviting him to the Christmas concert at the music school that used to be his family mansion. It sounded like a nice idea – perhaps he could take Heather along as a surprise?

And so they did, Heather arrived on the Tuesday and they drove over on the Thursday, Ivy was invited but went to see her family in Ireland.

It got dark relatively early and was difficult to see the roads in the darkness; Bart had forgotten what real darkness was like.

The house was still the same from the outside; the structure of it was so beautiful it would just have been ignorant to demolish it.

'This is it – I grew up here, Heather.'

'It's fantastic,' Heather answered, smiling. 'Bloody freezing though!'

And they made their way inside.

The pair were greeted at the door with quail eggs and champagne (which Bart refused).

Red drapes hung from the staircase and a Christmas tree speckled in gold and silver tassels and glitter balls filled the room. Holly and mistletoe hung in bundles from the arched ceiling.

Heather took in the size, popped a quail egg into her mouth, realized she didn't like it, spat it out into a tissue and slipped it into her father's pocket – it was easy – he didn't know how to tell her off.

During the concert Heather smiled and clapped and laughed and danced.

She is the most beautiful thing in the world, Bart thought.

'Hello, Bartholomew!' the old mayor welcomed. Bart couldn't quite believe how drastically the mayor now resembled a prawn.

'How are you? So great of you to come along, and this must be . . .?'

'Heather,' Bart and Heather chanted in unison, both awkwardly apologized and then laughed.

'A very close-knit family I see . . .!' the mayor grizzled.

'Father, may I be excused?'

'Certa—'

'Don't you dare listen to that old fool!' the mayor's red wine-stained mouth croaked. 'You do what ever you like, anybody as pretty as you should be allowed to do whatever they like in this goddamned universe. Now off you trot!' The mayor chuckled and patted Bart's back and he winked at Heather as she made her way to the toilet.

'Listen old Bartholomew, you have done a wonderful job raising Heather, unbelievable after everything you have been through. And it is Christmas after all and so we here at the Treasury have got you and your beautiful daughter some Christmas presents. Open them in the living room, won't you? Beside the piano, excellent photograph opportunity. It's like I always say—'

'Thank you,' Bart interrupted;

he never liked to be made a fuss of.

Bart was handed a basket filled with gifts, soaps and fruits, all wrapped in gold ribbon.

'I think I'll put them in the car, save them for Christmas Day.'

'Yes, you do that. Good chap,' the old prawn replied.

Bart left the house and breathed in the cold air. He made his way to the car and put the presents in the passenger seat. He was looking forward to Christmas with Heather. As he looked down at the basket of gifts, the fragrant soaps – he could smell them through the paper – the exotic teas and fruits and the fudge looked delicious. What a fantastic present, expensive too – the labels were from the best shops in London. But just as he was about to let himself out of the car he saw an eye, a pink cheek, a flower. Immediately his face turned to panic and anger, he ripped off the clear foliage and threw it behind him, the soaps, the shiny red apples and perfect plums rolled out of the composition, exposing her, the doll.

He began to unscrew the doll, tears began to fold from his eyes, and he became hysteric, 'No, no, no, no, please, no, no . . .'

He undid the top half of the babushka and this time the smaller doll sat, upright, boiled egg-like.

'Not again, not again.'

He unscrewed her, and as before sat the same happy face.

Tears streamed from Bart's tired eyes.

'WHAT IS THIS CURSE? WHAT DID I DO TO DESERVE THIS?'

And he went to the second smaller doll and opened her up, his eyes closed.

And then he heard a scream,

A scream so piercing, so mind-blowingly horrifying and deathly that the party jerked to a halt.

'Well, what the jolly is going on?' asked the mayor.

Bart ran to the door, 'Not my baby . . .'

He ran, pins and needles ate at this legs and arms. 'Please, no . . .'

He grabbed at the doorknob, his heart throbbing in his chest, rattling at his ribcage, every joint felt loose.

Inside the hall the guests' faces fell like paper planes, glassy eyes, ashamed and in denial, sunk low in tearful grey sockets. Shoulders came down like floating dead leaves.

But he already knew – the babushka had decided.

'Bart. I'm so sorry.'

Bart ran to the top of the staircase, a cluster of men gathered outside the entrance to one of the rehearsal rooms. One of them put their hand on Bart's chest,

'Please, don't go in there.'

Bart threw the hand off his chest and ran to the end of the room where the window was gaping open, the draft blew the music sheets into a gust, and three other gentlemen leant over the sill.

'Where is she? Where is she? Where is my girl?'

The men made way for Bart as he threw his head out into the frosty air and down, Heather lay in the finely trimmed holly bush below, the iron fence rooted in her stomach. Her hair in golden curls swam into nature's bed, her open happy glassy

eyes were peaceful and her nimble wrists bent up to the thick night.

She was still the most beautiful creature that village had ever seen.

'She threw herself, Bart,' one of the family friends muttered.

'We are so sorry.'

Bart screamed into the sky, his pain shuddered the mansion. He fell to his knees into a shock-filled fit; he passed out from terror.

That night he survived his first and last heart attack.

Ivy came straight back from Ireland as soon as she could, she offered Bart to come for Christmas but he said he would rather be alone.

He had lied.

A courier came over and brought round Heather's belongings from art school. She was so gifted, her talent swelled up Bart's flat like an overgrown garden, it leaked into the kitchen, spiralled around the drainpipes and all over the walls. It was too much. Bart received so many phone calls, apologies from friends in the past, cards, presents, letters.

Ivy knocked on the door, 'Bart. You called for me, sir?'

Bart didn't open the door.

'What do you think about onions, Ivy?'

'I use 'em, sir. They are good for flavour, sir.'

'Sure. What about the layers of an onion?'

'Shall I come in, sir?' Ivy started to enter.

'No need to come in, Ivy. Ivy, your work . . .'

He began to cry, he put his hand over his mouth, breathed, spoke, 'That's all for today now, Ivy. That's enough.'

'Okay, sir. Goodnight.'

'Goodnight, Ivy and thank you for everything.'

'Very well, sir. God bless, sir.'

Bart leaned back in his chair; he held the doll against his chest.

As soon as he heard the door shut he put a cellophane bag over his head and held it to his nose and mouth. He breathed

in and out,

in and out,

in and out,

and in and out

in long,

hard,

deep

breaths.

He began to get nauseous but didn't stop as he pushed the bag over his head, closer and closer. He became a deep-sea diver and saw colours, saw the water rippling over him, his weightless body floating into the empty sea, backing away into the depths of nothingness.

At last the doll fell from his hand onto the waxed floorboards, smiling, pregnant with the miniature versions of herself, rocking from left to right until finally coming to a halt.

'Bloody beautiful room,' the removal man said, wiping his chin with the back of his sleeve.

'Ain't it just?' his boss tutted. 'So unfortunate. He had no family left or nothing.'

'Where's all this going then, mate?'

'His housemaid.'

'Un-bloody-believable!' the removal man said, smirking, showing his collection of fillings and gaps.

'Eh-eh. What's this?' the removal man asked picking up an ornament he found on the floor.

'One of them Russian dolls, ain't it?' his boss replied. 'Do you like it?' he said, handing it over.

'Give us another look.' The removal man held it in dirty fingernails. 'Bloody stinks.' He sniffed it. 'Smells like . . . what is that? Onion?'

'You're an oddball, you are.' The boss frowned, disapprovingly. 'Come on now, either take it or don't. Get on with it.'

The removal man slipped the doll in his pocket; he would give it to his girlfriend as a present later.

Ivy thanked the removal men as they put down the last trunk of her belongings and closed her new front door. She went straight over to the trunk and opened it up, after removing all the white tissue paper and bubble wrap she took a breath in and blew the dust off the inside – revealing a trunk full of identical Russian dolls.

'Sorry as the day is long
As the sea is wide,
And the sky is thick.
Sorry as the ground is forever,
And the trees are tall
And the globe is round.
You will be sorry Bartholomew –
On your face – a frown.'
Then that old babushka cackled to the sky,
oh how that babushka cackled.

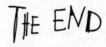

THE END

The Unmet

I have never met you enough.
I have never met you enough
and I know you exist as you ROAR ~~about~~ your way
into my life like a sticky thick relationship or an itchy
picnic blanket.
And I refuse to surrender- to fall in love.
I have never met you enough.
I have never met you enough
and you are not that dreadful really, just like the
dark and twisty turny path that nobody wants to follow.
Yet here I am doing everything to avoid you.
You remind me of catching the eye of a regular
Street weirdo- or an old friend's mum,
You are red wine, a cigarette, a lapse
a VOGUE magazine, a package to go get.
You are that clog of sick when you know you've left something on
the train- beating on the window as it peels away. leaving
me to conquer the day.
We must spend time, get together, get to know each other a
little better, you dark city,
You shady stranger- roll me under your wave and meet me.

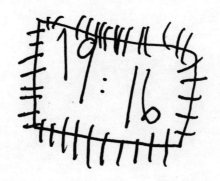

'Have you not got a lid that fits?' I say holding up the oversized tea lid. My words are scattered over the heads of the King's Cross commuters, blown like cotton from a dandelion and ignored.

'Never mind,' I say, just quietly enough to delude myself that I wasn't just having a conversation with myself – even though I was – I most defiantly was.

Taking careful pigeon steps, I take a sip of tea and burn not only my lip but also my tongue and the roof of my mouth. I stand shivering, waiting for the 19.16 train to Peterborough. I feel like buying a big sandwich and then remind myself I have already eaten and that I was only been gluttonous because I was bored. The gates are unlocked; the train is ready for boarding. The guards wait, grumpy and cold. I go up to the most miserable-looking one and show my pass.

I specifically ask to be by a plug socket, I usually have a laptop with me and the four-seat booths are the only ones that can fulfil this requirement.

I take off my coat,
hang it up on the little offering of a coat hook,
wipe my glasses clear,
relax.
My ticket,
I better have that ready,
I look for it.
Wrong pocket.
Relax.
Laptop, just lean down to reach the plug,
is it in?
That's not it,
have a look,
right,
yes,
in,
computer on.
May as well get started.

Christmas Eve. It's come relatively fast this year. Wonder what it will be like at my sister's this year. I knew I should have made a family, had a son. I could have got him a train set. I have a joke I say to myself every year whilst on the train at Christmas, 'Next stop, Daydream Central,' and that's what I do, I fantasize about a family that I don't have, in this I'm *DAD*. I'm the hero, the concrete, the foundation, and the core of a good family. I'm the battery in the back of the alarm clock. I come up with ideas like, 'Let's take the kids to the beach,' and my endearing wife will say something concerning like, 'But it's muddy and wet outside!' and I'll say something prevailing like,

'Who gives a damn?!' and the kids will jump up and down and out we shall go, plodding and squelching through the boggy, swampy mushiness until we are well and truly splattered. We are met at the door by my charming wife who beckons us inside and one by one drags off our caked wellingtons and soiled clothing and . . .

Just as I am about to slip into a chaos of loveliness and imagination, on step three girls.

They sit opposite me, all three of them squashed onto the same two-seater. They are young, say fourteen. The biggest of the three sits closest to the window like a dead octopus. Under her bramble of dark hair is a big, round, podgy face; over it is a grim smear of controlled terror, her eyes painted shut by the generous amount of make-up. It is clear this girl is the leader.

On the far side of the two-seater is a prettier girl with large eyes. Rolling round her head they are, searching frantically for a way out, an escape, tears on the end of each lash like a drop ready to jump free from the nose of a leaky tap. And in the middle of the two, a very small, pale girl, asleep. I wonder about the situation, how they ended up this way. I must be wondering too hard as the biggest one pipes up:

'Drunk, sir, collapsed at a party.'

'I see,' I nod, and open Word on my laptop.

I begin to describe the girls in words on the blank page; I imagine them out at the party, dancing, drinking, and having fun. It's difficult not to look at them again. I peer my head over the laptop.

'Maybe she needs some water, bread or something?' I enquire.

'Yes, she's had some, sir, thanks. We'll get some food for her when we get off.' She smiles and puts her small chubby arm around the sleeping girl, her squashy fingers bitten down, with fleshy folds flapping over the bitten bits, a line of dirt under each one.

'Very good,' I smile, minding my own business.

Some minutes have passed and I am writing but I am writing nothing. I am acting. I cannot think of anything. I worry about the drunken girl; will she make it home safely? Are these young ladies going to know what to do with her? What if she chokes on her own vomit? Or gets too heavy to carry home?

I have another glance over at her, closed eyes, milky and glued down almost under lids of swirly blue lines. Her hair is soggy and flat, greasy, her lips, cold. *A fly trapped in the jam,* I think.

'Are you sure she's okay, girls?'

'Yes, thanks, sir. Sure.' The octopus winks at me. I close off, dangerously, the wink was a threat, a caution I think, a warning. I am always wary of young girls and their trump cards, I have learnt to never underestimate.

Just before Peterborough, I switch off my laptop,

zip the cover up,

in my bag,

my coat,

off the hook and on my back.

The longest journey, stifling. Drunken teenagers, what a shame. I'm actually glad I'm not a father; too much responsibility, too cynical, I wouldn't allow my children to get drunk and get on trains with fat octopuses. Ridiculous. For a moment I feel switched off from the world. I'm the only one working whilst everybody else is at home making apple cakes and sharing beef bourguignon. I freak out at the sight of a drunken girl on the train. I'm boring; I don't know this world at all.

The train pulls into Peterborough, I wanted to leave the girls with a strong moral message but don't want to sound like a FRANK advert. It's dark, outside a blizzard is blowing, an upside-down snow globe, the white puffs turn in spirals. When the train doors eventually part, I collect myself to brave the cold.

'MOVE! MOVE! MOVE!' An angry squad of police tears onto the train. I'm thrown off backwards by one and nearly topple over. I pick myself up, find my balance and watch through the window of the carriage. They charge forward towards the girls, split them apart as though breaking a stiff rope. The drunken girl falls through the middle, clangs to the ground like a hot pan; droopy, she is like a stringless puppet. The army of police arrests the girls. The bigger one effing and blinding, screaming obscenities from the gut of her stout, beefy body. Refusing to be cuffed, she tries to run but she is battled and thrown against the glass window of the carriage. Our eyes meet. I watch her. She watches me. For a second I feel responsible for her.

The second, prettier one is removed from the carriage, her head low. I am asked by a policewoman to explain what I saw during the train journey and have to give over my telephone number. What a palaver over a silly drunken teenager.

I arrive at my sister's house, and have lots of embraces with lots of people whose names I can't remember. I sit down with a glass of dark rum. My mobile rings.

'Mr Weybridge? Hello?'

'Hello. Yes?' I attempt to sober up.

'We are terribly sorry to bother you at this time.' It's the police. 'Merry Christmas, by the way. Is there any more information that you can give us regarding the event that you regrettably witnessed this evening?'

'No, nothing else that I can think of, other than the three girls had been out, one had got drunk and they were taking her home.'

'Very well. Thank you for that information, Mr Weybridge.' The officer seems quite sincere, surprisingly.

I have a reasonably uneventful Chistmas. Lots of hoo-hah and leaving me out of situations I never wanted to be let into anyway. I have decided that mistletoe should be banned, it should be against the law to force people to make contact because of a plant.

On my train home, I sleep. My eyes restore faith in me.

Coming out, I gather my bearings and make for the Underground. But then there is this pillar of dread that sends me into a blank. A pillar, a peeling paint arch of the train station, decorated with this girl's face, this girl that I know, I know, that I know I have seen, that I have perhaps talked to, and below it flowers, flowers and cards and teddy bears in plastic wrapping with dramatic ribbon bows on top, notes scribbled by loved ones. I go over, there are people there already, including a news channel. Then it dawns on me. That girl, the broken stringless puppet on the train, the pale milky girl, the one that clanged to the floor, like an unwanted barrel. And now she is dead.

I feel sick, awful. Alcohol poisoning, I knew it. I just knew it.

But then I hear it, the reporter, on his yellow spongy microphone. 'Skye Phelps, murdered. Murdered by Miss Boyle and Miss Steele, murdered and then disguised as an intoxicated passenger by her murderers. A vindictive and calculating crime? Or a cry for help? The case continues.'

I find a spot to throw my guts up. I am sick because I am regretful and know that I could die this very moment and would have no pillar in a train station, no flowers, no notes from loved ones.

The End.

The tongue-Cut Sparrow.

Once upon a time, there lived a very poor husband and his very poor wife. They were both so poor life was absolutely impossible. The wife was so poor she had no shoelaces and most of her teeth were missing. The husband was so poor he often went hungry and his bones popped out of him as though he had swallowed a toolbox. The husband spent most of his days hanging around outside Starbucks – apparently they give their sandwiches away after 6 p.m. – and his wife spent most of her days cleaning and washing clothes.

Those days outside Starbucks weren't easy. The husband resented looking shady and snide and boy was it boring, kicking the ground, being pushed by the odd aggressive, angry man, shoved in the shins by a yappy toff with a pram (even the baby showed no remorse). Most nights, the husband would return home from begging, sling himself onto the makeshift couch and grumble.

'I don't want to do this anymore. It's an awful life, begging, it's vile. I hate being seen as such a leech.'

To which his brutal wife would roll up a newspaper, or whatever she could find at the time, and beat her husband silly until he apologized for even entertaining such cowardly thoughts. About as cuddly and as loving as a pinecone, his wife was a bit of a tyrant and was as frightening in appearance as she was in personality. It was fair to say her husband was desperately terrified of disappointing her, the punishment was always a kick in the teeth . . . seriously.

So the next day the husband would go out again searching the floor for odd change, lottery tickets, any-fucking-thing. Then one day he came across half a cheeseburger lying discarded by the side of the road.

'Oh Lord!' he grinned. It was perfect: a soft bun, sauce squeezing out of the sides and yellowy plastic cheese sticking to the beef. But being the kind husband he was, he wrapped the burger up in a scrap of magazine and popped it in his pocket to share with his wife when he got home. As he stood to leave, he noticed that there sitting on the ground next to the bin, was the most perky little sparrow scampering at the ground, he too was scavenging. The husband leaned down to the sparrow's level and put his hand out towards it, expecting the sparrow to flee. But the sparrow hummed to him and hopped about on his palm. The husband reached into his pocket and brought out the burger, snuck a chunk from the bun and placed it in front of the sparrow who nipped it up energetically and waited for more. The husband continued feeding the sparrow until nearly all the burger was gone. The remains were dragged off by the bird, tweeting graciously as he left.[1] But alas, the time! It was twenty to seven! The husband ran to Starbucks only to find the staff mopping the floor with vigour, the doors locked.

---

1 'OMG,' he twittered, 'I just met a bare safe human being, thanks life.'

'CRUMBS!' he cursed and had to go home empty handed.

His wife had never been so mad. She cursed, she broke the little furniture they had and told him he was an imbecile for making friends with a dirty rat with wings. The husband nodded, but really he knew the sparrow was not dirty; his name was Mr Sparrow and he was very charming indeed. They went to sleep hungry.

The next morning the wife booted her husband out earlier than the day before and told him to beg with more vim than he ever had before. She scruffed him up by running a blunt hand through his hair and even attempted giving him a nice black eye to finish the desperate look off even more, however her husband ducked, thankfully. If only she knew about the cheeseburger!

The husband enjoyed begging slightly more now that he had found a friend in the sparrow. Mr Sparrow was a very impressive singer and could match the notes of Daniel Bedingfield absolutely perfectly – these made the Starbucks shifts whizz by and, sometimes, when the time was right and their relationship was comfortable, Mr Sparrow would humorously imitate violin solos to add an atmospheric charm whilst the husband begged. Often this worked terrifically, reminding passers-by of one of those charity adverts on TV. The husband confided in the sparrow, telling him of how frightening and greedy his wife was. Mr Sparrow listened intently and offered to visit the house, he thought a bit of his singing could cheer her up whilst she went about her chores. The husband agreed that with a voice as melodic as his, it would undoubtedly work a treat.

And so, the next day, the wife set about her daily chores, her knees sore from scrubbing the day before, her back knotted and distressed from all the washing of clothes. She ground the old rice and left it to dry out on the windowsill as she went to heat the iron; the rice would do for starch. While she was gone, the sparrow came to the balcony of their flat to enchant the wife with his impressive pitch. And when he saw the powdered rice, Oh, what a sweet offering from the husband! he thought. Powdered too so it was easier for his tiny beak to suckle up; how thoughtful. But when the wife saw that coy, dirty sparrow pecking at the ground rice she was furious. Her tight wooden peg of a face twisted up into a goblin grizzle and in one swift well-practised move she grabbed the sparrow in her clenched fist and hauled him into the kitchen.

'You dirty rat!' she barked. 'How dare you eat that rice? That is for my ironing, you wretched thief!'

Mr Sparrow panicked and spoke, 'Please, forgive me, I thought it was for me, food left from your husband, he knew I was coming to sing to you, as a gift, to cheer you up, please do not hu—'

But before he could even finish the wife cut out his tiny tongue with a pair of heavy rusty scissors.

'Now be off,' she instructed and threw the poor sparrow out of the window. He fell towards the ground, all bloody and retching in a cloudy fog of rice powder that clung to his wounds, his eyes heavy with blobby tears and the ache in his heart enormous.

When the husband returned from a day of scavenging with two bags full of sandwiches and pastries, the wife bleated in delight and began unpacking the treasure. However, the husband could not eat.

'What's wrong with you?' the wife asked him, cramming egg and cress mix into her gnarly open trough of a mouth.

'I didn't see my sparrow friend today. I thought he'd be back, but he wasn't,' he grumbled.

'That stupid sparrow! Who are you, David Attenborough? Get over it, he is an evil thief, he has not one good bone in his teensy body. He stole food from our home so I taught that damn thing a lesson.' She spat a speck of egg onto her wrist and then fingered it back into her mouth.

The husband watched in panic, he knew what his wife was capable of. 'What do you mean?' he asked, a glue of worry filling his throat, rasping.

'Well, I cut out his tongue of course.' She bit into an apricot danish, the sheets of sweetness cracking over her lap; she brushed them off viciously and then mumbled in satisfaction as though she had simply mentioned she had topped up her Oyster Card.

'How cruel,' he muttered. He wanted to keep his own tongue but inside he was raging like a wild menacing sea.

The husband missed the sparrow terribly and could not stop himself from thinking of how much agony his little friend must have felt. Still, he did not want beatings from his mardy bitch of a wife and so kept schtum about it and went to beg as usual.

Whilst working, the husband felt a twig fall on to his head and he looked up to see Mr Sparrow there.

'Mr Sparrow!' he rejoiced. 'I am so sorry about what happened to you. My wife is an absolute monster for hurting you the way she did. Please forgive me.'

And of course he did, and even better, he invited the husband back to his home to meet his family. The husband was very nervous but accepted the invitation with gratitude and shoplifted a box of Roses from the newsagent especially for the occasion.

Mr Sparrow lead the husband, frail and teetering, on a long and treacherous walk through the brambles and thistles until they reached a tiny door in a willow tree that overlooked the most beautiful and calm lake. Mr Sparrow pecked onto the little door and a very feathery, delightful, larger sparrow tweeted at the door and beckoned them both inside. Mr Sparrow flew straight in and left the husband to squeeze in on his own. He wedged in, elbows first, shuffled, moved round, flapped his arms about – it wasn't going to work, so he thrust his arms out and in went his fragile head as he wiggled through to his brittle shoulders. And then UMPH. Stuck. Except this wasn't awfully uncomfy, what with the door being the perfect height for him to stand on his feet and he had an ideal spot at the table.

'Toodleloo!' the family greeted him from their cosy home. Mr Sparrow had twin daughters and a son from what the husband could make out. This was not at all what he was expecting, this was like a funny little doll's house: a toasty fire blazing in the corner, bamboo blinds, an oak table and even a mini television. The kitchen had a bright yellow Smeg fridge with magnet alphabet letters on it and a cuckoo clock. It was astonishing; the nicest house he'd ever popped his head into and certainly did not live up to the poor, hard-knock life he had visualized.

Mrs Sparrow presented a humongous bowl of hot sweet potato custard and large edible bread spoons to eat it with. It was the best thing the husband had ever eaten and he giggled with delight. Then they had slices of sugar jelly that was so sweet it made everybody giddy, and rock candy and bowls of hot starch sprinkled with sugar and they slurped this with chopsticks. Later they had tea and cake and Mrs Sparrow combed her glorious feathers and clapped her wings whilst Mr Sparrow played the guitar and danced and his daughters sang, their son curled up fast asleep on a silken cushion. The husband had not had so much fun for as long as he could remember and dreaded going back to his miserable bitch of wife so he decided to sleep the night, standing, his head propped in the sparrows' front door, and all sparrows snoozing around his dozy head.

In the morning, the husband woke to the smell of warm coffee and bananas and Radio 4. He ate muffins and nuts and drank fresh juice before saying his goodbyes.

'Wait,' Mrs Sparrow cried. 'Mr Sparrow has something for you,' she smiled. Sparrow nodded with excitement and urged the husband to look over.

Since the sparrow could not speak, having had his tongue cut out and all, he and his wife had learnt a special way of communicating. Mrs Sparrow translated as follows: 'Here are two baskets, one of which is heavy and one of which is light. Please choose one as a parting gift from us.'

And there, as the sparrow had said, sat two baskets. The husband, not wanting to be greedy, opted for the lighter one, excusing himself, 'My body is far too frail to carry such a heavy big basket back home but I take this lighter one with gratitude.'

The sparrow and the husband parted and the husband then unscrewed his head out of the doorway like a cork popping out of the neck of a wine bottle and waved goodbye.

By the time he reached his front door he was tired after walking such a long distance. He was met by a purple-faced, hot-tempered, angry wife screaming in his face, 'Where the hell have you been, you maniac?!'

So the husband told the story of his journey to Mr Sparrow's house, of the walk, the family, and the food and then finally the present.

'Well, let's open it then,' she huffed, expecting to find bread-crumbs as a simple sparrow offering. However, inside the basket were gold and silver coins, gems and precious stones, amber, crystal, coral and sapphire, and a countless bag of money sewn into a gold embroidered silk pouch. The wife gaped in awe and pleasure. She chuckled, hysteric with greed, and then she remembered what her husband had told her.

'And you mean to say he offered you two baskets, a heavy one and a lighter one and you, like a dickhead, took the lighter one? Do you have any idea what have could have been in the other one? You idiot!' she sneered. 'I'm going to that shoddy little sparrow's house right away and I'm going to bring back that heavy basket and you will realize what a weak man you really are!'

And she slammed the front door and left.

When she reached the sparrow's willow tree she was impressed by the location, the surroundings were quite incredible. She had never seen a place that was so defiantly wonderful, the colours of the fruit and flowers stood as though it were a perfect port-folio of nature's capability. For a slight snippet of a second, the wife understood the beauty of life and the universe, it sank her heart, and it made her feel as though she was going to pass out and then she realized that her face was being taken over by a smile. Still, no time for idle wandering. She instead decided to make use of the natural amenities and bent down to the lake and flecked some specs of water onto her eyes and down her cheeks. Then she knocked, frantically, onto the sparrows' door, pretending to cry, of course.

Mrs Sparrow opened the door humming a lovely love song. The wife thrust her head inside the sparrows' house, not waiting to be invited in. Mr Sparrow was angry that she had come.

'I'm so sorry,' the wife blurted. 'I cannot stop crying, Mr Sparrow. I feel so regretful of what I did to you; it just keeps going over and over, repeating in my head. How could I possibly be so cruel?' She wailed and dribbled all over the sparrows' expensive rug, that was handmade and from Morocco.

Mr Sparrow ushered his wife and children into another room, as he did not wish them to meet such a wretched woman. They did as they were told. Mr Sparrow offered the wife some water but that was all and he listened intently to everything, false or not, that the wife had to say before encouraging her to leave.

The wife could see she was not about to be offered a basket and so, discreetly, brought this up into conversation,

'Sometimes,' began the wife, 'it is polite, when you are normal and not just a sparrow, to offer one a parting gift as a farewell.' The wife's mouth twitched as she displayed a most artificial grin.

'Of course,' Mr. Sparrow said, playing along, and went to get the baskets. 'Forgive me, please choose a basket as a parting gift.'

'Hmmm . . .' The wife pretended to brew over her decision. 'I think the heavy one is probably best. My husband has the lighter, so best to have one of each.'

And she waved goodbye and eased her head out of the

doorway and scrambled home as fast as she could, laughing most of the way. As she walked, the bag became so very heavy it was difficult to manage, but she dragged it home, sweating as she did, completely driven but in so much pain. A polite passer-by offered to help the poor skinny wife with her load but she refused stubbornly, afraid of having to share her goodies with anyone.

She reached the front door and booted it hard. 'Let me in, you twat!' she hissed. Her husband obediently did as she asked.

'I'm so excited,' she sang, 'and I just can't hide it, I'm about to lose control and I think I like it!' She boogied her stiff, skinny body around the flat before settling down to open the basket. Her husband kneeled beside her.

'Go away!' she screamed. 'You've had your fun, this treasure is for me and for me ONLY!'

So the husband left her to her own devices and retreated to the shadows of their bedroom. Filled with disgust, he watched as his crabby wife threw open the lid to the basket. At first it appeared empty, and she put her bony knuckles to her hips and dropped her jaw, about to scream and accuse her husband of stealing the contents. But then, in an instant, in the flash of an eye, a cuttle-fish darted out, his snappy pincer grasped her neck and cut her throat. Her neck flapped and folded back like the opening of a heavy book, but it wasn't enough to kill her. Next, a skeleton tall and gangly prodded her so hard in the chest that it, like a hot rod, pierced through the skin and stabbed her, blood spat her in the eye. She howled in agony and cried for her husband who was stunned and frozen in terror. Then, a white-horned cow leapt from the basket, filling the room with his mightiness and burst her stomach with the tip of his horn, gutting her, her insides folded out into a droopy sack on the floor. She put her hands around her wrecked body and sobbed before, to finish things off, a slimy goblin serpent rose from the basket, his oily horse-haired spine coiled around the wife before he smothered her, squeezing out all of her breath before her eyeballs popped out of her head and rolled away, until she went blue and died.

The husband held his hands over his mouth. H did not know what to do next. He stood, motionless, replaying the incident over and over and over, wondering if he was hallucinating, as hunger pains had done such things to him in the past. But, as he blinked and re-blinked, he saw the bloody corpse of his wife, lying like a heap of rags covered in uncooked sausages, the smell was unavoidably vile and fermented. Then, as he watched, a host of gormless demons rose from the floorboards and ate the remains of her and her black soul.

Over. As though she never existed at all.

The husband, being such a dutiful man, still created a mini grave for his late wife, in a shitty, muddy car park. Then he lived harmoniously with a long sparrow friendship-injected life in a large extravagant house with a beautiful aviary and not a single pair of scissors in sight.

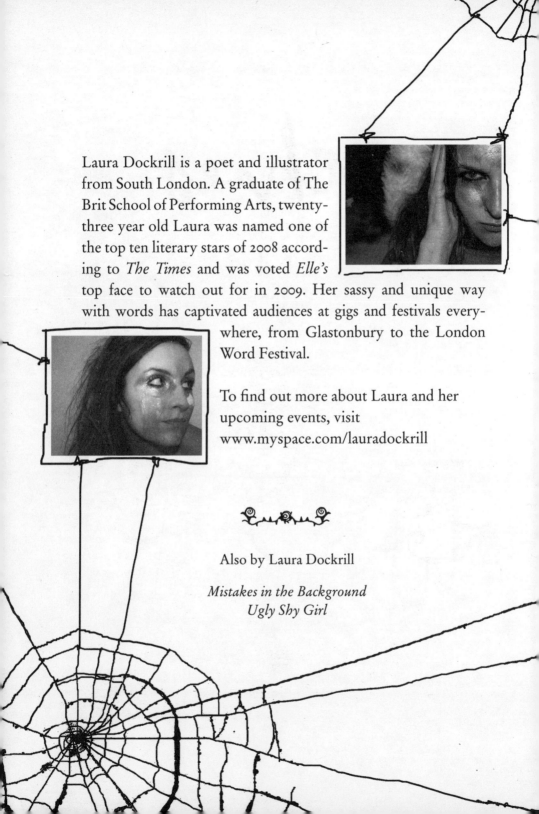

Laura Dockrill is a poet and illustrator from South London. A graduate of The Brit School of Performing Arts, twenty-three year old Laura was named one of the top ten literary stars of 2008 according to *The Times* and was voted *Elle's* top face to watch out for in 2009. Her sassy and unique way with words has captivated audiences at gigs and festivals everywhere, from Glastonbury to the London Word Festival.

To find out more about Laura and her upcoming events, visit www.myspace.com/lauradockrill

Also by Laura Dockrill

Mistakes in the Background
Ugly Shy Girl

THis book
belongs
to

....